NO

Denny was running away from the crushing weight of her mother, Isabel's, all-embracing forgiveness, and the knowledge of the pain that her perverse acts of rebellion caused Isabel over and over again.

Marshall was running away from the fact that the lost and lonely woman he first fell in love with had now learned to stand on her own two feet and speak her own ideas and emotions.

Isabel was running away from her doubts as a mother, as a lover and as a broadcast journalist competing in a man's world.

But there comes a time when everyone has to stop running—and start facing the cruel tests of life, the agonizing dilemmas of love and the ultimate truths about one another.

Charlotte Vale Allen

Running Away

MIRA BOOKS

ISBN 1-55166-150-0

RUNNING AWAY

Copyright © 1977 by Charlotte Vale Allen.

For Guinea Pig and Philpa

For Carine, Olga and Pauline

One

Returning from the kitchen for a second look just to be sure, Blake realized Denny wasn't just on the nod. He moved closer and felt panic clutch his insides as he saw how unnaturally pale she was, how shallowly she was breathing. As if she'd maybe stop any second.

"Hey!" he shouted to the ones out in the kitchen. "Something's really wrong! Somebody better call for an ambulance."

He dropped down beside the bed, and unable to think of anything else to do, started giving Denny mouth-to-mouth while Jude was calling in the kitchen. Scott and Freddie stood in the doorway for a minute watching what was happening, then turned, looked at each other, and tacitly agreed to split. Neither Jude nor Blake noticed them go.

Unsteadily, Jude replaced the receiver and hurried into the bedroom to kneel beside Blake, watching; not daring to speak for fear of distracting him; scared by the way he'd lost all his color and the way he was counting out loud as he bore down on Denny's chest, then went back to breathing into her mouth.

Scared. She'd never been so scared in her life. This was serious. Bad. She couldn't understand what had happened. She knew Blake couldn't figure it out either. He was keeping on and on with the mouth-to-mouth, and she stood up, her ears straining for the sound of sirens. She wanted to hear them, wanted them to get there now, fast.

God! she thought. What happened? Denny, what did you do this time? What?

Blake was sweating. He was scared too, Jude could tell.
God! What if Denny died? The idea of it terrified her. She
thought of trying to tell all this to Denny's mother, and suddenly wanted to cry, furious with Denny for doing whatever
it was she'd done, making all this happen. Denny's mother.
She'd . . . Wow! What would Mrs. Gary *do?*

One more thing Denny was doing that would put that awful, confused, sad sort of look in Mrs. Gary's eyes, the way
the things Denny did always seemed to. Because Denny,
without even trying too hard, was always fucking up, somehow winding up dumping on her mother, because it was all
she seemed able to do. Jude had never been able to understand how Denny could treat her mother the way she did—so
badly, so uncaringly—when Jude would've given just about
anything in the world to have a mother like that.

The ambulance arrived, and Jude ran out through the
kitchen door to show them the way.

"I don't think she's breathing," she told the two attendants, leading them to the house on the run.

"Grab an ambu bag!" one attendant shouted to the other.
"What else?" he asked Jude.

"Man, I *don't* know!" Jude cried. "She must've taken
something, or something. All she had with us was like one
beer, and then she got all weird and started nodding out, so
we brought her home with us. We only just got here like fifteen minutes ago. Blake said he didn't think she looked right.
You know? Peculiar. So, he went back to have another look,
make sure she was all right, and next thing we know, he shouts
out we should call an ambulance. He's giving her mouth-to-
mouth now."

The two attendants got Denny onto the stretcher, the one
in back holding this ambu-bag thing over Denny's face while
the other guy picked up the foot end and they carted Denny
out to the ambulance.

"One of you two better come along," the first attendant
called out. "We'll need some information, ID. This'll probably have to be reported."

Jude looked at Blake, who backed up a step, shaking his
head.

"Man, I can't!" he said, ashen-faced, on the verge of throwing up. "They need to know anything, I'll come around later. But I can't now. I can't!"

"Okay," Jude said softly, disappointed, climbing up into the back of the ambulance with the attendant. She looked out through the rear window, to see Blake with his hand on the fender of her VW, bent double, his back heaving. She was more scared than ever, her head messed with too many thoughts.

"Is she breathing?" she asked the attendant in a small, fearful voice, stunned by the enormity, the gravity of what was happening.

The attendant glanced over, saying, "She's breathing," in a flat, uncaring way. Then his eyes returned to the number he was doing with the ambu bag and the syringe he was trying to fill simultaneously. "What she do, OD?" he asked.

"I don't know," Jude answered. "She could've. But I don't see how. I mean, when? I know she didn't feel too well. She said that."

"One drink? She had one?"

"I saw her drink a beer. But I don't know what she had before," she said, badly in need of a cigarette but knowing it would have to wait until later. Maybe a lot later. "I mean, nobody could figure it out, you know? She didn't even finish that one beer. We were all set to order another round, everybody saying, 'Same again,' and like that, and when we got around to Den, her eyes were all funny and she laid her head down on her arms and said, 'I feel sick.'"

"What's she on?" the attendant asked.

"*On?* Man, I don't know what she's *on!* I mean, she like pops uppers, downers. But only sometimes, not like a regular thing. She's not into hard stuff or anything like that. I don't *think* she is. I don't know. I haven't seen her for weeks, until tonight."

"She have a bag, a purse?"

"Oh, shit!" Jude exclaimed. "It's back at the bar. We forgot all about her stuff, her bag."

"Probably ripped off by now," the attendant said knowingly, turning his attention to the driver, engaging him in what seemed to Jude a frighteningly technical, important-sounding dialogue. Radioing ahead, asking for a bunch of equipment on standby. With this fatigued air, as if they'd been doing this trip fifty times a day, every day, for a zillion years.

She'll be all right, Jude told herself, looking at Denny's arm hanging limply over the side of the stretcher, at Denny's exposed breasts and the little contacts the attendant was putting on Den's heart, his eyes watching the screen of this small machine. Then wrapping a blood-pressure gizmo around Denny's arm. These guys know what they're doing, she told herself. They'll make her better. I'll have to call her mother. What'm I going to *tell* her?

Every time, Denny. Every single time, you manage to pull off one really major downer, something positively guaranteed to make your mother crazy. I can't believe you haven't succeeded yet. But this time, this time it's heavy. You'd better not die. Man, don't die!

The flashing red roof light bounded off the walls of the tunnellike entrance to the energency room, and Jude followed the stretcher down from the ambulance and in through the doors, listening to them call for a stomach pump, calling for this, for that. Back to being scared again, her knees all wobbly. She was afraid she'd wet her pants watching them pile Denny on a trolley—loose-heavy, like a big rag doll, her arms and legs flopping—and push it off into an examining room. She didn't know what to do. Was she supposed to go in there with them? The door got closed in her face. No. She looked around, seeing nowhere to sit. She'd just have to wait. Wait.

A nurse came rushing past, and Jude put out her hand, wanting to ask what to do, but the nurse didn't see her, brushed past Jude's outheld hand, and kept going. All starchy-sounding stiff, smelling like disinfectant, like Lysol.

She had to go, would wet herself if she didn't. She moved on down the corridor, saw a door marked "Women," and pushed in. Her pants were already a little wet. She lined the toilet seat with paper—Christ! The things mothers taught you to do—and sat down, staring miserably at her dampened underpants. That did it. Really. Eighteen, almost nineteen, and she'd wet her pants, she was so scared. She wasn't some dumb little kid. She was grown, responsible for herself. But it was not understanding, not being able to make sense of any of this, that shook her up so badly. That and the idea of having to try to explain to Mrs. Gary, someone she really loved a lot, someone who'd take this right in the gut. She covered her face with her hands and cried so hard—so mad at Denny and so scared for her—that some woman just coming in asked through the door, "Are you all right in there?"

Jude wiped her eyes and nose on the sleeve of her denim workshirt and called back, "I'm okay." Then thought to add, "Thank you." Four little slippery squares of that useless institutional toilet tissue. She zipped up her jeans and flushed the toilet. The john was so bright. Like a spaceship. She stepped over to the row of sinks and washed her hands, then finally looked at herself in the mirror. I look scared, she thought. I actually *look* scared. She washed her face too. Then combed out her hair. Killing time. Thinking: Maybe by the time I've finished this, Denny'll be ready, waiting to go home. Maybe. I want it to be that way. Please make it be that way.

She went back out into the corridor to look up and down. Nothing. It was too quiet. She made her way to the emergency desk and had to stand for a couple of minutes while the nurse went on shuffling through a stack of papers. Making Jude wait. They always did that. You're a nothing kid, so you just wait while I do my ultraimportant gig here, show you what kind of heavy-duty superstar I am, what kind of power I've got over little-type people like you.

"May I help you?" the nurse asked finally, looking up at Jude with aggie eyes. You could still buy a bagful for twenty cents at the newspaper store near the high school.

"How is Denny? You know? She just came in on the ambulance."

The nurse stared at her blankly, the eyes as depthless and opaque as stones. Marbles were prettier than that.

"My *friend*," Jude repeated. "Denise Gary. The ambulance just brought her."

"You'll have to wait," the nurse stated.

"Where?"

The nurse chose to ignore this question, returning to her papers. Jude backed away and turned to look again down the corridor toward the room where they'd taken Denny. She inched her way down the corridor until she was opposite the examining room, and stood for a long time staring at the door, thinking every couple of seconds the door would open and Denny would come out looking angry and confused, the way she always did. But it didn't happen. Jude slid down the wall and sat on her heels, keeping her eyes on the door, waiting. A whole hour, and nothing. Thinking this, that, remembering all kinds of things—little-kid stuff they'd done, years and years getting big together. Saturday-afternoon movies with their knees up against the seats in front, boxes of popcorn—they both hated it buttered; bike rides all over town; checking each other out when they first started growing breasts, laughing like crazies but a little scared about the whole thing too. And now this. I can't just sit here doing nothing, she decided, searching her bag for a dime. I've got to call her mother.

She got to her feet—her legs felt sore, too weak from squatting for so long—and headed back to the entrance, looking for a pay phone, trying to think how she'd put it, what she'd say. Goddammit! Poor Mrs. Gary. She wanted to start crying again, thinking about how rotten this would have to be for Denny's mother. It wasn't fair. It really wasn't fair of Denny to do something like this.

She was always keyed up when Marshall was due back in town. He spent so much time traveling that the time they had together always seemed too short and they tried to cram too much into it. Tried via plans. But without fail, the elaborate plans they'd make for the three or four days they'd have together would get put aside—as tonight—and they'd wind up not going beyond the front door of her house. She was both angered and elated by the consistency with which Marshall deftly shelved their plans.

For him, in the course of the two-and-then-some years they'd been seeing each other, it was a case of his attachment growing until he'd arrived at a point where he was seriously considering either relocating on a permanent basis or changing fields altogether. The separations—usually of a week's duration at the least, and more often two or three weeks—were a hardship. Each time he arrived back at the airport, his first steps were in the direction of the bank of telephones close by the arrivals gate. To call Isabel. He'd hear her voice, and any thought he might have had about going first to his apartment evaporated, and he was on his way to her.

For her part, knowing he was due to arrive in town momentarily somehow coerced her into keeping within range of the telephone, even leading her so far as to take the telephone off the hook while she was in the shower. She felt a niggling obligation to be there when he called, an irritation with herself for performing these minor acts of availability. She did want to be there when he called, but disliked that something inside her that responded so obsessively to his pending arrivals. But she'd spent too many years alone since Howard's death. And now that Marshall was in her life, her focus had been allowed to shift to him. Willingly. Intentionally. Because he seemed to be what she'd been needing for a very long time. Time's passage, she'd found, seemed to have a way of whittling away the decorative niceties embellishing basic needs, so that she found herself less reluctant to perform in the way she did with Marshall now than she might have, say, even five years before.

Marshall. Forty-four years old. An environmental-research biologist flying here and there across the country, across oceans; advising communes or foreign governments, speaking to anyone willing to listen; trying to save the air, the water, the planet. Saving her, she thought, from loneliness, from slow-building desperation, from the onerous daily process of making-do in every way; offering her different perspectives, encouragement, and his undivided attention. She sometimes, guiltily, felt the weight of his attentions to be a little heavier than she could bear. But she kept telling herself that his contribution to her life more than compensated for his usually rapacious sexual single-mindedness.

She'd been almost thirty-eight when they'd met. At his urging—he seemed to have taken great delight in helping redirect her life—she'd returned to school, completed her long-ago-started graduate degree, and ultimately been hired, minus illusions, as the token female on the production staff at the local TV station. The station being a not-so-small cog in a conglomerate wheel.

Her job for the first six months had seemed utterly meaningless, and the corporate tokenism did take a definite toll on the men she was obliged to work with. They were divided. The majority of men—the producer of the show she worked on, the makeup man, several others—regarded her as merely another employee and offered her the benefit of their experience and knowledge as they would have to another man. The minority—Jerry Brenner, the star of the show she worked on; one of the cameramen; and a particularly taciturn electrician—condescended to explain details to her with an air of wearied boredom that caused her to perspire heavily beneath her simple but attractive "work" clothes while she tried to pay close attention to what she was being told. It was that majority group who'd finally managed to help her gain an understanding of the inner machinations of the show's programming, advertising time-slot power, and the actual production of the show itself. Management. It had all seemed, initially, like so much note-taking and hustling bravado performed solely for the sake of the self-aggrandizement of those of the men whose faces or voices ultimately got sent out along the airwaves for public consumption. In particular, for the sake of Jerry Brenner. She could not make herself like him, found it a struggle to keep her features bland when it was necessary to speak with him. His chauvinism extended far beyond the realm of women, right into the ranks of his peers. Jerry Brenner.

She'd stood on the periphery for months, listening and watching, until finally being assigned to Ash Stevenson as his production assistant on *Mid-Morning,* a two-hour talk show that aired at nine, immediately after the end of the national network morning show. She then spent more months dashing about in the early-morning hours with clipboard, stopwatch, and list of scheduled guests, frantically trying to coordinate, mediate, and placate. Coordinating the time slots

and commercial breaks, mediating between Jerry Brenner and
Ash, and placating those of the guests who saw fit to take offense at Brenner's calculated rudeness.

Unquestionably, the best part of the job was the time she
spent with the guests. She enjoyed people generally, enjoyed
these selected people especially. And found it effortlessly
pleasurable to distract them from their immediate, chafing
dislike of Jerry. Isabel couldn't quite see how he managed to
hang on to his job, managing as he did to alienate such a large
number of people on so many different levels. And being as
busy as she was, she couldn't afford to spend undue time an-
alyzing this. She was too busy scurrying here and there inside
the studio, helping to get the show on the air; confirming
times and dates with certain of the show's guests; seeing to it
that those guests—when they did arrive—were comfortably
ensconced in the Green Room with coffee while waiting to go
on.

Finally, collapsing one day at show's end for five minutes'
breathing space, folding into an available armchair in the de-
crepit Green Room, sighing exhaustedly over the surprisingly
successful completion of yet another day's cross-purpose efforts, she was joined by the seldom seen Ash, who observed,
"I like the way you handle yourself, Isabel. The guests. The
show's getting a little lopsided with Jerry carrying the whole
thing. Would you be interested in taking a stab with a guest
every so often?"

"On camera?" she'd asked, sitting up a little straighter.

"I've been running it around," he'd gone on. "You've got
a nice way of handling people, getting the best from them."
He studied her face closely. "Watched you on the monitor this
morning during the commercial break. You look good. I think
it'd be kind of interesting."

"But I'm not an actress . . ." she began, finding it difficult
to imagine herself playing the role of a female Jerry Brenner.

"That's the whole point," Ash had said, lighting a cigarette. "You're *not.*"

"I don't know. I mean . . . when?"

"Up to you," he'd said. "It's a gut feeling." He'd looked
beyond her at this point, into space. "The ratings are drop-

ping a little more every month. There's no *contrast*. The
thing's turning into Jerry's personal hate trip. People at home
watching don't like it first thing in the morning. Can't get off
on that before they've had their second cup of coffee. Women
calling in saying, 'Does he have to be that way?' Well''—his
eyes had returned to her face—''let me know. I'm high on the
idea of a woman's viewpoint. For the audience reaction.''

"But what about this?'' she'd asked, holding her hand over
the clipboard and stopwatch sitting on the arm of her chair.

"Oh, that.'' He'd looked at the clipboard, then at his
wristwatch. "We can get another girl. I've got to go. Some
stuff upstairs, then a meeting over lunch. Think about it,''
he'd said again. "I ran it out upstairs a couple of weeks ago
and got the go-ahead, so it's up to you. If you choose not to,
at least we can get you a couple more bucks for the leg-
work.'' His way of being complimentary.

"All right,'' she'd said, her heart racing. "I'll think about
it.''

She did. For a solid week. Day and night. Trying to imagine herself sitting with some measure of composure up there
beside Jerry in one of the captain's chairs, interviewing some
guest. The idea of it appealed to her greatly. But the idea of
having to contend with Jerry on a direct, daily basis made her
uneasy. Yet, why not? Why not try?

She'd caught Ash on the fly as he was about to hurry off to
the Press Club, and told him she'd be willing to try. He'd
glanced at her, not seeming to hear. But within another week
there'd been someone new running around with clipboard and
stopwatch, doling out cups of coffee. Annette. Appearing to
thrive on her confrontations with Jerry. And Isabel was lining up her questions, reviewing the advance promotional
material for her first week's guests. She'd have a fifteen-
minute interview segment each morning. On her own. Without Jerry. In a separate corner of the studio with a new set.

Jerry'd made a pretense of ignorance, making it seem as if
she wasn't happening to him. Privately considering this another personal affront. And stood beside the monitor on the
morning of her first show, chatting with the lighting man
while the taped commercial was running. Isabel carried on a

whispered conversation with her guest—a toy manufacturer, elderly and amiable—trying to put them both at ease. And then they were on camera and it was easy. Easy. Asking the questions, getting the answers, finding further questions to ask as a result of the answers given, loosely following the guidelines she'd laid down in preparation. And then saying, "I've been talking to So-and-so, who's done Such-and-such. Thank you very much for being with us today on *Mid-Morning*." Easy.

She'd received a new salary check at the end of her second week—the station paid twice a month—that sat her down in sudden surprise, not sure a mistake hadn't been made. But no, Ash had presented her with a contract requiring her signature. And the annual figure was commensurate with the check she'd received.

Seeing her expression, Ash asked, "Not enough?"

"More than enough," she answered, reaching for a pen. A year's contract with an option. She was now, with her MA in education—she'd thought she might teach, only to find herself disenchanted after a half a dozen trial classroom sessions—a TV talk-show hostess. And thought to herself: Welcome to Fantasy Land.

So, tonight, after this morning's contract signing, she and Marshall had planned to celebrate by going out for dinner, dancing. She'd dressed accordingly in a pair of high-waisted black crepe evening trousers, a long-sleeved white silk shirt slashed daringly to the waist and secured halfway by a somehow suggestive-looking red-silk rose. She'd coiled her hair into an elaborate chignon, taken a good deal of time over her makeup, applied her favorite perfume liberally, and they'd gone nowhere.

He'd arrived laughing, depositing his attaché case and suitbag on the floor of the front hall before enveloping her in a giddying embrace that succeeded in unhinging the rose, thereby revealing a good deal more breast than she'd intended. From the front hall to the bedroom had taken no more than two minutes of "But, Marsh, we're going out. I'm ready." And "You're beautiful. Just for five minutes." And "You do this to me every single time." And "I can't help it.

It's been two weeks." Hence to the bedroom. Still laughing, he'd called her "Star." He had not yet seen the show.

In the course of their two years together, they had, through Isabel's patient teachings, arrived at a substantially gratifying series of formulae that delivered to each of them a considerable amount of pleasure. For him, it was the most stunning experience of his life.

Having suffered through eleven years of a marriage he'd been certain would bring about his eventual annihilation—or possible emotional castration—he found Isabel to be the woman he might have dreamed of, had he dared to dream. He'd managed to survive the marriage and ensuing divorce, feeling that the only part of himself left intact was his attaché case. And moved into life as a bachelor with little or no motivation toward ever again involving himself in another marriage. But Isabel came like something of a reward for those eleven years of tuning-out, self-defensive tactics and bouts of severe depression.

He'd caught sight of her early one evening in the parking lot of a nearby shopping center and did something he'd never done before in his life: went marching boldly across the macadam to stop her as she was getting into her car to ask, "Are you married?"

She'd looked at him blankly, wondering if something violent was about to happen. Yet, incredibly—she'd never know why—she'd answered him.

"No. Why?"

"I was just driving out, and I saw you. I think you're beautiful. I've never done anything like this before in my life, and probably never will again. Will you come have a drink, talk to me?"

And still without knowing why, with no reason to, she'd believed him and had nodded her head, trancelike. Whereupon he'd closed the door of her car, gently taken her arm, and led her into a bar three doors down from where her car had been parked.

They'd talked without strangeness, like old friends who hadn't met in years. Isabel had sat studying him, listening to him, all the while hearing a voice in her head saying: You've got to get involved again sooner or later. It might as well be sooner. And certainly he was more interesting, less pretentious, more attractive than anyone else she'd encountered since Howard's death. She had nothing to lose. She'd come around to thinking: All I've got left to lose is my life. If I'm going to be murdered, I'll be murdered. I might as well take the chance.

They'd agreed to meet again, same place, same time, the next evening. They did. And went from the bar to his car to his apartment to his bed without ever discussing it. The progression seemed so inevitable, she simply went along with it.

He found her almost too beautiful—something inside him wanted to break down at the sight of her—with her mass of thick black hair and round dark eyes, her white skin with its blue-veined tracings, her quiet voice and sensuous mouth. Everything about her struck him as perfect, awesome. She was very tall—almost five-nine—but elegant with it, and her large-boned body was wonderfully proportioned. Neither too fleshy nor too bony. Just right. With rather large breasts that he felt were redeemed by their firmness and their failure to have begun to sag. Surprisingly youthful breasts. In contrast to the beginning-to-age quality of the flesh of her belly—''a little too soft'' would have been his only criticism—and her inner thighs. As far as he was concerned, she was as close to perfect as a woman her age was likely to come. And he was damned lucky to have found her. Frequently he wondered aloud, ''What are you doing with me?'' to which her constant reply was, ''The same thing you're doing with me.''

She did, in truth, find him appealing, well above average. Although there were times when she wasn't sure that her thoughts of him when he was away weren't better than his reality. But with too-straight hair of medium brown, and hazel eyes, a tall, lanky body, trim mustache and indented chin, along with a tendency toward laughter, he touched something inside her that had been lonelier, even emptier than she'd realized.

Their first few skirmishes in his bedroom had been cruelly disappointing. She'd been reluctant to express her feelings, but gradually, testing the ground and finding the reception good, she began attempting to work things out; discovering his preferences, trying to indicate her own. Stifling a feeling of mingled sadness and demoralization at having to become an instructor at her age. But touched nonetheless by his daring to say, ''Please, for God's sake, tell me! Tell me what and where and how! Eleven years of indignant silence have made me kind of scared. I'm too old to be blundering around hoping it's all right. I *want* it to be right! For you. Because it's fantastic for me.''

So she whispered signals, closed her eyes to the mechanics, forged a route to pleasure, and told herself she'd been fortunate in finding him.

Her only problem was Denise.

Denise had been eight and a half when Howard died. At the time, she'd seemed bewildered, completely disoriented by her father's illness and resulting death. Yet displayed what Isabel construed as a legitimate absence of understanding. After all, Isabel had to force her own understanding, when she'd have preferred to hide from the reality of what was happening. What did alarm her, though, was the way in which Denise slowly became drained of energy and interest. And all of it seemed to stem from the advent of Howard's illness.

Denise entered into adolescence docile and uninterested, and emerged at sixteen caustic, critical, and hostile—in particular toward Isabel, who tried to be reasonable in coping with her daughter's exaggerated highs and lows, attempting to logically attribute these up- and downswings to a natural change in hormones as well as to a healthy, full-functioning intelligence. Denny was, without doubt, fiercely—almost defiantly—intelligent.

Working to reason it through, Isabel acknowledged that she herself wasn't so far removed from her own very rebellious teenage years that she couldn't remember the miseries and attendant confusion of that period. She tried to be sympathetic, available, but Denny wasn't having any. ''Leave me alone!'' was her standard cry. ''Just *leave* me *alone!*''

It hurt every time. And as a result, Isabel suffered through lows of her own, wondering time and again if having a father mightn't have altered this phase of Denny's life to an appreciable degree. She spent weeks, months trying to reach an understanding of why Denny was so alternatingly withdrawn and antagonistic. There didn't seem to be an answer. So it was best, Isabel decided finally, to do as Denny had asked, and within the bounds of common sense, leave her alone.

Isabel wasn't surprised when, upon graduating from high school and having—at least outwardly—calmed down quite considerably, Denny sat down with her mother and quietly explained why she felt it would be best if she didn't go on to college right away. She didn't yet know what she wanted to do, and thought a year off from school might clarify her thoughts, help her decide. And, she continued, it would be better if she had a place of her own. Denny sounded in control, sensible, appearing to have come through the worst of whatever it was she'd endured. So, unable to find any critical holes in Denny's arguments, Isabel agreed to have the room over the garage completed and made into a separate apartment. With an entrance inside the house and another outside. It was done. Denny moved in, stayed a little over a month, and then announced it wasn't far enough away. She wanted to move all the way out. Resigned, Isabel provided her with several hundred dollars to help her get started.

And once she was living away, with her friend Judy and another girl, she seemed to evolve into a close fascimile of a friendly relative. She telephone regularly a couple of times a week, came at least once a week to dinner. And on those occasions when she came to the house and encountered Marshall there, she did try—despite her initial claims to loathing him—to be polite and friendly.

Isabel, greatly relieved, settled down to her work at the station and to Marshall, happy that things seemed to be sorting themselves out at last. She loved Denny deeply, devotedly, and tried to temper her attachment with reason and as much objectivity as she could muster. It was anything but easy, but it looked as if the end results would be worthwhile. If Denny could only determine her values and finally begin putting her intelligence to good use.

But then, something else happened. Isabel had no idea what. But something happened, and Denny was gone again.

Moving rapidly away from the tentative understanding they'd been approaching. Trouble time again. Would it never end?

Her black trousers and white shirt now lay in a heap on the floor beside the bed, tangled in and around Marsh's discarded clothes. They'd been—atypically—engaged in preliminaries for close to an hour and were both at fever pitch.

"Let's get married," he said unexpectedly, following the particularly well-defined vein running the length of her arm to her wrist with his thumb.

"How?" she asked, disconcerted. Why did he choose this moment to spring that on her? "It's impossible. You're never here." I don't want to talk, she thought. "I'm not sure about marriage."

"I've had a good offer to head up a group here. If you wanted to offer me a little incentive, I might be able to work it out so that I *am* here."

"Let me think about it," she said, shivering as his fingers began tracing the veins in her breasts. She was terribly excited, unusually so. If he touched her too importantly right now, she'd come. And she wanted to wait. This was one of the rare times when she knew she'd be able to come with him inside her. "Could we talk about it later?" It had been two incredibly good, satisfying weeks; so many new things happening. A feeling of regenerated self-confidence, quietly inflowing. Images of the growing self flashing rewardingly against the blurred screen of thought pictures.

"Would you let me move in here with my spare lenses and microscopes and sampling kits?"

"I need to think, Marsh. I can't *think* right now."

"It's a good thing," he said softly, for perhaps the hundredth time, "your mother never warned you about strange men in parking lots."

"Oh, she did," she said, feeling a banking impatience. *No more talking.* "I simply forgot that day, that's all."

At last he was silent. She could push away the abrading impatience, their mouths meeting with mounting hunger. It was going to work this time. She could feel the pressure at once, that pleasurable weight at the top of her thighs.

She was gone, volunteered away. Into exquisite grinding madness accelerating without need no need thank God for signals rising rising floodtides cresting. She was just starting the glorious lazy descent down to the cooler calmer regions when the telephone rang.

She hung up and sat very still for a moment, her body fighting its way up out of the aftermath of pleasure into the hypertension of fear. Denny, Denny. What have you done this time? Why does there always have to be something that you do that's guaranteed to rip into me, into my life, as if I, my life, were as gauzy and insubstantial as cheesecloth?

"What is it?" Marshall asked, placing his hand on her spine.

It would all go now. Two weeks of success, of gratification. Already going. She could feel it leaving her.

"Denny," she said, her voice gone husky. "She's in the emergency room at the hospital."

"What happened?"

"I don't know. I've got to get down there." I'm so tired, she thought, suddenly feeling it in her joints.

"I'll take you. You go ahead and get dressed. I'll run down and use the other bathroom."

She dropped the soap. She dropped the towel. After that, she dropped her hairbrush. Moving too quickly, in a state of panic. She was dropping everything. Her hands wouldn't work properly. But an inborn sense of decorum dictated she simply could not go to the hospital and her child directly from her bed without first making the most basic attempts to erase the scent of fresh sex from her skin. And as she fumbled through these ritual cursory acts of cleanliness, her brain was chanting out a message that said: Something's happened again. Everything will be changed again. Again. Always. Never a chance to rest, relax, and enjoy the minor gains. Never. She was frightened for Denny, for herself, for Marshall. For Judy too. Judy had sounded terrified, her voice small, staccato.

She pulled on a pair of Denny's discarded jeans and a sweater—no time to waste on underwear—pushed her feet into a pair of loafers, caught her hair back with a rubber band, and raced down the stairs to grab a jacket and her handbag.

Make sure you've got the medical card, the voice alerted her. She slipped through the compartments of her wallet, finding the identification card issued with the station's group-insurance policy.

Marshall came flying down the stairs, snatched up his keys from the hall table, took her arm, and hurried her out to his car.

"Did they tell you anything?" he asked, barely stopping for red lights, braking only enough to see if there was any on-coming traffic.

"Judy didn't know. She said something about going out for a drink, and something else about Blake giving Denny mouth-to-mouth. She was a little incoherent." I'm scared, she added silently. Every time, it gets a little worse. You keep thinking it's got to end, but it goes on and on, and there's never an end. You get to be a mother for the rest of your life. Your heart thudding to a stop with every fall, every new cut, every fresh spill of blood.

"It may just be nothing," he said, trying to reassure her.

"It's not nothing. I can feel it." Don't die, she thought. Please, don't die! I wish— Oh, Lord, I wish I knew what you're trying to say with all of this, Denny!

He reached out to take her hand. It was cold, unyielding. She let him hold her hand, her attention on the deep breathing she was doing. The actions she was performing tricking her mind backward to the labor room. Holding on to How-ard's hand, trying to smile, doing the deep breathing, count-ing. Scared. But not really. Nothing could go wrong. Except that it was all going on too long, too long, and she was so tired and wanted to see the baby, wanted it out of her and into the air. The baby. Her body grotesque, huge; seared with pain, the mound of her belly taut, hard.

Then her mind was bringing her forward in time, so that she was standing beside Howard's bed. And his hand, all bones, was closed around hers, like steel. Nothing recognizable left of the man, all his flesh eaten away from the inside out, his face cadaverous. Thirty-four years old, he'd looked eighty. His hair gone, fallen out after the radiation treatments. Howard. "I want to die," he'd moaned, tears sitting in the sunken wells beneath his eyes. "God, let me die! Tell them to leave me be, let me die!" She'd told them. They'd discontinued everything but the painkiller. And finally, finally, he'd died. The pain of missing him just a little less than the pain of eighteen months watching him die.

Now Denny. Please, not Denny! She's too young. Eighteen isn't old enough. Thirty-four wasn't old enough. But eighteen . . . She has to have a fair chance to find out why. . . .

"You go ahead in. I'll park the car."

She got out and pushed in through the doors, to see Judy squatting against the wall halfway down the corridor. There was no one at the desk.

"Judy," she said, touching Jude's shoulder.

Jude stood up, her eyes stark, and draped her arms around Isabel, crying, "I'm sorry, Mrs. Gary. I'm really *sorry*."

"I know that, Judy. Just tell me what happened. Where is she? Has anyone told you anything?"

"Nothing! I don't know what's going on."

"No one's spoken to you, told you anything at all?" Isabel asked, wiping Jude's eyes with a tissue she fished out of her jacket pocket.

"Not one thing. They've been in there"—she pointed at the closed door—"for hours. It's freaky. A whole bunch of people went in. Not one of them's come out yet. And you know they're not going to tell me anything, Mrs. Gary. They think everybody under thirty's a moron. I'm sorry."

Marshall came down the corridor.

"There must be someone who'll tell us what's going on." Isabel was struggling to stay calm.

"Let's go find out," Marshall said, almost cheerfully, steering her back in the direction of the nurses' station. Isabel looked at his profile. He seemed too hearty. Too something.

The same marble-eyed nurse materialized behind the desk and looked at the three of them doubtfully.

"I'm Isabel Gary. My daughter . . ."

"She's still in—"

"I understand that," Isabel cut in. "I wish to know her condition."

"They have been in there quite a while," the nurse conceded, her eyes moving to the closed door. "You fill these in, and let me go find out." She pushed some forms across the desk to Isabel, then pivoted neatly around the corner of the desk and squeaked off down the corridor, to disappear silently through the examining-room door.

Isabel wrote quickly, automatically, filling in the blanks, inserting information in the spaces provided. Hearing the eerie voices broadcast over the PA floating disembodied along the deserted middle-of-the-night corridors.

Within five minutes the nurse reappeared in the company of a tall gray-haired doctor in his early fifties.

"You are the family?" he asked, taking the three of them in with sharp, intelligent eyes.

"I am her mother," Isabel said, freeing her hand from Marshall's grasp. She wished he'd stop grabbing at her.

"If you'll come with me," the doctor said.

She followed him down the corridor and into what was evidently some sort of staff lounge, where, without inviting her to sit down, he leaned against the closed door and said, "I'm Dr. Raymond. I do not advise you to see your daughter tonight."

"I don't understand," she said, her brain fuddled. Too many things going on.

"She's very weak. Her stomach's been pumped."

"Why? What did she take?"

"She took something," he said, his features softening somewhat. "Several somethings, as a matter of fact. We can't seem to pinpoint what, precisely."

"May I see her?"

"Mrs. Gary"—he sighed wearily—"she doesn't want to see anyone right now. She's managed to be very specific about that, if nothing else. They're moving her now. I suggest you go home and try to get some sleep, then come back here around noon. Give her a chance to rest, calm down."

"Moving her to where?"

"Just upstairs. We'll keep her a few days. That's all."

He studied Isabel's face for a moment or two, trying to relate the two people involved in the terrible sameness of the situation. Two or three times a week the children were brought in to have their stomachs emptied or their veins flushed clean. And the parents came wearing their expressions of disbelief, their eyes round and sorry and dismayed, their words accusing, guilty, and bereft. This mother, he thought, was more in control, more rational than most.

"It'll be all right, Mrs. Gary," he said quietly. "She's overwrought. And angry."

"Angry." Isabel nodded her head. "Oh, yes. Do you feel angry?" she asked him, noticing a white scar on his throat.

"Oh, frequently," he admitted. "Nobody knows how it happens. I've got kids, too. Sometimes you get lucky. Sometimes not. Do you care?"

"I care," she said tiredly, feeling it in her spine. "I care this time. I cared the last time. I'll care next time. But all the caring doesn't change anything."

"It might. It could. In the long run. I'll have someone stop by to talk to Denise in the morning," he offered.

"She doesn't like psychiatrists. We tried that once."

"She won't like this one either," he said. "But we try anyway." He put his hand on her shoulder and opened the door. "You keep on trying," he said, directing her out to the corridor. "I haven't yet heard about anything else that works."

He turned and went striding across the corridor, back into the examining room.

"I won't be seeing her until tomorrow noon," she told Marshall. "I'll come back in the morning."

"What did he tell you?"

"She doesn't want to see me."

The nurse came bustling out of the examining room, saying, "Mrs. Gary, if you'll come with me to the desk, I'll just have you complete the admission forms."

Isabel looked at Marshall helplessly. He took hold of her hand. On the pretext of getting her pen from her bag, she freed her hand and followed the nurse. Jude tagged along.

The forms completed, she scrawled her name at the bottom, barely able to write. The nurse whipped the papers away, and that was that. They were dismissed.

"The doctor," Isabel said, "said I should go home and get some sleep. Why do they think people can simply go to sleep when the worst things happen?" She looked past Marshall at Jude. "Come on, Judy," she said, seeing the distress wrinkling Jude's small face. "We'll take you home."

Holding Judy in the circle of her arm was so different from holding Denny. Judy was all tiny sparrow's bones and surprising softness. Like a small child. Denny was bigger, harder, too elusive ever to be held for more than five seconds. The texture of her hair different, too. Judy's hair feather-soft. A little bird. But one with a profoundly well-developed sense of responsibility, a maturity far beyond her years. And she'd always been this way. As long as Isabel had known her, which was most of Judy's life, the girl had been fun-loving, effortlessly good-natured and fair-minded, delightfully imaginative, and steadfastly responsible. She had never as a small child carried tales or tattled the way some other of Denny's friends had. She'd never cried unless she'd sustained a genuine injury. And she'd never instigated trouble. She asked a great number of questions, talked a lot in her schoolgirl's high-pitched voice, and derived perhaps her biggest pleasure in life from the replies she received to the questions she asked. Of all Denny's childhood friends, Judy was the only one still around, still loyal. And obviously still responsible.

"I feel so terrible about this," Jude was saying. "Did the doctor say she's going to be all right?"

"They'll keep her in for a few days," Isabel answered.

"Oh!"

Marshall squeezed Isabel's hand. A signal: We'll talk when we get home. She squeezed back halfheartedy but this time did not disengage her hand.

"Where are you staying, Judy?" she asked the girl.

"Could you drop me at Blake's place? My car's there. I've been kind of been staying there," she admitted rather shyly.

"Was he with you all evening?"

"He was the one who realized something was wrong. You know? We thought she was just like tired or something. She had this one beer, didn't even finish it, and the next thing we knew, she went all stoned and dopeylike, and laid her head down on her arms. So we took her back, and me and Blake put her to bed. We were all out in the kitchen, and Blake came out with this strange look on his face, shaking his head, saying she just didn't *look* right to him. So he went back to have another look and shouted we ought to call an ambulance. So I ran to call, and when I got finished calling, everybody else had split, and it was only me and Blake. And then Blake wouldn't come to the hospital. He got sick. And the other thing," she said miserably, "we forgot Den's stuff at the bar. I phoned there while I was waiting, and they couldn't find it. I feel just *terrible* about that."

"Thank you." Isabel hugged Jude tight against her side. "You did everything you could."

Marshall pulled the car over to the curb, and Jude turned to put her arms around Isabel's neck, their cheeks pressed together.

"I'm sorry," she said. "But I'm glad we were with her. You know? Will you call me, let me know how she is?"

"I'll let you know."

Jude removed her arms, and sat looking into Isabel's eyes thinking: I'd never dump on you like that. You didn't do anything to deserve it. You never do anything to deserve it. But Denny *thinks* you do. "Okay," she said softly. She slid out of the car, and Isabel watched her walk around to the side of the house.

They drove the rest of the way back in silence. Marshall put his car into the garage beside hers, then went back to close the garage door while she let herself in through the kitchen. She walked in, flipped on the light, stood looking blankly for a moment at the tidy kitchen, then slumped down into one of the kitchen chairs.

"I'll make some food," he said. "Something to eat. Some coffee."

"I couldn't eat," she said absently.

"Listen," he said, dropping down in front of her, taking hold of her hands. "By tomorrow it'll be all good news. So don't go to pieces now that the worst is over."

She sighed, freeing her hands, looked at him, wondering why he seemed to be radiating a kind of satisfaction at his involvement in this situation. No, she was reading it wrong. She drew his head against her breasts. "The worst seems to keep on happening," she said. Then shivered and tightened her hold on him.

"Don't anticipate," he cautioned. "You could drive yourself crazy that way. Maybe this time she'll see she went too far and start pulling herself together."

"Marsh, it's more critical than that. I keep trying to think up answers for Denny, why she is the way she is. But there aren't any. It's a dreadful feeling, over and over... She hated me for sending her to the psychiatrist, hated me for going along to see him myself. Hated both of us for wanting to help her. She hated me for not giving in and buying her a car. For not giving her the thousand dollars to go with that group from school to Europe. For the way I decorated the garage apartment. For *everything*."

"There was an Irish poet who said, 'There are no answers to real questions.'"

"Cold comfort. It doesn't solve my problems."

"Why don't you fix us a couple of drinks while I put some food together?" he suggested, sounding to her as if her recitation of past failures was too boring to be allowed to continue.

You don't understand any of this, she thought, getting up stiffly and walking through the darkened house to the bar in the living room. The irrational idea that she should have been with Denny tonight was fixing itself in her mind. Somehow, she thought, if I'd been with you, none of this would have happened. But no, that's nonsense. Children grow up, grow away. You can't hover over them, warning them to be careful.

But, Denny, how did you come to be someone who lives away, stays away, prefers to keep distances between us? It was never what I wanted, Denise. But you wouldn't be held, couldn't bear sitting on my lap as a small child. Finally couldn't stand being in the same house with me, you said. And I'll never know why. I've tried to be tolerant, open-minded. But no matter how much I've agreed with you or offered my help, it hasn't been what you've wanted. It's never what you want. Always keeping a good distance between us, your eyes wary, as if I might finally remove my mask and reveal the real monster underneath, the one you've always known, believed was there. What do you want, Denny? What do you need that I can't give you? And what happened tonight? All the way up to the doorway of death. I don't want you to die, Denise. What was it all for, if you have to die to prove your points?

At Marshall's urging, she ate half a sandwich without tasting it, unable to tear her eyes away from a spot on the kitchen wall just above the sink. She could *not* stop staring at it. A smudge. Or a cooking spatter. Her eyes refused to move.

"Come on," he said. "Let's go up. I'll clean up in here tomorrow."

"The show!" she said, her eyes snapping back into focus. She got up and went to the telephone to leave a message for Ash with the night engineer. Hearing the soundtrack from the late show in the background. She wouldn't make it for tomorrow's show.

"The doctor said to come at noon," she told Marshall, her hand still on the receiver. "I can't wait all morning."

He couldn't think of what to say to her. Having no children of his own, and having taken an immediate and thorough dislike to Denise, he was having a hard time summoning sympathetic responses.

She stood beside the bed staring down at her crumpled evening clothes. Crushed. Like the good feeling she'd carried with her these past two weeks. Marshall came over, saw the direction of her gaze, and bent to pick up the clothes, laying them carefully over the back of the chair by her desk.

"Come on, sweetheart," he said, turning her around, starting to undress her. She let him, her mind a logjam of snarled thoughts, memories, fears. She climbed into bed and lay gazing up at the ceiling until he lay down beside her and gathered her into his arms. The contact relaxed her fractionally. She wanted him to say and do certain things, hoped he'd seek to offer what she felt she most needed at this moment. Tell me what I need to hear. Say it, talk to me. Don't let me down now.

"I'll stay a few extra days," he said. "So don't worry. I'm not going to leave you on your own with this."

It wasn't quite what she'd wanted. He held her against his chest, stroking her, so that, gratefully, she began to feel drowsy and closed her eyes. Her head was aching, pounding. She thought of getting up to take an aspirin but lacked the strength to move. Only two weeks, and already she was letting them down at the station. She could just see Jerry, hear him making little acid comments about the wonderful dependability of women. Don't think about it! she told herself. Marsh's hands were soothing her, lulling her into sleep.

Then the movements changed, became more direct, more focused. She opened her eyes to look at him, wondering how he could be aroused at so inappropriate a time. I can't do this, she thought. Not *now*.

He was looking at her questioningly, the telltale signs of desire turning his mouth loose.

"Maybe we should get married right away," he said.

"How can you think that?" she asked, feeling panicked anew. Was this real? What switching circuitry in his mind led him along these devious byroads?

"Because you need someone around. Two have more strength than one."

That's not true, she thought. And you don't even *like* Denny. You're not telling the truth. "Marsh, it's impossible."

"It isn't. Not really." He waited for an answer. She didn't have one. She couldn't honestly conceive of being married to Marshall.

"Think about it. You'll see I'm not wrong. You can't go on handling everything alone." He smiled coaxingly, his eyes straying from her eyes, looking quickly, guiltily at her breasts.

"Yes," she said, latching on to that. "Let me think about it. Let me do that."

She closed her eyes again, hoping that would be the end of it. But how could it be, when he was butting gently but insistently against her thighs? You truly do not understand, she thought, feeling suddenly very desperate. Horribly, anxiously intimidated. Because he was here in her bed for the night, and there was no way she could, without seriously hurting him, ask him to sleep in the guest room or even to go back to his apartment. He was here and determined, and she had no immediate alternatives.

Do I owe you this? she wondered. Will it help you in some way I can't fathom? All right, Marshall. Anything. To be left alone. To have room for thinking.

She rolled over onto her back and spread her legs, tensed. He came down on top of her, his mouth hot, urgent.

"Just *do* it!" she whispered, making herself available but not assisting as she usually did.

He pushed into her, and she cried out. Pain. She wasn't ready, didn't want to be doing this, couldn't understand any of the things that had happened and kept on happening.

As he thrust into her, her mind returned to the hospital, stalking the deserted corridors. This is no good. I can't involve myself. Not when my child is lying in a hospital bed having very nearly succeeded in killing herself. Intentionally, unintentionally?

She wished she could cry, or that Marshall, instead of doing this, had opted for further conversation. About anything. Ask me how I feel, Marshall. Ask me if I'm deriving something from this. You're depriving me of the one thing I most hoped you'd offer: comfort.

Feeling used, the reluctance of her interior; feeling him striking hard against the unyielding fist of the cervix. At least, she thought, feeling agonizingly labored in the motions, say you love me.

She lay blinking at the ceiling, feeling the awful rawness all down the back of her throat where they'd forced the tube down. And the aching pain in her stomach. Glucose dripped intravenously into her arm, and the nightlight turned the ceiling a sick yellow color.

She'll come tomorrow and tell me how much she loves me, and look at me, all expectation, wanting me to respond to the magic formula. She says she loves me, and I'm supposed to turn into a good little princess. Leave me alone! I didn't ask you to make me, didn't ask to get born. So why should I love you just because you look at me the way you do and hope I will, expecting me to?

Groggy. The ceiling was starting to fuzz, to take new life, with strange pictures. Last time. Bailing me out of juvenile hall. Smart. No recriminations. No big affronted-parent number. Just "I'm sorry, Denny." Taking it all. Bend your back a little more, Mom, I've got these two fifty-pound bags I want to dump on top. Shit! I hate hospitals.

Forever fussing over low-grade accomplishments, making it such a big-deal thing! If I laid open my head and put down a few thoughts, you'd snap out. Because it's some kind of game. Just 'cause you haven't done your number—your big major number—on me yet doesn't mean you haven't got it there, saving it. All the same, all of them. Mothers. Granny Gary was just as half-assed about the whole thing when she was still alive. Making out like "dear Isabel" was like some kind of grafted leftover from poor dear Howard, her *baby*. And Mom playing it all kindness and patience. "She's old, Denny. She hasn't anyone else." Good old Mom.

You'll come tomorrow and lay your love down like a blanket, making me too hot with it all, smothering me.

Hate hospitals.

Denny, you know you're full of it? That fucking little-kid voice. Shut the fuck up! Shut yourself up, moron! You just can't wait for her to get here so you can check out the damage. Pretend you're suffering when she puts her arms around you. When—you're such a godamned liar!—you know damned well if she didn't come you'd freak right out of your stinking skull.

You'd just better *be* here.

Tears collected in the corners of her eyes, and she let them, continuing to stare—unblinking now, as the sedative crawled through her system—at the shimmering ceiling. Mama! Tears, rolling down the sides of her head. So that they dried on her face, leaving minute snail's tracings on her temples.

Two

She insisted on going to the hospital alone. Marshall prepared breakfast, stood over her to make sure she ate it, then kissed her good-bye. At nine-fifteen he telephoned his office to explain the situation. And said he might stay out as long as a week or two.

That done, he went upstairs to tidy the bedroom, pausing beside the bed, hearing her whispering, "Just *do* it!" Bewildering, alarming. She'd slipped to some sort of primitive level where niceties, preliminaries, failed to exist. But perhaps, he thought, it's just that animal pain requires animal remedies. Whatever the reason, he was bothered by the coldness of last night's connection. Through the things she hadn't said and hadn't done, he'd received the decided impression she'd been expecting him to say and do certain things he'd failed completely to realize. The truth was, he hadn't, then or now, any idea what needed doing or saying.

He sat down on the side of the unmade bed, his hand on her pillow. One long strand of her hair lay coiled like a question mark in the indentation where her head had lain. He sank down, pressing his face into the pillow, breathing in her scent, the illusion of her warmth. He was very distressed.

She was moving away from him. He could feel it. Less than two years at the station, and already she was appearing on television. He couldn't see how that had managed to happen. Without thinking, he got up and turned on the little portable set, watching the picture take focus; sitting back down in numbed surprise. She was there, talking to some woman. He upped the volume, his heart racing, realizing it was a rerun of a show she'd done at some earlier point in the past two weeks.

But look at her, listen to her! Her voice, her face, her gestures. Real. He could feel how real she was.

"How do you feel about women's lib?" she asked the woman. "Do you think perhaps organized groups are applying too much pressure to the individual?"

The woman answering. But see Isabel's eyes.

He turned down the volume and sat watching her, stricken when she turned at last to smile into the camera. And then vanished. Her image replaced by the craggy, grinning face of a man whose head seemed to be too large for his body. A man whose whitely capped grin was somehow—indescribably so—repellent.

He switched off the set, then once more returned his face to her pillow, where he remained for quite some time. He had the frightening feeling he'd accidentally triggered some extraordinarily potent weapon—done it by eagerly encouraging her to go out, go to school, put her intelligence and energy to worthwhile use—and now, powerless, he was going to have to sit by and witness the ensuing explosion. There was no way to hurry backward and deactivate the thing.

At length he got up, squared his shoulders, made the bed, tidied the room, and went downstairs to make some more telephone calls on his credit card. They'd never be able to get married now. And it had seemed the perfect time, a time when she needed someone stronger to help her through; assist with that wild-haired, wild-mouthed delinquent. He felt unutterably let down, disappointed, as if he'd lost something crucial to the continuation of his life. And he experienced a brief, but seismic desire to do away with Denise. Erase her, obliterate her. But even as it swept over him and on past, he knew it was only partially Denise. The rest of it was Isabel. And her face, her voice coming out at him from that small screen.

She drove along to the hospital, thinking about how tired she felt and about the way Marshall had taken her so close to sleep, then entirely destroyed her ability to get to sleep. His reaction to what was happening was diametrically opposed to what she'd have hoped for. She had, until last night, found his sensitivity to be his most appealing quality. Suddenly it was gone. Quoting lines at her from obscure Irish poets, talking clichés about two being stronger than one, when none of that was what she needed or wanted. And what was happening to her? All at once she couldn't bear his grabbing for her hands every few minutes. She'd set up a quota of interior demands, none of which he was satisfying. She'd have to work at maintaining some sense of proportions, of reality. If he was suddenly failing to live up to her expectations, maybe it was because her entire perspective had been—again, again—sharply altered. Denny had dragged her out of romance into drama, and she seemed unable to reconcile the lack of boundary between the two. While Marsh seemed completely unaware of any transition having been made.

She parked the car and entered the hospital, going along the now busy corridors, past West Indian cleaning ladies lyrically murmuring to each other over their buckets, past scurrying nurses and interns, to the coffee shop.

She sat down at a table with a cup of coffee, staring at the smeary surface of the chipped formica-topped table, her thoughts traveling backward again.

She hadn't been afraid at first. But in those random lucid seconds after the contractions peaked, she could tell—even though he said nothing—that Howard was becoming alarmed. And angry. When the obstetrician arrived, Howard took him out to the corridor. And their voices had drifted back in to her, mingling with her counting, the breathing. Howard's voice abnormally high, taut with nervousness. The doctor's voice low, placating. And with a look of grim resignation on his face, Howard returned to the labor room, resumed holding her hand. His vigil. Yet his eyes strayed repeatedly to the door. Hours. She hadn't had any idea how long it was lasting. But the thought was very clear in her mind that she was dying, would die. It was visible in Howard's eyes. No sense to it, no logic. But she was dying. Her pulse rate and blood pressure dropping steadily. Bleeding steadily. Her strength flowing away with the blood. And then, suddenly, her body had ceased resisting, and Denny had been born.

Those hours spent in labor lost their significance in the face of the baby's reality. She'd remained awake long enough to drink some juice and then to clasp Howard to her with trembling arms—exhaustion rattling her body like a chill—both of them laughing exultantly. "I was so worried," he'd admitted. "But I didn't want you to be scared, too."

Nevertheless, there were blood transfusions and two weeks' stay in the hospital and twice-monthly visits to the obstetrician for close to a year afterward. She'd arrived at the gate to death with all of her refusing to pass through. She refused to die. Suffered the endless internal examinations, the medications, the suspension of their sexual life for months, until told it was safe to resume. And there was Denny.

A pleasant, relatively uneventful childhood. They'd been very happy, a tight little unit, taking the baby with them almost everywhere they went. A laughing, greedily hungry baby who slept when she was supposed to and was content to play quietly in her crib in the mornings until Isabel or Howard awakened. All so easy. Years doing ordinary things, deriving pleasure from the simplest outings. A picnic in the park, visits to the zoo, drives in the country, an early dinner out somewhere. Easy. Too easy.

Denny was seven, and Howard was dying. They agreed, both of them at first reluctant to accept the diagnoses, to accept the inevitability of his death rather than grasp at the slim possibility of a hope for a cure. And spent their final months together exercising every ounce of their awareness of the aspects of their life they most valued. And it had been, except at the very last, a good end. A respectable death. With dignity and a minimum of ceremony.

Adamantly refusing to allow each other to nurture any false optimism or to harbor unstated anger, they'd seen it through. She'd grieved his death, his awesome absence from her life. But she'd believed, and still did, that they'd faced and met death naturally, realistically. Being firsthand witness to his destruction had been a harrowing and gruesome experience from which she'd suffered nightmares for years afterward. Nightmares primarily revolving around the last weeks, when he'd begun turning into a skeleton, when the air around him had started to reek, when he'd commenced claiming his right not to prolong the suffering.

In the aftermath, she decried the disease, the atrociousness of cancer. But not the death. She accepted the death. For her not to have accepted that as the final outcome would have meant additional pain she'd have been selfishly inflicting on Howard. And not only did he not deserve that, she couldn't have continued living knowing she'd actively contributed to his pain.

In the years following, she'd worked very hard not to neglect Denny or omit her from the memories. Denny was a part of Howard. Denny also had rights. And the right to display sorrow was one of those. Except that Denny didn't. She did, though, say several things—innocent remarks having to do with wondering where Daddy had gone and if he knew she was in grade three now—Isabel found heartrending and close to impossible to respond to. But she tried, responded, and did the best she could. It wasn't easy. Nothing was easy then.

Accepting the insurance money, the social-security benefits, was anything but easy. It seemed as if she was, in some macabre way, being paid off for Howard's death. But through Howard's attorney's patient explanations, she was able to gain a different, more rational understanding. Because she was now dependent upon that money. She needed it in order to live, in order to support Denny. And Howard had taken exceptional care with the arrangements of his estate, risking converting all his whole-life policies into higher-value term policies in order to provide a very large lump sum of money in the unlikely event of his sudden death.

She hadn't realized the extent of the damage to her own self until, several months after the funeral, an old college chum and ex-roommate of Howard's came to town and invited Isabel to go out to dinner, to talk. He came to the house to pick her up, and they sat in the living room talking—Denise being away for two weeks at summer camp, her choice—reminiscing, when Lew laid his hand on her arm to emphasize some point he was making. She responded to his hand on her arm as violently as she would have to an electrical shock. And understood she hadn't died with Howard after all.

There was a moment of mutually stunned silence. And then they were in each other's arms, kissing wildly. Lew had demonstrated commendable kindness and understanding, met her sudden dreadful need with just the right amount of abandon, and taken her upstairs to bed instead of out to dinner. To make love to her throughout the night, until, both exhausted, they said good-bye the next morning. And never saw each other again. Although his wife saw to it that Isabel remained on their Christmas-card list. Isabel sent cards in return. Once a year remembering, gratefully, his perception and the renewal of her own life.

Denny.

Without any warning or discussion, she stopped talking about her father altogether, making it appear as if she'd given up believing he'd ever existed. She also omitted all mention of death and dying, and never again was willing to talk openly about it. Until a few years earlier, when Judy's father underwent a lengthy, painful death and Jude came often to the house needing to talk out her reactions, her feelings. Her mother having died when she was eleven. And Denny and Denny's mother being the only people to whom she felt really close. Jude had talked quietly, calmly. Her voice losing its schoolgirl high-toned pitch, sinking permanently to an ear-pleasing contralto. And Denny had reacted to Jude's continuing narrative with surprising passion, profoundly shaken by this second confrontation with a prolonged death.

Because it had been so rare a display of Denny's usually buried feelings, her outburst at that time stayed in Isabel's mind. And she thought about it from time to time, forced over and over into wondering if the things that had gone wrong between them hadn't stemmed from omissions unknowingly made while Howard was dying. Because somewhere, *somewhere* along the line, the circuits had managed to get closed. And every time Isabel was obliged to chastise or reprimand Denise for some typically childish misdeed, she felt vaguely guilty for doing it. But it was useless trying to reason with a child who—at nine, ten, eleven—hadn't yet developed any talent for reasoning. A whack on the behind got the point across without undue pain, without undue loss of the child's dignity.

There had been, too, a few occasions when, driven frantic by Denny's stubbornly ceaseless demands for candies or something else she'd been told she couldn't have, and her refusal to quit, Isabel had responded with the only weapon instantly available: her superior strength. She would, at those times, take hold of Denny forcefully by the upper arms and literally throw her out of the room. At once, having done this, she'd feel horrible, knowing she'd accomplished nothing. She'd have succeeded only in sending Denise into a thumb-sucking pouting session and herself into a state of anger at herself for having been so easily manipulated. Because it was all manipulation in one way or another—demands for attention at the most inconvenient times, those times when it seemed Denise knew absolutely that an approach on her part would guarantee general pandemonium. Isabel would tell herself: I should know better, then calm herself down and go to sit with Denny to try to talk the whole matter out.

Like trying to squeeze a rock into a different shape with merely the strength of your fingers. Slowly, inch by agonized inch, Denny would allow her feelings to be drawn forth. And once her thoughts had been aired, she'd then be all hugs and smiles and promises. I'll be a good girl. Whereupon would follow several weeks of relative peace. Until the next episode. Each one worse than the one before. It seemed as if Denny had managed to locate all Isabel's most vulnerable spots and was determined to spend the rest of her life pressing and probing to see how high and how far her mother would jump.

The year Denny was eleven was a memorable one. Denny seemed to have given up her button-pushing and whining demands for things she didn't really want, and mother and daughter spent two weeks in June camping out at the side of a lake in Algonquin Park in Ontario. They'd slept together in the rear of the old station wagon, cooked over a small spirit stove, and swam together in the breath-stoppingly cold, pure water of the lake. They'd hiked through the park, gone canoeing on the lake, and returned home promising each other they'd do it again the following year.

But by the end of that year, Denny had changed again. She suddenly started growing in all directions at once. She shot up to five-eight, grew breasts almost overnight, developed a truly lamentable case of acne, began menstruating, and refused to leave the house except when she absolutely had to. She played truant with such manic regularity, the school principal threw up her hands and stopped requiring notes from Isabel. It was a pointless exercise. Denny was positively masterful at forging them, had notes covering every conceivable disaster, from the hideous deaths of fabricated relatives to extended trips to New York. She spent her time upstairs in her room writing off for free samples of skin-care products advertised in *Glamour, Mademoiselle,* and *Seventeen.*

When asked where she spent all those illicitly acquired hours of freedom, Denny admitted to passing the majority of her time in downtown movie houses, frequently sitting through two and three showings of the same film. Isabel deprived her of pocket money. Denny didn't have quite enough courage to steal. So she started going back to school.

At twelve, she was the tallest girl in her class and one of the youngest. By the time she turned thirteen—having abandoned all hope and given up writing for free samples—she was morbidly self-conscious, overweight, argumentative, sloppy, and disgusting in her personal habits. Isabel was forced to sneak into her room at night to collect Denny's dirty clothes. Otherwise, Denny would go on wearing them until they were filthy and stinking. Isabel was sickened by the condition of Denny's underwear—swore under her breath finding repeatedly worn, heavily stained pairs of pants shoved into the corners of dresser drawers or tossed under the bed—but tried not to go overboard reacting, gritting her teeth as she dumped Denny's clothes into the washing machine to do a double-soak cycle.

At fourteen, all at once acutely boy-conscious, she asked to go to a dermatologist, took an overwhelming interest in clothes, and began bathing and changing her underwear with that same manic regularity she'd previously applied to school-skipping. Boys began calling and appearing at the house by the carload. Isabel didn't know whether to be pleased or further frightened, so held her reactions in abeyance. Waiting to see.

By the time she was fifteen, Denny's face had cleared almost completely. She took to using dark blue eyeshadow and gooey-looking mascara to emphasize her eyes, glossing up her mouth so that it invariably looked sticky, and began staying out later and later on her frequent dates. In secret, she took herself off to a family-planning clinic and obtained a prescription for birth-control pills. Isabel accidently discovered a half-used packet of the pills in Denny's top drawer and guiltily put them back precisely where she'd found them before taking herself downstairs for a stiff drink and a close examination of her feelings.

The fact that Denny had the pills and was taking them didn't necessarily mean she was actively engaged in sexual endeavors. But it certainly meant she was very obviously aware of the possibilities and considering them seriously. Isabel was both upset and reassured. If nothing else, at least Denny was using her common sense. The idea, however, of her fifteen-year-old daughter out making love on these dates she accepted so blithely wasn't exactly thrilling. It wasn't easy to face the probability that Denise had chosen to surrender her virginity, but Isabel had no alternatives. She did wish that Denny would come forward and talk about it. Because there was no way on earth Isabel could talk about what she'd discovered without having Denny bombard her with accusations for snooping, prying. "I've got no goddamned privacy!" Denny complained regularly. Denise never mentioned the pills. Isabel felt aged by at least ten years.

That same year, having realized she was nearly as tall as her mother and certainly bigger, Denise decided it was her prerogative to speak her mind on anything and everything. Beginning by informing Isabel that she'd figured Isabel would find the pills. And she hadn't bothered hiding them, because she'd *wanted* them found. "Don't go out of your gourd," Denny said calmly. "I knew all about all of it two years ago." Then she watched Isabel's face to see how that registered. When she failed to get the exterior response she'd hoped for, she redirected her attack. To criticizing anything and everything. Being typically hypocritical for her age, she denounced Isabel's skimpy social life and the men she dated, making almost unbearably accurate yet scathingly lewd assessments of their sexual potential. On those occasions when Isabel had a few people in to dinner and the conversations got a little loud or the music and dancing a little frenzied, Denny would make a point of calling down the stairs in a voice laden with derision and sorely tried patience, "Would you *mind* not making so much noise? I'm *trying* to study." The sort of nasty, condescending little remark tossed like a grenade into the stairwell, sure to put Isabel into a temper. But Isabel refused to rise. She'd gaily call back up the stairs advising Denny to close her bedroom door if she was bothered by the noise. And then she'd return to her guests. But there was a war going on in the house.

Denny reciprocated by going off for a ride with a bunch of "the gang," and found herself handed off to juvenile hall, arrested for being in a stolen vehicle. Isabel went down, heard Denny reprimanded by a kindhearted judge, who, offended and alarmed by Denny's animosity, made her probation contingent on regular visits to a child psychiatrist. Terrorized, Denny kept the first few appointments, then uncharacteristically, pleaded to get out of the visits. Isabel took a trip to see the doctor herself, listened to him diagnose Denise as "suffering nothing more severe than acute growing pains," accepted his decision that he could offer her little if any help, and returned home to tell Denise she was out of it. Two months of quiet in the house was Isabel's reward.

That year was definitely the worst. Denny went back to demanding things she knew she couldn't have, wouldn't get. A car. A trip to Europe. Clothes. A horse, of all things, when she couldn't even ride. One after another, demands. Making Isabel feel even guiltier than ever.

Isabel had, shortly after Howard's death, returned to school, taking afternoon classes at the university, working toward her degree. But abandoned her efforts when life with Denny became gradually more emotionally charged. She simply couldn't handle both Denny and her studies. So the studies went. Until Marshall happened along. Denise took one look at him the first time he came to the house, made a disgusted face, and said, "Anybody ever tell you you've got really *sad* taste in men?"

Denise turned seventeen and lost some of her tendency toward icy criticisms, offered occasional perceptive comments about general affairs and certain political issues, took up with a junior at the university with whom she declared she was having a very "meaningful" relationship. It lasted for three months. And then the junior was gone and she was once more accepting dates. She came and went as she chose, disregarding Isabel's quiet requests for her to come in at a decent hour. She never went so far as to stay out all night, but came infuriatingly close, and Isabel felt they'd finally lost all contact. Denny's only requests were for money now. Isabel doled out the dollars helplessly, wishing she knew how to find a route through to Denny.

After graduation—a minor miracle in itself, this accomplishment—too soon, Denny was gone. But at long last some sort of communication slowly began to develop, and Isabel was openly delighted every time Denny turned up unexpectedly at the house. They were learning to talk to each other, finding common ground. And then that something—that mysterious something—had happened, and Denny began rapidly sliding down and away into a state of mind and being Isabel couldn't begin to identify or comprehend. She was having a difficult enough time trying to adjust to her new career.

She glanced at her watch. Too early yet to go up.

Drugs. Do you take drugs, Denny? Obviously you must. Why? All so strange, hearing Judy talking about you "nodding out." And Blake. I must thank Blake. But what happened? Am I losing my mind? I don't understand any of this. Is it me you're trying to hurt, Denny, or yourself? Will it turn out to be an entire lifetime of screaming alarms that send me leaping out of bed in the middle of the night? For the first time in such a long while, I'm doing something that has meaning for me, working, enjoying it. Do you sense these things from the distance and do a war dance while you think up something new and more self-destructive than the last time?

How on earth could I get married to Marshall? How could he think of something like that at a time like this? Maybe he thinks an offer of marriage constitutes a show of good faith in a critical time. Critical. I don't want this to be happening. I feel as if I'm getting too old to keep on coping. Denny.

Have I been a fool, done everything wrong with you? I've tried to do my best. But being a mother isn't a child's storybook. It's so difficult. So much easier handling other people's children, because you know whatever faults and problems they have are through no omission you've made, no fault of your own. And they go home after a while. They don't stay. You're not compelled to suffer through their agonies of puberty and growth.

You think I don't know, but I know how you felt being the tallest, the youngest. Did it never occur to you, did I never tell you, I went through all of it just the same? It's why I never did confront you with those pills, never waved your foul underwear in your face, never insisted your performance be to my specifications. I was there, willing to listen, to try to understand. But you've taken and taken, always grudging with your affections, refusing even to admit those feelings existed. I want to believe, have for so long, that one day you'll see me as a friend, someone who loves you; not someone you believe was designed specifically for your torture. I know that feeling. I felt that way about my own mother. The criticism, the disgust seeing the mistakes she made. Both of them. My mother and father. Just people. And not the shining wonder-people the child me had thought them to be. I'm just me, Denny; someone who's tried to the very limits of my ability to be sincerely good for you, helpful to you. Am I blind, deficient? What *is* a mother, after all? What? Someone who cares even when the child makes caring an obstacle course. Very little of it's been the way I expected it to be, Denny. I'm as disenchanted with the experience as you are with me. I've watched you holding yourself farther and farther away from me through the years, and despaired. Having you blame me for all sorts of things without bothering even to enlighten me as to what those things might be. Never able to defend myself, justify my actions, or even talk to you, because you've held your hurts, your antagonism up in front of your face the way you used to hide behind your tattered bunny as a little girl, so that there was no way I could get close enough to whisper it away, kiss it better, hug away the bad dreams.

I knew. I've never pretended you were happy. I gave you eight solid years of my sole undivided attention. And it all turned stale, yellow at the edges, because you've gone on refusing to come forward, to take even half a step toward an understanding. Did I do this to you? Was it Howard's death? Do you blame me in some way for the loss of him? Had I had the choice, I would have kept him. But there were no choices then. There are none now.

The logical, reasoning part of my brain insists there was never anything more I could have done for you, Denise. But the illogical, unreasoning, always-loving other part of me goes on feeling guilty, convinced there's been a way all along but I've simply failed to find it.

She looked again at her watch. Her heart lurched. Time to go up.

I'm afraid ... I'm so afraid. Get well, Denny. I don't want to lose you. Find yourself. I want a chance to know you.

Her insides quivering, quaking, she pushed her chair away from the table and got up to go. She felt so suddenly dizzy, the room seemed to tilt, the walls rushing away from her. Fortunately, the sensation lasted only a moment, and then everything settled. The walls returned to where they were supposed to be, the floor was once more level beneath her feet. Tired. She hadn't slept at all, but had stayed awake beside Marshall's sleeping form thinking about that ludicrous first meeting in the parking lot.

All those years. Of men. She'd given herself, after Lew; mortified by the mechanics, unable to feel. Occasionally responding with an orgasm because it had been there inside her waiting through a dozen prior unsuccessful encounters, and the next one to come along activated the system, released the catch, and she fired. But no feeling, no emotional involvement. A sort of sad sisterly/motherly affection for those men

with their obvious eagerness for her body, her face. But no
real desire to find out if there was anyone living behind that
face, inside the body. Searching only for the unconstrained
availability of her breasts—their faces going soft, their
mouths hungry for her breasts—the access to the interior of
her body. She'd always despised the social standards that early
on established her as being more than pretty. And wished
she'd been born less pretty, less appealing. Just to have it end.
To see an end to the parade of men all determined to unbind
her breasts, unlock her thighs. Until Marshall.

Everything had fallen so neatly into place. He claimed to
see the person in her, demonstrated recognition. And she'd
wanted so much to care about someone again. He told her,
"There's something about you. I saw it as I was driving out
of the lot. It was as if you were walking inside a bubble of
bright light. Or an aura. I can't explain it, really. But I had to
stop you, try to talk to you. And when I got up close enough
to really see you, it was almost a shock seeing your face. Because I hadn't been thinking about how you looked so much
as how you *felt* to me."

How unusual, she'd thought then, hearing him say all this.
Someone whose eyes were open, who was using them for more
than a direct hotline to his genitals. She'd listened to him talk,
and felt more relaxed all at once than she had in years.

That second evening, she'd been there too early, so anxious to find out if the feeling would be the same. And it had
been. They hadn't even finished their drinks, but had gone
directly out to his car. And she'd rested her head on his
shoulder while he drove, allowing herself the rare luxury of
trusting the direction, the control to someone else; not having to be responsible for her own safety or making the decisions for just a few blessed minutes.

They'd undressed in his bedroom, and she'd started to go
into the bathroom, but he'd asked her not to.

"I'm not peculiar," he said. "Nothing like that. I just want
you to be the way you are right now. I want us both to be as
we are. Can you understand that? Nothing manufactured or
deodorized, sanitized out of recognizability."

This had rocked her. Because for all those years she'd been availing herself of soap and water whenever possible, or in advance of an evening's encounter, in order to submit herself anonymously. But here was Marshall claiming he was prepared to seek out her identity not only through her words but her body as well.

Uncertain and detached, she'd watched him put his hands to her body, watched him breathe her in and take her from the tips of his fingers, declaring he wanted her exactly as she was, loved her precisely the way she was. Her detachment and uncertainty dissolved, and for the first time since Howard, she was able to slip inside someone else's feelings as well as her own and dispense with the protective passivity that had been her armor for so long. Her disappointment in his lack of skill didn't matter. She could guide and instruct and allow Marshall to make an impression upon her senses, because her needs had built to a point where they'd been threatening to topple and suffocate her. And Marshall had displayed such an intense interest in her psyche and its well-being. How, now, in the course of one night, had they managed to move so far apart?

No. He loves me. I'm expecting too much of him, asking too much right now. I love him. Perhaps I should have asked him to come with me this morning. No. I couldn't handle that right now. The very idea of him at this moment bothers me, makes my jaw ache. Angry. Calling me "Star." It's a job. A job that pleases me. I don't denigrate your planet-saving project, Marsh. Stop! I'm overreacting, tired. How do I handle this?

They took away the glucose drip and told her she could get up and go to the john, have a shower if she wanted to. She sat on the toilet, suddenly very dizzy, and couldn't get up for a while. So quiet in there, the nurse yanked the door open, asking "You all right?" All the blood rushed up into her face, feeling like such a fucking moron, no goddamned privacy anywhere, people marching right in on you, even when you were sitting on the stinking john. "I'm fine," she answered, and the nurse went away, closed the door. But now she couldn't go, and was hurting, trying to force herself. So she took off the scratchy hospital gown and took a long shower, using the crummy hospital soap to shampoo her hair. But feeling better after that she put the gown back on and got into the freshly made bed. Gagged over the breakfast tray, and they had to take it away.

Then the shrink came. One of the low-key, soft-spoken types. A dude who liked to peer earnestly into your eyes while he asked his bullshit questions. As if, if you didn't say what he wanted to hear, he might see it go across the bottom of your eyes like a message flashed across the tube in the middle of some program. Storm warning. Or: Special announcement. He went away finally, heavily bugged by his lack of success.

People. One after the other. Coming around. Gray Ladies to offer library books or magazines. Or maybe you'd like to buy a little needlepoint kit to keep your mind off the fact that you nearly made it over to the dark side on a couple too many of those little white jobbies.

She's coming. She'll be here. She'll come in with apologies written all over her face, all tucked up in her long, hesitant hands. If you could just once see me instead of looking and seeing what you want to see instead of what's real, what's me. We can't talk. If I talked, I'd break you into little bits with all the words... I don't even know what I'd say, and you already see me—it's just that I can't show you the me I want you to see.

I hate hospitals! God! The stink of this place. You could die in a place like this, even if you weren't sick but just visiting. It's getting late. Where *is* she? Probably with that moron Marshall. Or into her new gig. Jesus, was *that* ever some trip! Walking past a goddamn TV and appliance store, and there she is rapping away with some lard-head chauvinist, laying down her points. My heart turned right over. And for a minute there, like some dumb "Hey look at me!" number, I had this big thing inside my head about stopping people in the street and saying: What the hell! What d'you think of that? That's my mother! Yeah, that's right! Right there on the tube, yakking it up with that nerd. Can you feature that? My god-damned *mother*.

Where is she?

Three

A wall of interns and doctors barred her view. The voice of one of the doctors reciting information about this "case," the treatment. Isabel stood in the doorway, seeing Denny's feet moving impatiently beneath the blankets. Denny wasn't liking this. Isabel took shallow breaths, holding herself together, tensely prepared for the group of people to move on, continue their morning rounds elsewhere.

The bodies separated, people moved out of the small room, and Isabel stood at the foot of the bed. Denny's face, eyes angry. Always angry. What do you want, Denny? Ask me, tell me. I'm a reasonable person. I don't demand miracles. Just something small. Some recognition? I was so like you, Denny. There's such a lot we have in common. We both tossed over religion. What was it Marshall said about religion? Absurd answers to profound questions. Do I believe that? I wish right now I believed in something uplifting, spiritual. But I can't believe in what I can't believe. When I was eight years old, I knew. Praying one night to God to give me a bicycle. And suddenly, hearing myself whispering, "Dear God, please give me a bicycle," I thought: This is silly. And saw that I was only praying to myself for cleverness, the cunning necessary to convince my parents how desperately I needed that bike. I somehow couldn't believe in that white-haired man in the sky with his hundred-thousand-pound book of deeds and misdeeds. I was disappointed and angry not to be able to believe then, because something inside me had very much liked the idea of being watched over, praised and rewarded for my good deeds. I'd be eight years old again now if I could believe, have something to assist me into believing in possibilities. But I can't now, at forty, believe in God or possibilities; not standing here faced with your anger, your indignation.

"How do you feel?" she asked, placing a smile on her mouth.

"Shitty," Denise answered, examining her mother's face, the smile.

Nothing's changed, Isabel thought. Tired, she sat down in the chair beside the bed. Denise turned slightly to look at her.

"What happened?" Isabel asked quietly, unbuttoning her coat.

Denise shrugged. You look tired, she thought. But even tired, you look like a face you see on the tube. Something about the way you look makes me so... What? I love your goddamned face. But you just make me feel so mad. I don't know. Shit! Her hands were suddenly sweaty. She wiped them on the blanket. Her stomach hurt.

Don't let this be another fruitless, frustrating confrontation, Isabel thought; another one where you sit barricaded by silence, refusing to volunteer anything at all; making me wring it out of you one word at a time. Everything I say probably serving only to send you deeper into the storeroom of your grievances. Like some beautiful miser, hoarding your complaints, checking off the rows and rows of them, anxious to be certain they're all there where they're supposed to be. Beautiful. How beautiful you are. The intensity of the pleasure I've always derived simply from the sight of you—ignoring the infuriating everyday bickerings—joy at the sight of you. Is that my vanity? Or is it aesthetic? Have those young men haunted you, tormented you, demanding you offer up your body, your beauty? Have you had any chance at all, taken any time to try to discover the self inside you, Denny? I'll go mad sitting here watching your eyes shifting away from mine, avoiding me, already wishing I'd go away. You've been losing weight. Much thinner. Mother love and home-cooked dinners. How do I get through the brick wall of your defenses?

Look at you, Denise thought, off on another guilt trip. *What did I do wrong?* Her interior voice mimicking: *How did I fail you?* I wish to Christ you'd stop all that shit. No, that's not true. Something in me really gets off on you doing it. And something else in me hates that part that gets off on it. Shit! I'm probably psycho. But if only we could just say the real stuff to each other . . . I know, I know. It's my fault we can't. Why can't I just *stop?*

"Can we talk?" Isabel asked.

"Not if you're going to do your famous big number on how I'm wasting my life, my intelligence, my potential. No."

"I've never said anything like that to you."

"It's what you think, though."

"Is that what *you* think?" Isabel asked.

"It's what *you* think I think," Denny countered. Look! Here we go, doing it to each other again. "I caught your act on the tube," she said, remembering, turning a little more toward her mother. "How'd you manage that number?"

"I'm not really sure," Isabel answered truthfully. "But I'm liking it. It means something to me."

"I could *tell* that," Denny said, her words delicately underscored with the faintest sarcasm. "You into some kind of star-type ego trip?"

"It's a job I like." Anger, like a needle, slowly piercing the base of her spine. She kept her voice carefully controlled. "What are you going to do now, Denise?"

"Do?" She looked slowly around the room, then let her eyes return to Isabel's face. "Get the fuck out of here for openers. I hate goddamned hospitals."

"And where will you go?"

"Well, I'm not coming home, that's for sure," Denny said quickly. "So forget that!" She saw it strike, registering in her mother's eyes, and felt at once both gratified and sorry. I don't really want to keep doing this to you, but I can't get myself to quit. Right now, I wish to Christ I could just quit. For the space of several seconds while she watched the hurt spreading over Isabel's eyes like a membrane, she wished they could all say the real things, the true things, and stop all this other stuff. She wished she could be little, starting all over again, a baby crawling up onto her mother's lap to hide her face against her mother's shoulder and feel the good feeling of strong arms protecting, comforting. I hate the way we are to each other. No, not the way you are to me. The way I am to you. I'm tired of being this way. I want to stop.

"They lay a lot of political shit on you on this gig?" Denny asked, curious about the inner workings, the kind of scene she was into at the station.

"Political political or inside political?" Isabel liked the question, relaxed somewhat.

"Inside stuff. I mean, you're not an actress or like that. Are they really coming on to you there? Mouthing off, handing down a lot of flak?"

"There's going to be some from Jerry Brenner, I think," Isabel said, putting into words what had previously only been a nagging sensation, doubt. "He doesn't like having to share the spotlight. He especially doesn't like having to share it with a woman."

"You'll handle it," Denny said ambiguously, so that Isabel wasn't sure of her intended meaning.

"I suppose I will."

"Yeah," Denny muttered, looking down at her hands. Got to stop biting my fucking fingernails! It's so gross. Thinking: You always handle everything. Isabel Gary, the Handler. Come on, handle me. Get the old adrenaline pumping, jump up out of that goddamned chair and surprise the hell out of me. You're coming home with me, and that's enough of this shit! Do that! I'd get off on seeing you do a number like that.

"Denny"—Isabel drew Denny's eyes back to her—"just until you're feeling a little stronger..."

"No way!" Denny said sharply. "I'm not... Oh, *shit!*"

Marshall had appeared in the doorway. Isabel turned and stood up abruptly, her coat and handbag sliding to the floor, her eyes large, very dark. *I told you not to come here!* she silently screamed at him as he came around the side of the bed to stand beside her, looking at Denny, taking hold of her hand. Isabel wanted to strike him, knock him down; felt she could, the intensity of her anger giving her the illusion of superhuman strength. Anger that could kill. Because she and Denise had been creeping toward a small communication, and he'd arrived in time to ax-murder it.

"How are you?" he asked Denise, who rolled her eyes at the ceiling, looking agonized.

"Get him out of here, will you?" she asked Isabel, keeping her eyes fixed on the ceiling.

"I see you're your usual eminently lovable self," Marshall observed.

"Marshall!" Isabel was staggered by what appeared to be the complete loss of his prior sensitivity. Or did he reserve that only for people he wanted to win over? "Please wait outside. I'll be out in a few minutes. Please!"

"I'll wait outside," he said as Isabel impatiently twisted her hand out of his. He looked at her meaningfully—she hadn't any idea what the look was supposed to convey—and went out.

"Why the *fuck* did you bring that moronic turkey here?" Denny demanded, irate. "What's the matter with you, for crissake? Can't you do a goddamned thing without that *fool?*"

"Denise, I'm sorry. I didn't know he was going to come here," she apologized, as angry as Denny, for almost the identical reasons. They'd been so close to it, and he'd destroyed the opportunity for them to meet.

"Don't you have to go to work or something?" Denny's eyes were on the window.

"We have to talk." Isabel touched Denny's arm lightly. "We've got to. I'll come back later, this evening. We'll talk."

"D'you have any cigarettes?" Denny asked, looking at Isabel's handbag. "My stuff got ripped off or something."

"I'll leave you some money," Isabel said, feeling dejected, knowing she'd been dismissed. Marshall had totally destroyed the mood. She took a ten-dollar bill from her wallet and pressed it into Denny's reluctant hand. Leaning across the bed, she extended her hand, turning Denny's face to her. "Denny?" Isabel whispered. Denny's eyes slid slowly around to meet hers. Flickering with resentment and childlike misery. "I don't want to lose you. Feel whatever way you like about me, but don't die to make a point. I'll be back later, and we'll talk. I am sorry about Marshall. He hadn't any right to speak to you that way."

Denny's eyes widened, then narrowed as Isabel kissed her forehead, then once again scanned the depths of Denny's eyes before gathering up her coat and bag and leaving. Denny watched her go with a constricted feeling in her chest, her throat. She heard her mother's and Marshall's voices in the corridor, and the constriction turned to anger. She wrenched open the drawer to the bedside table, dropped in the money, then slammed the drawer as hard as she could. Wishing Marshall would drop dead out there. How could she *ball* a moron like that? How could she even let that creep put his hands on her? She wanted to take her mother by the shoulders and shake and shake her. Could see herself doing it, hear herself shouting: Don't you know *anything?* Don't you know that creep's a parasite, a bloodsucker? *Mother!* That guy's *nothing!* You don't need a shiteater like that. Christ! He probably doesn't even know where to put it. Goddamn damn damn....

"I said I'd come *alone!*" she said, walking rapidly down the corridor, battling down what looked as if it might blossom into full-scale outrage. "And how *dare* you speak to her that way! This is a *hospital!* Denise had been *ill!* My God! What were you thinking of?"

"Take it easy," he said. He assumed she was simply redirecting her anger with Denise to him.

"I don't know what to do," she said, fastening her coat. "What should I *do?*" she asked the air, pushing through it. Even the air felt heavy.

"I don't know," he said, feeling inadequate; hating it.

She bit back the words rising into her mouth. Words about respect and privacy. Words that sounded ominously like Dennyisms. She was so tired, she couldn't stop trembling, and yet so strangely energized that her mind was flashing and ticking like a computer. She thought of the station, work, preparation for the week's shows.

"I think it might be a good idea if you tried to get some rest this afternoon," he said, taking her arm. "You're exhausted."

She shook off his hand. "I am. Yes," she agreed. Tired of you, suddenly. And victimized by my anger. Raging anger. At least she'd have fifteen minutes to herself in the privacy of her car, driving home. Fifteen minutes in which to think.

"I'm going to see Mrs. Gary, talk to her," Jude was saying, sitting cross-legged on Blake's bedroom floor, chewing on the side of her thumb. "I mean, I know Denny won't talk to her, and she'll want to talk to someone."

"I don't see that," Blake said doubtfully. "I don't see it'll do any good, probably getting her more worked up than she already is."

"Denny's my *friend,* man. So's her mother. It bothers me this happened. It *has* to bother Mrs. Gary. It seems to me it's only... I don't know. If it was me, and Den was my kid, if I couldn't talk to Den, I'd want to talk to someone who could like relate to what was going on."

"I think you'll just be sending her on a big downer, Jude. I mean it. And I'm not with you. It's Den's business, not her mother's. You're wrong. I think you're way out of line, interfering."

"I don't *believe* you!" she said, looking at him in surprise. "I thought you were the one who believes in playing it straight, doing it with truth, no cons or copouts. It is *not* interfering. You want to know *why?* I'll tell you this little story, okay? I'll tell you what kind of lady we're talking about here, okay?

"After my mom died, like maybe a couple of months later, I got this whole thing figured out how I could put the world back together again. What I'd do, I'd get my dad to marry Mrs. Gary, and then he'd be happy and I'd get a new mother and a sister, too. Everybody'd be happy. Beautiful. Perfect. So I went over there after school one day. Man, I remember this so totally! I can even remember the way the sun was shining in the kitchen, how really bright everything looked. Anyway, she gave me a glass of milk and some cookies. Den was out somewhere. At the library, I think. Somewhere. So, anyway, I was sitting there having my milk and an Oreo, and Mrs. Gary was sitting there with me at the table. Smiling. She always seemed so super nice to me, you know? And I figured she'd probably think the whole idea was just as neat as I did. So I started laying it on her about how if she and my dad got married he'd be happy and she'd be happy, I'd get a sister, Den would get a sister, and everything would be just perfect. She sat there and listened to every single dumbass word I had to say. And then you know what she said? She said, 'Thank you, Judy.' No talking down, none of that stuff. Said it was probably one of the nicest things she'd ever heard about, and how touched she was that I'd want her for my mother. A little bit about how marriages didn't get arranged quite the way I thought they did. But she said, 'No matter what happens, Judy, you can always come here. We'd always want you here.' That's all. No big fuss, no put-downs. Just thank you.

"I wanted that lady for my mother, man. No way it's interfering. No way. And anyway"—she lowered her voice—"I want to know how Den's doing today. I mean, God!" She shivered. "She could even have died or something, and I wouldn't know."

"If she'd died, you'd have heard," Blake said calmly. "You're dramatizing. And I'll tell you what else you're doing."

"What's that?"

"You're still trying to get that lady for your mother. Don't you think you're like a little old for that?"

"I think I'll just get my gear together and split," she said quietly, getting to her feet, looking around the room.

"How's that?" He looked stunned.

"I just found out I don't like you very much," she said, moving quickly, pushing half a dozen textbooks into her shoulder bag, making it enormous. "You like to talk big about a lot of things, but when it comes right down to it, you don't care too much about people caring."

"Where are you going?" he asked, confused.

"I don't know," she said, collecting her things hurriedly. "I'll know after I talk to Mrs. Gary."

"Don't do it," he warned. "You shouldn't mess into other people's problems."

"I thought I just explained to you how it's my problem too. You're scared to get involved," she said. "You don't even know Mrs. Gary. And I don't care what you think my motives are. She's the only person I've ever known that I've never heard talk down to anyone. Because she doesn't *think* down. Well," she said, her arms filled with clothes, giving the room another quick check, "I'll see you, huh?"

"You don't have to split, you know."

"No, I do. I don't much like where your head's at. But I'm glad you took care of Denny the way you did last night. Mrs. Gary said to thank you. That was good, Blake. The rest of it—your ideas, being scared of getting involved—that's all warped. You shouldn't be worried about that kind of stuff—staying safe, out of things. That's not where it's at. Where it's at is making some kind of real contact. I might actually be able to help Denny's mom. Fill the gap or something. There's nothing wrong with that. Maybe it's something I need too. It's not like it's a sin or something to want to help, to maybe make things a little better for somebody else. I thought we had some of that happening here. But we don't. I can see that now. So, I'll see you."

She carried her things out to the kitchen, unearthed a shopping bag, shoved everything into it, and went out.

It *is* right to be involved, show you care, she told herself, dumping the bag in the back of her VW. She felt a pang of guilt thinking about Blake having to bus it to work tonight. She shrugged. That's the way it goes, Blake.

She stopped at the doughnut shop to telephone Mrs. Gary.

"How's Denny? Did you see her? I thought if it was okay and you're not too busy, maybe I'd stop over for a little while to talk."

"We'll talk when you get here. How long will you be?"

"Twenty minutes?"

"That's fine. I'll see you then."

Jude hung up, listened for the dime to drop, and then, on impulse, bought a box of doughnuts to take along with her.

She sat for a long time staring at the doorway, chewing on her fingernails, while this crazy, heavy-duty need to move crept through her veins and arteries. The lunch tray was brought in and set in front of her. She looked under the lid at the pallid, gravy-drenched food on the plate, gagged, and replaced the lid. Pushed the tray table away from the bed and wrapped her arms around her bent knees, trying to think, trying to get it straight.

Why the *hell* had that fool, that moron, that pathetic fucking sadtimer had to show up? If he'd just stayed away— from both of them—everything might've been okay. She'd felt herself on the verge of giving in. And it hadn't been such a downer, either. A little more rapping, and she might've let herself be persuaded to come back to the house for a little while. She'd been thinking about it, about how maybe it wouldn't be so bad. Now that Mom had that incredible gig on *Mid-Morning* and was getting into some very interesting shit. But no. He had to go and push himself right into the middle. And what was *wrong* with her? How could she have let that zero get so far into the inside of her life? Couldn't she see what a positive nerd, what an absolute fucking zero, he was? She couldn't believe he'd lasted this long. Two years, for chrissake. Where's your head, lady? Don't you have eyes for *decent* dudes? Shit, that brings me down!

I've got to get out of here.

She looked at the closed closet door, at the door to her room, the door to the john. Doors. Just open one and walk through. Change the scene, change your head. What was there to stop her from getting dressed, just walking out? Nothing. She had the ten. That would get her... Where? Think! Lane. For a couple of days, until she could get her act together and decide. It wouldn't kill her for a couple of days.

She swung her legs over the side of the bed and stood up. Light-headed, weak. She had to put her hand on the bedside table to steady herself. Eyes closed, waiting for the balance to come back, feeling so goddamned *puny*. No way I'm going back to the house with that turkey there. Rather die first. Almost did die. That's heavy. Stinking stomach hurts, throat too. Kill you to get you better. I'm getting out of here. She counted to five, then opened her eyes and moved on strangely disembodied legs to the closet.

* * *

"Your lady friend's time of the month, sweetheart?" Jerry grinned.

Shove it up your ass, Brenner! "Her daughter's ill," Ash said without inflection.

"Listen, seriously..." Brenner moved conspiratorially closer. "She fuck ya for it? Spread it with promises?"

"Jerry," Ash said patiently, "could we just stick to business? I've got another meeting in twenty-five minutes, and we haven't finished the rundown for tomorrow's show."

"Big broads're always out for your balls. Ever notice that? It's the nice little ones want to rub your tummy and play nice. You've gotta watch out for the big ones. She'll be producing the show, next thing you know. Better keep your eyes open."

"How many minutes can we get out of this beauty queen, do you think?" Ash tapped the eraser end of his pencil on the desk.

"She better not fuck with me," Jerry said, losing his grin. "Aggressive, opinionated bitch."

"She's an intelligent, *dignified* woman who happens to have opinions. And you're wasting my time."

"Okay, Okay." Jerry pulled the page over in front of him.

The sight of Jude with her box of doughnuts stabbed through her. She opened her arms and held on to the girl as if this act might somehow bring her closer to Denny, nearer to an understanding. Holding Judy, she could pretend for a few seconds that life hadn't gone so far beyond her grasp finally, pretend Denny would be on her way in from the car, bringing the coffee. How many Sunday mornings had the two girls arrived that way, with coffee and doughnuts? Coming to sit over the Sunday papers and eat the breakfast Isabel prepared to go with the offerings they'd brought. And throughout the morning, the girls had laughed or talked or gone suddenly silent reading some article one had pointed out to the other. A burst of laughter. Or sudden, animated conversation. Isabel had enjoyed the one-day-a-week luxury of remaining in her dressing gown with her hair hanging uncombed, sitting with them and working at the crossword

puzzle, a cup of coffee beside her. Having them both there
had been so satisfying, had held such family feeling.

When had it stopped? Months. At least four months since
they'd come here together. Jude sometimes dropped in on her
own. But it wasn't the same. They both felt Denny's absence. Still, Jude's arrivals did bring a good measure of that
warm family feeling back. And just now, Jude's presence did
to some degree reduce the starkness of the past twenty-four
hours, relieve the weight of Denny's absence.

"I'll put on the coffee," Marshall said.

"Will you stay for dinner?" Isabel asked her, all at once
fervently wishing Marshall was on one of his three-week trips
to Europe or Uganda or Tasmania.

"Well, that's sort of what I wanted to talk to you about,"
Jude said.

"Let's go sit down."

"How's Denny?" Jude asked, as they settled themselves in
the living room; furious with herself for not putting Denny
first.

"All right," Isabel said, unable to put into words just how
Denny was. "I'll be talking to her again later, when I go back
after dinner."

"Oh." Jude nodded.

Isabel looked down at her hands. No rings. It was still
something of a shock after all these years to look down and
see her denuded fingers. The wedding and engagement rings
were upstairs in the top drawer of the dresser. She'd never
been quite certain what to do with them, had entertained the
vague notion of one day giving them to Denny.

"She's going to be okay, then?"

"She's going to be just the same as she's always been," Isabel said. Then stopped, hearing the bitterness in her voice
like an echo. "I'm sorry," she apologized. "It's the tiredness
talking. I'm tired."

Jude put her hand on Isabel's arm. "Why I came," she
said. "I was thinking. I mean, I don't know how you'd feel
about it, but I thought if I could, I'd stay and do the cleaning up, the cooking, and like that for a while. Or until Den
comes back. I'm still working Saturdays, Sundays, and

Thursday nights at the supermarket, so it's not as if I'd be around all the time getting in your way or anything like that. But I thought maybe we could like trade off, you know? I could do all the household stuff, and you wouldn't have to think about any of that or anything, and I'd have a place to stay... I mean..." All of a sudden, it felt weird what she was asking.

"You're welcome to stay here," Isabel said, fascinated by Jude's hand on her arm. So small and delicate, smooth and soft. "Have you had a falling-out with Blake?"

"A disagreement," Jude answered, thinking: If you were my mother, if you... I'd never want to leave here, leave you, never. How can Denny be the way she is with you? You're so... gentle. Hurtable. "The thing is, there's some stuff. About Denny, you know? I think maybe you really should know. That's what we disagreed about. But I think... I mean... It could help to get it all straightened out."

"What stuff?" Isabel asked, looking into Jude's eyes. She had the feeling she was about to have shattered the illusions she hadn't known she possessed. A terrible apprehension. She wanted to hear but didn't want to know.

"Blake said I shouldn't get involved, interfere. But it seems to me I'm already involved, so it isn't interfering."

"What stuff?"

"Well, like there's this guy."

Marshall came in and set down a tray bearing cups of coffee. He took a cup of coffee and sat down in the adjacent armchair, crossing his ankles. Was about to lift the cup to his mouth when he looked up, seeing Isabel and Judy both watching him.

"I've got a couple of calls to make," he said, getting up, carrying his coffee out to the kitchen. Thinking about the horrible sameness of these kids. All of them. This one wasn't any different from the other one.

Jude watched him go, thinking that, even trying to be fair, she could see what it was about him that turned Denny off so hard. He had positively no sense of timing.

"This guy," Isabel prompted, as if Marshall had never been there. She had an odd sensation in her lungs. If only everything would stop, just stop for a while. She needed time, more time.

"Lane," Jude said. "Lane something. I can't remember his last name. Lane what?" She shook her head. "Anyway," she went on, "he and Den were having this thing, you know?"

"Go on."

"Well, she moved over to this Lane's place. But it didn't last very long or something. I don't know. I heard a lot of different things."

"And?" Isabel asked, her voice wispy.

"Well, the thing is, everybody kind of knows Lane's a dealer. And a lot older. Like maybe thirty-five. I don't really know too much, except that I saw her one night a couple of months ago... oh, more than that, maybe four months ago, out at Nighthawkers', the bar, you know? Out on the old Shore road? Anyway, she was really down that night, looked just terrible. When I saw her, naturally I went over to talk to her. I was so glad to see her. Because she'd just moved out on me and Anne, and I was kind of worried about her. So I asked her how she was and like that, and she started telling me this big confusing story about how... God! I really don't want to bring you down telling you this. It's like I'm ratting on Den and doing a number on you, too. Maybe Blake was right. Maybe he was."

"It's all right," Isabel said. "Tell me."

"Well . . ."

"Go on," Isabel urged.

"From what I could make out," Jude said carefully, "she'd been hanging out with this guy before she met Lane, you know, and she got VD and had to do a number at the free clinic, getting shots or whatever, and giving out a list of her, um, contacts. She said Lane was going to throw her out and wouldn't give her her stuff. Something. Maybe I've got it wrong. She wasn't making a whole lot of sense. But the thing was, this Lane really bounced her around, I guess, for giving out his name and like where he was hanging out. And because of that, he had to move his whole gig to somewhere else. It really sounded like a big mess."

"What does he deal?" Isabel asked.

"Oh, anything, everything. I've only ever seen him this one time. He's a great big dude, wears these tacky silk suits and Italian shoes. And he'd got this whole gang of guys who travel around with him like bodyguards. They look like real motorcycle hoods."

"And that's where she's been staying, with this man?"

"As far as I know."

Isabel sat back, staring at Jude. Just staring. It gave Jude a rotten feeling.

She felt so tired, so paralytically tired, she didn't want to have to speak or react or think or feel. She couldn't. She heard Judy's words spinning around and around inside her head, and thought: I'm going to have to pretend I don't know about any of this when I talk to Denny tonight. More things we can't talk about. I can't think about this now. I can't.

"Thank you for telling me," she said. "I have to lie down for a while." With a deep sigh, she got up and went out of the room, upstairs, to lower herself on the bed, appreciative of the cool pillowcase against her hot face. I can't, she thought. I can't right now.

She was almost asleep when she remembered and lifted her head to call Marshall.

"What is it?" he said breathlessly, having torn up the stairs three at a time.

"Tell Jude she can move into the garage apartment. That way, she won't feel she's intruding, imposing."

"Okay," he said. "I'll tell her." He felt stupid, standing there watching her drop her head down on the pillow. Stupid because he'd thought she was calling him about something important. "I'll wake you when dinner's ready," he said, wanting to stay up here with her, to exchange confidences, talk intimately.

"Mmm," she murmured, her eyes already closed, so that he felt coldly left out.

He returned downstairs to the living room.

"Is she okay?" Jude asked anxiously.

"She said to tell you you can stay in the garage apartment. Need any help getting moved in?"

"No," Jude said. "Thank you. I've stayed there before."

"Oh? When was that?" He hadn't known that.

"Last year. I always sort of come here when things fall apart or go bust. Like home, you know?"

"Sure," he lied, not knowing at all. He wished she hadn't come, bringing her bad news. It had to have been bad. All of it was. Couldn't she see Isabel didn't need this? "How's school coming?" he asked, politely disinterested.

"Slowly," she replied. "I can't afford to take more than a few credits every semester. But maybe I'll be able to get a good job this summer to pay for a few more courses next year."

"Maybe," he agreed. And maybe, he thought, we'll all be somewhere else next year. Then, excusing himself to check on the food, he wondered why he'd thought that, why all his thoughts seemed to be turning so negative.

Six cameras. All on. The round red lights glowing with life while she stared and stared at the clipboard on her lap, at the list of prepared questions. Unable to read. Her mouth open, her features slowly turning pale under the heavy makeup. Pan-Cake. And thick bands of orangy-red slashed over her cheekbones. It was all melting, oozing down her face as she sat openmouthed trying to get her brain to begin working. Laughter. Jerry, beside her, had lit a cigarette and was sitting smirking at her, offering his favored profile and perfect teeth to the cameras. She couldn't speak, couldn't read, was dying a public death. And Denise was standing by the studio door, arms folded comfortably across her chest, a wicked beaming smile in possession of her mouth, as she, too, watched, enjoying the shameful spectacle.

Marshall lifted an escaped strand of hair away from her face and stroked her cheek. The sensation grated. She moved her head to escape it.

"Dinner," he said, sitting down on the side of the bed, waiting for her to surface. "Time to get up, Is."

Is. She hated that. She turned onto her side and opened her eyes, shoving the dream away from her. For a moment, Marshall looked like someone she'd never seen before. His face above hers was slightly asymmetrical, the right eye fractionally larger than the left, the right side of his mouth a little fuller than the left. There were discolored shadows beneath his eyes, the flesh there crinkled, crisscrossed with thousands of miscroscopic lines. His eyelashes a golden brown color, white at the tips, very straight, very long. She looked at his mouth again, noticing the pink of his lips—not really pink, but a color somewhere between pale pink and a light red-brown.

She wet her lips and blinked several times, swallowing, trying to bring herself back to reality. Why did everything look so distorted, misshapen?

"Jude's setting the table," he said, tracing her eyebrow with his thumb. That grated her too.

"Marsh, I know there's no reason for it now, but I'm afraid."

"That's understandable," he said, glad she was voicing her fears to him. It gave him some semblance of a feeling of control. "Kids're a scary business."

"You think so?" She turned over a little more to free her hand from beneath her. It was numb, sensationless from her having slept on it.

"The whole thing's scary," he said. "Drugs and overdosing. It's hard trying to make sense of things like that. And we always want to try to make sense of things so we can adapt to a situation. This is pretty damned hard to adapt to."

"Tell me why you think that." She wanted to keep him talking, hear someone else's reactions, thoughts.

"It's the sort of situation that's bound to make those involved feel . . . inadequate. Because there's no logical progression of actions. There's no logic, period. I think anybody faced with end results for which he can't provide causes feels minimized, ineffectual. Because no matter how hard you scramble mentally trying to come up with answers, there's almost no chance at all of satisfying that need to know."

What he was saying sounded nonsensical to her. Book-learned lessons that had no real-life application.

"I've thought about it," she said, hoping to soften her words by talking softly, touching his cheek. She felt a sudden terrible fondness for him. The way she'd once felt as a very small child about the old family dog, patting him, knowing he was going to get put to sleep. "There's no possible way I could even consider getting married at this time. There are just too many problems.''

"I guess you're right," he said, looking wounded. "It was reaction, I guess. I shouldn't have started blurting out the first things that popped into my head. But I did work out a few things this morning, and I'll be able to stick around for a couple of weeks. A month if I squeeze it. By then, things should be fairly well settled down, back to normal.''

"Perhaps they will," she said, astounded that he hadn't consulted with her on this decision. She wasn't at all sure she wanted to have him around for an entire month. Not sure she wanted him even for a week. Denise wouldn't come anywhere near the house as long as he was here. And she wanted Denny to be willing to try staying at home for a while.

"Once things do settle down," he went on, oblivious of her tightening features, "we can talk about getting married. In the meantime, I'll pick up a few more things from the apartment and stay right here with you."

She nodded, preoccupied, her mind on her pending visit to the hospital. Then, returning from that thought, thinking: What can I do? I can't tell him to take his love for me and pack it up with the rest of his things. It's too cruel, too sudden.

"Let's go down now," he said, encouraged by her silence. "You need to eat something."

"I'll be down in a few minutes," she said, trying to think what inducement she could offer Denny, what words, what incentive. What?

He went on down, and she got up and walked into the bathroom, her eyes bothered by the brightness of the light. She'd been intending to change the bulb to one of a lower wattage, but it was one of those things she'd been thinking of doing for ages but kept forgetting. So simple, really, to change a lightbulb. So why couldn't she hold the thought long enough to actually do it? How many other things needed doing that she kept on forgetting to remember?

Her skin felt strange to her fingers as she splashed cold water over her face. Her fingertips seemed to have become supersensitized, and she seemed able to feel every pore of her skin, the definition of the bones beneath. She dried her face, gazing at herself in the mirror, continuing to do so as she picked up the hairbrush and swept the hair back from her face, holding it at the nape of her neck with one hand while she reached for a narrow gold barrette with the other. Her eyes stayed on that face in the mirror. As if she'd become someone else and her eyes simply could not recognize the woman reflected.

How, she wondered, can you continue to do these ordinary things? Washing your face, brushing your hair, being neat, tidy. But what should I be doing? Life continues, and it's that that stuns me. How can I be here washing my face, brushing my hair, when my child almost died and now can't or won't talk to me? Has never talked to me. How do I save her? How do I save myself? It does no good at all reminding myself of all the other mothers, other daughters suffering similarly. No good. Because this is *my* situation, our situation, Denny's and mine, and I don't know how this happened or why things are the way they are, and hearing about other people's problems of a like nature does nothing to make me feel any better about mine. I don't *care* about mothers, other daughters. I care about this mother, my daughter.

The barrette in place, she dropped her arms, continuing to stare at herself in the mirror, but seeing Denny there now. In a smocked pinafore dress and new sandals, carrying a miniature handbag. All readiness. Where had they been going? We'd been on our way to somewhere. A summer morning. The air sweetly cool, billowing through the house, sending the curtains dancing, lifting the newspaper where it lay folded on the kitchen table. A moment of pure silence, touched only by the flittery-whisking sound of the newspaper. Howard coming into the kitchen. Not yet dressed. He was supposed to be dressed. *Howard!* She ached all over suddenly, remembering.

He was supposed to be dressed. But he was still in his robe, his face utterly without color, his hands clinging to the doorframe. He'd urinated blood. And been so alarmed at the sight of it, he'd forgotten himself, lost control. There was blood all over the floor. He was sorry, ashamed, frightened. And before she could be stopped, before we even realized where she was going, Denny was in our bathroom, gaping at the blood, nudging the toe of her sandal into the trickle making its way along the floor to the doorsill.

"Daddy doesn't feel well. Let's call up Auntie Sue and see if you can't go over and play with Leslie for a little while."

"But we're going to the zoo, and then we're having lunch out. At a restaurant. You *promised!*"

"I know we did, darling. I know that. And I'm very sorry. Truly sorry. But Daddy isn't feeling well, and we're going to have to go another time."

"*Why* isn't he feeling well?"

"Because he isn't."

"But you *promised!*"

She hadn't wanted to answer Denny's questions, try to explain. She'd wanted to hurry her out of the house, get her safely out of the way so she could telephone the doctor, get Howard attended to. And Sue, a nearby neighbor, had welcomed the opportunity to have Denny come and play with her daughter. Denny had burst into tears upon being deposited at Sue's front door, her face twisting miserably. Isabel had felt like a complete monster. But Sue had waved her away, saying, "You go on. She'll be all right," and had enticed Denny into the house with promises of stories and ice cream. Isabel raced home feeling cruel at having to do that to Denny, but so worried about Howard she couldn't stop to think further about Denny.

A week, and there was the prognosis: inoperable cancer. Terminal. Spread out through his kidneys, his bowels, and rapidly moving. But they'd given him treatments—chemical and radiation—to arrest the cancer's progress. A week. And their lives were upended, turned sideways, reversed. Nothing was the same. Nothing. Yet, there were the routines, the damnable routines. You got up every morning, went to bed every night, and in between, readied meals to be eaten, tended to your body's needs, and tried to move forward into the next day and the next. Because there wasn't anything else to do. Holding each other in the night with anguish leaking out of their eyes, out of their mouths, holding on. Because as long as there was breath in the body, as long as there were words and hands for holding on with, life continued. Life transformed into a nightmare of hospital visits, aborted outings with Denise, sudden terrifying attacks of infantlike weakness that put pinpoints of horror in Howard's eyes and sent fear—that it was too soon, that it was ending—rushing through her system like cold water being flushed through her bowels.

And what had it all done to Denny? She'd taken all of it as a full-scale planned rejection. "You don't love me anymore," she cried, rejecting comfort, rejecting explanations, rejecting embraces. And from that time to this, Isabel could count on the fingers of one hand the number of times Denny had allowed herself to be shown affection.

Just once, about six months ago—was it anything to do with her decision to move in with this Lane person?—Isabel had felt the beginnings of hope, finally close to being in touch with Denny.

She'd been home alone on a Saturday—Marshall being away for two weeks in England—when Denny had let herself in and dropped down on the sofa beside her mother with a sigh, lighting a cigarette.

"I guess," Denny said surprisingly, as if continuing a monologue Isabel had missed the start of, "I've always given you a rough time. I never could figure out how you could still keep on telling me you love me, putting up with all the crap I hand you."

"But I do love you," Isabel had said, with the tentative uneasy feeling that one false move would scare Denise away. "You're very important to me."

"Yeah, I know that. Sometimes, I just wonder why you bother. I'm not worth it."

"Yes, you are. I know how hard it is, Denny. I've been there. I do know."

"I get this feeling, you know, that my life just isn't going anywhere. This feeling like if I maybe stopped all the stuff I'm doing now and got my act together, I could put it all right. Things I could get into. Issues. Politics. Stuff that matters. *Doing* things. But then, when I think about all that, I just feel tired. Is there anything to eat?"

And that was the end of it. Two minutes. But it gave Isabel such hope. All the caring, the concern, hadn't been in vain. There were still opportunities for change, some hope.

Now, she thought, is this the way it's going to be forever? Up one minute, down the next? What am I supposed to do, write Denny off as some kind of perpetual ongoing accident and turn the feelings on when she happens to come around? I don't know how to make her not matter to me. I don't know how to relegate a child of mine to obscurity, discount her.

There's my job now, too. I have a career. Just. If I don't stay on top of everything, stay aware of what's going on at the station, I'll find myself back in production or even out altogether. Jerry. I'm going to have to watch him very carefully. He doesn't like me, doesn't like my having a segment of the show. He'll try to get rid of me. . . .

But why do I care? Maybe it would be better to be like Denise and just let things happen to you. Go along and let life carry you through, whichever way it wants to take you. But I *can't!* I want my daughter, my career, my life. Some peace.

At dinner, Jude asked if she might go with Isabel to the hospital. Isabel agreed. Marshall, excluded again and feeling the sting, asked casually, "Has anybody been around to where Denny was staying to pick up her things?"

"I don't know where she was staying," Jude said, embarrassed. Here she was supposedly Den's best friend, and she couldn't even say where Denny lived. "She never told me," she said.

"Someone must know," he said. "Why don't I take Jude around tomorrow, talk to a few people, see if we can't find out?"

Jude looked over at Isabel to see how she responded to that. The idea of going anywhere with Marsh gave Jude very bad vibes.

"Marshall," Isabel said levelly, "where do you think I'm going to be while you're out playing Sam Spade?"

Sensing instantly he'd again blundered, he said, "I assumed you'd be at the sta—"

"Stop, please, taking independent steps, Marshall," she said. "I am not an invalid. And certainly not in any way incapacitated. I intend to allow Denny the same privacy I always have. If she doesn't choose to tell me where she's staying, I've no intention of snooping around trying to find out behind her back. And she certainly wouldn't appreciate *your* doing it."

"I'm trying to help," he said, keeping his voice equally controlled.

"I know that. I do know that. I simply want you to keep in mind the fact that my faculties, as far as I know, are not impaired. I *know* you meant well. I *know* you thought you were being considerate. But we're talking about *my* daughter, *my* problem. I'm directly involved. You can't protect or shelter me because you might think I have enough to cope with or perhaps think I'm coping badly. Whatever. I don't happen to be in need of that. Do you understand?"

Jude slipped silently away from the table, out of the room.

"You're angry," Marshall stated. "Acting angrily, talking angrily."

"I'm *thinking* angrily."

"Not of me. Not with me. Being angry with me doesn't accomplish anything."

"Marshall!" she cried, losing her patience. "I'm only human. Stop expecting quite so much of me! This isn't a time when I have the time or the energy to stop and analyze how what I'm saying and doing is effecting you. I can't afford that right now. Aren't you big enough to take it? Can't you see the situation and go along with it without taking an arbitrary stance? Don't be hung up on the mistake of my face, Marshall. I'm not one of the beautiful dummies. I'm scared and I'm angry. I'm all kinds of things. So would you be if you'd spent more than eighteen years of your life worrying and watching and hoping and waiting with a child of your own, wondering every day of your life if you were doing the right things, making the right moves, or if you weren't maybe totally screwing up, doing everything absolutely wrong. Forget the way I *look* and what it is you want from me, and think about how I *feel!* My daughter nearly died! That *matters* to me, Marshall. I have to do what I can for her, help her. She's *important* to me! Think about that before you suggest taking any more unilateral steps that have to do with Denny's *life!*''

''Why direct this at me?'' he asked, red-faced.

''Oh, *Christ,* Marsh! Aren't you the one who's been talking nonstop about getting married? This sort of thing goes on in a full-time relationship, Marsh. It isn't all just highs, you know. It isn't all just cozy dinners and a lot of lovemaking.'' Her eyes held his for a moment longer; then she looked away.

''Okay,'' he said. ''Okay. I didn't know how you wanted to play it. So now I know. We all have different ways of handling things, you know.''

''I know that. And I'm touched by your wanting to be here. But . . . Never mind. I'm sorry I shrieked at you.''

''We're both sorry. We'd better get going. Do you want me to drive?''

She looked at him again piercingly, thinking: What's the *matter* with you? ''I'd prefer you didn't come. It would only upset Denny, and I think she's upset enough. But,'' she went on, ''if you *were* coming, I might like having you drive. The point I'm trying to make, Marsh, is you've got to remember that *I* know how to drive. Do you see what I'm getting at?''

''I got it the first time around. You're jumping on everything I say.''

''Try to understand,'' she said, exasperated but keeping a lid on it. ''I'm not suddenly crippled because Denny's managed to get herself in trouble again. I wasn't the last time, and I won't be the next time.''

She was right. He'd been wrong. But he still couldn't help feeling hurt by the way she'd attacked what he'd considered innocent remarks. He reminded himself of the strain, the pressures on her. But he still felt hurt. And knew that no matter what he said, it would only serve to make matters worse between them. So, obviously, the sensible thing to do would be to forget the incident, put it out of his mind. Not easily done, though. Because it was the first time in two years that he felt they'd failed to understand each other. He felt frustrated. He'd displayed good intentions, and she'd interpreted them as being designed to exclude her. When the truth was, he was the one being excluded. And all he'd wanted to do was make things easier, a little less difficult for her. It'd blown up. Right in his face.

Trying to help when he didn't even like the kid.

He sat trying to sort everything out in his mind, telling himself Isabel was behaving the way she was because she was being forced by Denise and her actions to exist under tremendous pressure. She wasn't usually defensive, angry, hypersensitive. She was angry, admitted to that. But would I be? he asked himself. Would I take it out on everyone around me? Maybe.

I'm reacting childishly, he chided himself, glancing across at Isabel's set profile, at once softened by the sight of her. Even with her hair pulled back severely, without makeup, she was beautiful. He saw her face again coming out at him from the screen of the TV set and felt a thrill of desire for her.

Forget the way I *look* and think about how I *feel!* The way you look has to do with the way I feel about you. I can't separate you into sections and react to a program. I love all of you, and your beauty is part of that. Am I supposed to become suddenly unable to see you, and focus solely on your emotional identity? Or your intellectual one? I'm not sure I know specifically what those aspects of you are. I feel the way I do because of ... You're asking me something that's impossible. Forget the way you look. How? You're a beautiful woman. Am I supposed to just go blind suddenly?

Denise. Surly, unpleasant kid. I can't even force myself to feel sorry she got herself into this. If she was a kid of mine, what I would've done years ago, I'd have put her over my knee and whaled the living daylights out of her. Spoiled rotten. How the hell could anybody love a kid like that? So damned surly. *Get him out of here!* Who the hell does she think she is? Snotty kid.

Your feelings are hurt, Isabel thought, accurately reading his look of thoughtful concentration. I'm sorry for that. I don't think you deserve to be hurt. But you've got to understand that passivity on my part right now would be some sort of prelude to my death. I can't allow myself to stop functioning, turn myself over to you like some brainless, useless dish-

rag. That's death. And I don't want to die yet. I don't want
Denny to die. But Denny seems to be caught somewhere in the
middle—between her desire for life and a perhaps uncon-
scious longing for death. And I want her to move toward life.
I'll do anything to motivate her toward life.

So, if it comes to making choices, if you force me to choose,
Marsh, I'll choose Denise every time. Maybe other mothers
wouldn't. I don't know. I don't care. It doesn't matter. But my
allegiance is with Denise. And you're beginning to believe
that, aren't you?

"I'm not giving you no more stuff, kid," Lane said,
smoothing down the pocket flap of his jacket.

"I don't want any of that. I never did in the first place. You
gave it to me, remember? I just need a place to crash for a
couple of days. Until I feel better."

He didn't want to do it, she could tell. And felt so scared.
He had to let her stay. If he didn't, she'd either have to call
Blake or go home. And no way was she going home with that
moron Marshall there. Why the *fuck* did he have to be there?
If he wasn't there, she could just go over, let herself in, crawl
into bed. Mom wouldn't do any hassling. She wouldn't, when
I feel so rotten sick.

Lane eyed her appraisingly for several long moments. "You
clean?" he asked finally.

She nodded, humiliated. She hated him, hated herself for
having nowhere else to go.

"Okay," he said, draping his heavy arm across her shoulders and dragging her over against his side. "For a couple of
days."

He laid a wet slobbery animal kiss on her, and she wanted
to cry. Just sit down on the floor and cry. She should've
known he wouldn't let her alone. Stupid! No way he'd let her
crash without making her pay. For a second, that little-kid
voice inside her head wailed *Mama!* and she wanted to be
home. Wanted it harder, worse than she'd ever wanted anything in her whole life. What was she doing in this tacky
Cadillac with this low-life hood in his tacky silk suit? Why
couldn't she climb off and close down the ride?

* * *

Isabel stood and listened in appalled silence as the duty nurse told her that Denny had simply walked out of the hospital. Listened, unable to speak or respond; turned to lead. Like a programmed robot, she signed the release forms, laid the pen down carefully on the counter of the cashier's desk, and walked back along the corridors to the main entrance and out. Her heartbeat hurting. Each beat knocking painfully. Jude followed after her in frightened silence.

In the car, Isabel fitted the key into the ignition, then sat with both hands gripping the top of the steering wheel, staring into space. Jude watched her every move, wide-eyed.

"There's nothing to do," Isabel said finally. "Nothing. I can't think of anything. What can I do?" She turned to look at Jude. "Where did she go?"

"I don't know," Jude said, her voice croaky.

"Why does she *do* these things?" Isabel asked, searching Jude's eyes. "Do you know why?"

Jude shook her head. "I don't."

"I'm her mother. Am I supposed to know?"

"How could you?" Jude near-whispered, dry mouthed. "She doesn't make any sense. Not doing something nutty like this, just walking out of a hospital."

"There's nothing I can do," Isabel went on, as if she hadn't heard. "Just my life. Keep living my life." She looked back at the windshield. "I have to go to work in the morning. I really ought to stop by the station tonight, see what's on the lineup for the week. I missed a production meeting this morning. But I don't feel like it. Did you ever," she asked, turning once more, "not feel like doing things?"

"Lots of times."

"Right now"—Isabel took a deep breath—"I feel like lying down somewhere, closing my eyes, and just sleeping all this away; waking up and having it all finished. I'm tired of trying to figure it out, tired of thinking. I love her, and I've gone on and on thinking if I keep loving her, keep *telling* her I love her, it'll finally penetrate and she'll walk out of whatever it is she's caught up in, and start living some kind of rational existence. But perhaps she's never going to do that.

Perhaps she won't. I've never been willing to admit that before. Maybe I couldn't. Or was afraid to. I don't know. But I'm admitting it now. Because I have this ugly feeling she just might be this way forever."

"What do you want her to be?" Jude asked softly.

"What? I want her to be . . . *fair*. Just fair. To do whatever it is she does without somehow directing it back at me. To be Denise in whatever she wants. But not to spite me."

"I guess that's reasonable," Jude said.

"Do you think so?"

"I think so."

"Why is it," Isabel asked slowly, "that *you* are the way you are and Denise is the way she is? What makes you you and approachable and makes her her and untouchable?"

"You know I can't answer that."

"I know. Lord, I'm so *tired*." She turned the key and started the car. "I feel as if I might just feel tired for the rest of my life."

"You won't," Jude said kindly.

"No. But it's funny," she said almost inaudibly. "I can't help thinking it."

Maybe, she thought, reversing out of the parking lot, maybe Denny's managing to bring me around to her apathetic way of living. Because I don't feel like going to bed tonight and getting up at five-thirty in order to make it to the station by quarter to seven. I don't feel like sitting in that squalid little makeup room with a paper cup of coffee, my hair in rollers, and Lenny putting Pan-Cake makeup all over my face, turning me into a television character. I wish I could sleep until seven, do my own makeup, and arrive at the station ready to go on. A few minutes' quiet talk with my guest, a cup of coffee, and on with the show. Instead of having to overhear Jerry trying to talk Ash into moving my spot, making veiled threats about contract violations because there was no second spot with a female signed for the show when he autographed the contract renewal. Tired. And Marshall will want to make love. I never felt less like making love in my entire life. Never. I actually hate the idea of it. Want to sleep alone, wake up alone, get myself ready for the day alone.

How could she just walk out of a hospital? How? And where has she gone?

As if sensing the course of Isabel's thoughts, Jude said, "Things'll work out. Denny's just trying it all on. And you know how she hates hospitals."

"I know." Hates them because they kept her out when her father was dying, wouldn't let a little girl in to say good-bye to her father, because some officious fool was worried about *germs*. I know.

Four

The next morning, Jerry charged into the tiny changing cubicle just as she was stepping—bare-breasted, wearing only tights—into the dress she was going to wear on the show. He smiled at her startled reflection in the mirror, said, "Oops, sorry!" and ducked out again. She told herself it was an accident but knew it wasn't. He was trying either to undermine her confidence or rattle her sufficiently just prior to airtime so that she'd blow her interview.

She finished dressing, hurried down to have Lenny brush out her hair, then went back along the corridor to the Green Room, planning to have a pre-show chat with her guest, only to find that Jerry had decided to take the man on an impromptu tour of the studio, pointing out this and that in flourishing arm movements, propelling the man farther and farther beyond Isabel's reach. She stood with her clipboard tucked under her arm, finished her coffee, watching. Knowing Jerry would keep the man with him until the last possible moment. She was convinced now he was launching a full-scale war of nerves.

Luckily, she'd read all the advance promotional material a week earlier, as well as having sampled the guest's product—a low-calorie, high-fiber bread new on the market—and was able to lead him through the interview without any embarrassing pauses.

But she was now completely on her guard.

The next day, Ash caught up with her after the show to say, "We've got a sponsor for your clothes."

"Sorry?"

"Changing the image a little. Getting a little viewer feedback saying, 'We like her a lot. But why doesn't she dress up a little?' So we've got a company who's going to supply your wardrobe for a tag credit."

"But what's wrong with my clothes?" she asked, wondering if Jerry had had a hand in this.

"Too drab," Ash declared summarily. "They've set up some time for you this afternoon for fittings."

The morning after that, when she appeared wearing one of her new outfits and saw the expression on Jerry's face, she at once understood he'd had nothing to do with arranging her "change of image." His eyes narrowed, and he wolf-whistled embarrassingly, patting her on the behind as he passed her on his way to the coffee machine. She stood very still and watched him pour himself some coffee, wishing he'd scald himself. She was learning to loathe him.

Jerry Brenner. All of five-six, with his hearty gung-ho on-camera vitality that came across as charm. Off-camera, deadly. Stocky, with a too-big head and too-long arms, calculating eyes. Famous for badmouthing everyone from production assistants on other shows to passersby touring the station. Famous for his crudely delivered invitations to girls at the station, equally famous for his decimating comments and cruelty to those same girls when they turned him down. As most of them did.

A former not-very-good song-and-dance man, he'd been around for years performing in revues, then on a weekly variety show at the station, finally somehow working his way up to the host of *Mid-Morning*. He had the ability to recognize talent in others, and always did his best, when forced to share the spotlight with someone of talent, to insidiously, deviously make that talented performer look less. He'd perfected any number of techniques over the years. With women, it was fairly simple. He'd make bold invitations, lewd sexual overtures. When turned down, he'd become sweetly nasty, casually dropping harmless remarks about So-and-so around the station. It worked nine out of ten times. With men, it was a little more complicated. He'd become Good Old Jer, the guy's best friend. He'd share his girls, his booze, his dinners, all the while gradually pinpointing the other man's weaknesses. And then, at an opportunely public moment, shoot him out of the sky with the dexterity and deadliness of a sniper. Nobody was going to get in Jerry's way. It had taken him too long to get where he was, he'd worked too hard to perfect his protection. Nobody was innocent. Everyone harbored secret ambitions revolving around desires to knock Jerry off his perch.

Isabel had seen him in action enough times in the course of her two years at the station to know his capabilities and dread them. He was the kind of person she instinctively kept away from. Small in mind and body, mean in spirit, megalomaniacal. With hints of paranoia. He was out to get her off the show. She had no doubts. And wondered how she was going to deal with him. She wished she didn't *have* to deal with him, wished he didn't exist. But he did. And he'd use every dirty tactic conceivable to push her to the point where she'd either walk off the show or throw a typically "female" scene, with attendant tears and borderline hysteria. She'd have to cope. She had no intention of being bullied off the show. Her only weapon was not to react. To say nothing, do nothing, show no response, whatever he did.

Jerry was very subtle. So subtle it was difficult to determine if things he did were intentional or actually accidental. Bumping into her as they passed each other in the narrow opening between one of the cameras and the lectern where he read the news. An elbow in the breast that caused tears of pain to gather in her eyes. She continued on up to the set, having only thirty seconds in which to get herself and her guest into their chairs, clip on their mikes.

Mistakenly picking up her clipboard instead of his own, so that she had to work her way through an interview without notes, without points of reference. An unnerving experience. Because that particular guest offered monosyllabic answers to her questions, thereby prohibiting her from following the guest's response into the next logical question. After that show, she calmly, quietly retrieved the clipboard from where Jerry had left it beside the coffeemaker and then made her way upstairs to sit in Ash's empty office for ten minutes telling herself she would not rise. Nor would she go to Ash and complain. She'd handle it.

She overheard Jerry arguing with Ash on several more occasions. Claiming she was receiving the cream of the guests, while he was getting the dregs. She boldly stood outside the control room listening while Ash dutifully explained how the interviews were being set up. Concluded by saying, "Isabel's segment's working. Viewer response is good, our ratings are up. Leave a good thing alone."

Satisfied, Isabel continued on her way.

After three more weeks, she felt herself becoming inured to Jerry's connivances. Telling herself over and over she would not be defeated by him. Because more each day she liked her work, enjoyed taking home the biographical material and advance copies of books, product samples, preparing her questions, her notes. If Jerry would back down, she thought, I'd actually be happy with this job.

But three weeks, and no word from Denny. Nothing. She was becoming daily more concerned for Denny's well-being. Her concern for Denny growing almost in direction proportion to her liking for her job. Like thermometers side by side, the two segments of her life growing more heated. Denny's prolonged silence, her continuing absence, seemed daily more unpromising. And Isabel couldn't help speculating aloud on the various possibilities, finding it eased her somewhat to give voice to her speculations about just where Denny might be and what she might be doing, the state of her health.

Marshall had the nightmarish premonition this present state of affairs was going to go on and on for months, years, with Isabel worrying either about her job and Jerry Brenner's latest offense or about Denise, speaking of little else. And he faced the prospect of returning to his own work, his travels, secretly ashamed at being relieved at the prospect of escaping—even if only temporarily—this high-tension living. Being ashamed of both his selfishness and his desperate desire to get out and away, he attempted to compensate by trying to anticipate anything and everything Isabel might need, taking upon himself every odd job that needed doing, any errand needing to be run. Anything. There was no job he was unwilling to perform, no task too trivial he wouldn't gladly undertake. Anything to ease the failure he saw in his longing to get away and his crashing disillusionment with this, his first long-term exposure to the interior workings of Isabel's life. She'd certainly been right about that, he thought miserably. It wasn't all highs and lovemaking. It was none of either. He tried to lose himself in odd jobs.

Unfortunately, there was little for him to do. Jude, with what he viewed as maddening competence and meddlesome interfering, went quietly through the house dusting, vacuuming, making trips to the laundry, the cleaners, the supermarket. She cooked and cleaned and conscientiously kept out of the way, spending three afternoons a week at her classes and the majority of her evenings diligently studying in the little apartment over the garage. He'd hear music from her radio trickling faintly around the edges of the upstairs door to the apartment and feel inordinately irritated. Why the hell was she camping out here? Why couldn't she find someplace else to live? And why on earth did Isabel tolerate her? Want her? He'd come across the two of them sitting close together on the sofa, talking softly, and feel like grabbing the kid by her streaky blond hair and throwing her bodily out of the house.

Like Denny, Jude made him uncomfortable. It was something about the self-containment, the nonchalant disrespect they displayed toward him. Their refusal, too, to conform to any decent sort of standard in their dress or behavior. Their insistence on being where they weren't wanted. Their way of speaking politely but displaying visual insolence. The one hanging around, making her presence felt. The other remaining conspicuously absent.

They were all this way, the kids. You couldn't tell the boys from the girls. You'd see some kid ambling along the street with a headful of gorgeous red hair, a long slim torso, and look on admiringly, only to come up close and, in passing, see you'd been ogling a teenage *boy.* How did they tell each other apart? Or did it even matter to them? A whole generation of ambitionless, unmotivated drifters, all casually indulging in sex or drugs; not one of them possessed of any meaningful goal or intelligence. Off to live in communes, to breed frowsy-headed filthy little ragamuffins who'd grow up exact replicas of their parents: without manners, goals, or the ability to talk coherently without resorting to meaningless euphemisms.

Staying in school just to keep on getting the payoffs from their parents. Filling the classrooms, depriving the few really motivated kids of their proper places. It was no good having kids. You got no returns, no gratitude. You couldn't even get respect. Look at Isabel. Driving herself into a state of near-illness and complete distraction for weeks fretting over a snotty, arrogant little bitch like Denise. And what did it get her? Nothing. The crummy kid didn't even have the decency to phone home. Not only did he fail to understand Isabel's devotion, he was entirely bewildered by this secondary attachment to Jude. Because it was certainly obvious there was an attachment. A substitute daughter? He couldn't make sense of any of it. He needed to get away for a while.

In the meantime, his moody presence in the house was slowly driving Isabel crazy. She didn't know why he was staying on, couldn't understand why he didn't leave. And finally, midway through the fourth week, she said, "I think the practical thing now would be for both of us to get back into our routines, for you to go back to work." She stopped, studying him carefully. "You're surprised," she said. "Why are you surprised, Marsh? Did you think I was unaware of your feeling? I know you're anxious to get back to work."

"I honestly don't know what I thought," he lied, glad she'd created this opening. "But I would like to get back to work."

There was a lot, also, he'd have liked to talk about. He wanted to tell her how he felt about her appearing on television every day, how it felt seeing her, and the odd, twisting discomfort that bit into him a little more every day, watching. He also wanted to ask her if they were going to continue this way right till the day he left—sharing a bed, sleeping side by side without touching. Because it was more of a temptation, more deprivation than he could handle for very much longer, sleeping beside her night after night without making love. He'd kept on waiting and waiting for a signal, but none came. And the more time that passed with no encourage-

ment from her, the more inhibited he became about initiat-
ing lovemaking. He couldn't get started. Was afraid to,
somehow.

She watched his face, waiting for him to talk to her, hoping he might at last air some of the things that were bothering him. If he would, she might then be able to explain to him
how she felt she was going dry inside, how she seemed daily
less able to feel anything. To talk about why she couldn't cry,
and how she wished she could. It would help so much to be
able to really open up and let her reactions pour out, her
thoughts about Jerry's nonending subtle torture and her
growing fear for Denny. Any number of things she felt she
couldn't discuss with Jude. Perhaps because she disliked the
idea of burdening a young girl with so many emotional issues. It wasn't fair to Jude. And there were things she wanted
to say to Marshall. She wanted to say: Until this all happened, I'd been toying with the idea that it might be nice to
have another child, nice perhaps to have your child. But now
I'm so frightened by all the aspects of childbearing, child-
rearing—the failures and crushing disappointments—I can't
even *imagine* having another child. And there's the way
you've changed, Marsh. As if stress has dredged up all the
insecurities and inhibitions you'd claimed you'd recovered
from after the divorce. These things are only part of it.

I don't *feel* anything. Not sexually. I'm not interested. I
can't want someone I can't talk to, someone I can't let go
with, someone with whom I have to censor every thought entering my mind. Or is it only that I no longer feel for you?
Whatever the cause, her desire was gone. Gone. Nothing
aroused her or brought her even close to a dim interest. And
she longed to have him speak out, so she'd be able to break
the silence finally. But until he volunteered his feelings, she
simply couldn't talk about her own. So she sat waiting, hoping. And at last couldn't wait any longer. Now.

"Talk to me," she said, knotting her fingers together.
"Please. Don't leave me out this way, Marsh. Weeks, and all
we've talked about are generalities and the guests I've had on
the show. One-word answers to one-word questions. Talk to
me! It's inhuman, living this way!"

"You've turned off," he said. "It's inhibiting me."

"I can't help it! I'm worried. Surely you can understand that."

"About what?" As if he didn't know.

"About everything. Denise vanishing. That despicable little man. The only person I've encountered in weeks who speaks to me as if I'm real and not some sort of threat is Judy."

"That's because the only person you're halfway willing to talk to is Judy," he accused.

Jude paled. Isabel was disgusted. He was jealous of Judy. She was so angry she couldn't speak. She pushed her chair away from the table and bolted out of the room, all the weeks of accumulated complaints throbbing in her temples.

"We shouldn't have started all that in front of you," he said to Jude.

"Forget it," she said flatly, starting to collect up the dishes.

Hopeless! he thought, getting up from the table to go after Isabel.

She was lying on the bed staring at the far wall. Wondering what it would take to simplify her life, clarify her life. He sat down beside her, determined to make one last stab at resolving this.

"You talk to me," he said. "Let's try to talk to each other. This is turning into some kind of crazy kids' game: you tell me, then I'll tell you. We've never been like this."

"I don't feel real," she said, her eyes still on the wall. "Nothing feels real. If I'm real, how can I be here? If I'm not real, how can I make love to you?"

"You're real to me. Am I real to you?"

"No!" she said, her eyes on him now as she sat up. "No, you're *not* real! It isn't real to play caretaker. It isn't real to rake up the leaves and carry out the garbage, wash the cars, get them gassed up, have the oil changed, see they're winterized. It isn't real to do those things and just wait around like some kind of executive handyman hoping I'll be the first one to break and start revealing how I feel. That is not real. You left me. I took my anxiety and anger out on you because you did several things without bothering to discuss them with me

first. You reacted by saying let's forget it, and that's exactly
what you've done. You forgot all of it, erected a block. And
included me on your list. You've put me in a vacuum. And
turned into some . . . You moved out and left your body here
to look after what you think needs doing around the place. I
can't communicate with that! I can't talk to someone who's
handling this situation with all the finesse of an attendant in
an insane asylum. I can't talk to someone who's given no in-
dication whatsoever that he wants to know or hear what I've
got to say. What have we been doing these past two years,
Marshall? I get the feeling we were two robots turning each
other's keys. Not people. Not in touch. Machines. Burying
our real needs, mouthing a lot of platitudes, pretending we
were skimming off the cream of a relationship. It hasn't been
real. And neither have you, these past weeks."

"Am I supposed to respond to that truthfully?"

"Yes! Yes, you are!" She searched his eyes. "You don't
want to be here, Marsh. You said you did. But you don't.
You've been unbelievably dishonest."

"Being truthful, right now I *don't* want to be here. I need
a break. I need some air. I feel as if any minute now I'm going to need some help breathing. Because you're not giving me
air to breathe. Love. Loving you has given me air, something
to stay alive on. This business with Denny, then there's your
show, and the next thing I know, you've gone underground.
I don't even know why. What'm I supposed to do, shout
messages down the hole to you?"

"Yes! If you love someone, you try to understand what's
happening to that person, giving her a chance to understand
it herself. I try to understand you. I *try.*"

"Just *how* are you trying? You roll away from me and sleep
on the edge of the bed. I get the feeling if I touch you, you'll
kill me. What'm I supposed to do about that?"

"You want to get out. I can understand that. I think you
should. Go on, Marsh! Get out, get yourself some fresh air!
I hope you get all you need to keep breathing, to stay alive.
Because you're right. I have gone underground.

"You don't like Denny. I know that. But you didn't *make*
her, Marsh. You didn't carry her around inside you or re-

joice when she was born. You can't be expected to love her or
care about her now. I know that. I don't expect it of you. But
it isn't me rejecting you. It's the other way around. And has
been since the night Denny went to the hospital. You refuse
to see I can't aggressively pursue you in any way right now.
You simply will not see that, won't acknowledge that for all
sorts of reasons I'm being forced to take it one day at a time
right now. Until Denny comes home or calls, something. Until things at the station ease up a little and Jerry lays off. I
didn't want to believe that about you," she said sadly. "But
it wasn't me after all, was it? It was my housing. You fell in
love with the packaging, Marsh. I apologize for looking this
way. I *do* apologize. I can see how misleading externals must
be for you. But I'm not responsible. You'll have to blame my
parents, their genes. I didn't know how close to impossible it
would be to live, just live, with customized packaging. Had I
known, I think I would've tried to have a lot more accidents
as a child, mess it all up a little. At least that way you have a
decent chance of knowing where the attraction lies and you
don't delude yourself into believing you've finally found
someone who sees past your skin and into the person. I don't
think you realize that *I* don't see the outside of me, Marsh.
I'm inside in here, just *being*. Inside here, I look and feel and
think and act just like everybody else. It's only you out there
on the outside who's been taken in by whatever it is you see
on my face. Go on, Marsh! I understand. I know. I do."

"No," he said angrily. "You don't know. You don't know
at all. It's too easy to say I'm hung up on your looks, your
body. It's not the truth. But two people, both holding back on
revealing what they know, what they're seeing and feeling,
wind up two people buried. Not just one. I know it's childish
to hope for a relationship without problems. I've always
known that. And I think until this past month we've had a
great relationship. Really great. But I can't help feeling you're
sitting on top of a big bunch of accusations you're ready to
make if I take one false step. And I know you're sitting there
waiting to pounce, so I'm afraid to do or say anything for fear
of starting a major battle with a lot of casualties. Does it all
have to fall apart now? Does it have to turn bad because of

something that's beyond the control of either one of us? Because there's no control, you know. I hope you see that.''

"What are you talking about?" For just a moment, she was positively convinced he was mad. Nothing he said seemed to make any sense anymore.

"Of course you know it!" he insisted. "But you want to go on believing you have the power to bring her back. And the truth is: nobody does! She's not coming back to you. Not ever."

"Damn you!" she cried. "My child! You're talking about *my child,* not some lost dog!"

"She's not coming back," he repeated. "It didn't work. Why don't you admit it? Admit it! Maybe then we can get back together. But until you do, until you face the fact that she's going to stay away, we're going to keep on going deeper and deeper underground. Whether or not it is or isn't your fault."

"How can you want to hurt me this way?"

"You're wrong," he said, seeing that he had hurt her. "I'd rather have my legs amputated than knowingly hurt you. There isn't anything I wouldn't do if it could spare you pain. But truth is truth, Isabel. And the way it looks right now, she's gone and she's not coming back. I'll be glad to stay here with you for as long as it takes. But you can't ignore it. That's the truth. That's real."

"Do you know what you're doing to me? Do you *know?*"

"I'm giving you what you asked for, in the only way I know how. I'm trying to tell you how I feel. Truth. This minute, I despise the truth. I love you, Isabel. But I can't stay here watching you pretending, trying to convince yourself there's a miracle going to happen that you ought to keep believing in. Because there's no miracle, and it isn't going to happen. And watching you agonize over that girl is no pleasure trip for me. You're a hell of a lot more than a face to me, and you know it. You mean everything to me. But we've all got problems one way and another. I'm not happy about leaving, but I've got very little choice in the matter. She'll take me to court, put me in jail if I miss an alimony payment. I'm no good to anybody in jail. And you're up to your ears with the TV thing. We've got to pick up our lives and keep going.''

"Marshall, I'm very tired.''

"I know. I'll bed down in the guest room tonight, let you get some rest. It's been a long day, and you've got to be up damned early.''

That small resentful note right there, coloring the reference to her job.

He sat a moment longer, then got up and went out.

She sagged suddenly, drained. And leaned back against the headboard. You consider Denny dead. And you'd like me to think of her that way too. Because you think somehow if you can manage to convince me of that, the two of us will be back to where we used to be. You're mad! And not just about Denny. But you practically choke every time you refer to my job. It's too much. She wished she could cry. But there seemed to be nothing left inside. Just a resigned weariness. The only times now she felt even remotely alive, functional, were when she was preparing her interview notes, immersed in the inner workings of the job she was being paid so ludicrously well to do. She felt completely removed from Marshall, from any feeling for him. In fact, was struggling not to despise him. Who are you? Thinking of how he'd groped for ways to explain and justify himself, only to have ended up attacking her and Denny, even Judy. Who have I been loving these past two years? You? Or my love of love?

It's been a long day, and you've got to be up damned early.

Indeed I do. And indeed it has been. A long day, a long year, a long decade, a long life. Forty years. And the jealousy that had flared in his eyes when he'd looked across the dining table at Judy.

Judy. Bless you. You're the only one who seems to see me now, the only one who seems to know without having to have a diagrammed set of instructions, the only one not clutching at my hand, demanding attention. Eighteen, you've been through two unpretty deaths, and you will not be put off by life's situations. Asking nothing. Volunteering insight and words in your mellowed voice, with your wonderful mind. You're the only one I can think of at the moment without wincing, without feeling I have to climb back into the sentry box and stand guard. The only one who doesn't give me the feeling I'm a failed mother but simply someone trying to do her best in an impossible situation. Judy.

Denise walked away from you, too, leaving you out. But you took the trouble to pursue her, to carry your friendship to her with both hands, making a splendid effort to understand her ways and meanings. Yet you haven't been any more successful in finding a route through to her than I have. That tells me something. But what?

I can't feel, can't cry, can't even think. Marshall's finally leaving, and it makes utterly no difference to me. I still care about him. But distantly. Very much removed. Like sitting on the top of a hill deciding which farm I prefer. An odd, misty vantage point from which I look down, unable to declare my preferences. The only preference I'm aware of possessing is the one that's grateful Marsh is leaving.

Not a bad man, really, nor unkind. Just a man who, no matter how hard he tries, can't seem to comprehend the subtleties of what it is I'm trying to convey to him. Never having had a child of one's own. Does it ensure a lack of sympathetic response, of understanding? Or is it simply that Marshall has always sought to protect himself from being obliged to take his caring beyond the immediate range of one-to-one responses? I can't think. I only know he's done something tonight, something to my brain. Like slamming a door in the face of a salesman. Feeling both guilty and justified. Guilty because the man out there's another person and you're aware of the lousy way that has to be to make a living. But justified because it's your right to refuse to be solicited. I've slammed the door on Marshall's prediction, on Marshall. Done that and managed to lock out my feelings, leaving them out there on the doormat to watch the salesman pick his way through the puddles en route to the next house.

VD. How ashamed you must have been. Poor Denise. Why didn't you come to me? Why haven't you *ever* come to me? I wouldn't have blamed you. I've never been able to blame you.

She looked down at her legs, her knees. Then at her hands. Studying the changing flesh on the backs of her hands, the texture changing.

Is there something seriously wrong with me that I can't cry? I am so afraid, caught in a state of fearful dread. But I can't cry. Not even at the possibility of your never returning, Denny; or Marshall's going away. It feels as if my chest, my lungs, are filled with sawdust. My head foggy, the machinery up there running without oil. If I did cry, little wooden pellets might drop out of my eyes. When I do speak, it's with amazement that I hear my voice, my anger. VD. Denise. The more I find out about you, the more I'm forced to acknowledge how little I know you. How did it come to be this way? Why?

If he didn't leave her alone, if she didn't get some rest, she'd snap. Like he was trying to prove what really bad shape she was in by intentionally dragging her around everywhere, pushing as hard as he could to convince himself she really wasn't well. Making her pay for the food he half the time forgot to buy for her, for the privilege of the few hours' sleep he'd let her have. Only because his own energy finally ran out and he forgot about her. But not before wearing himself out on her like she was some kind of gymnasium. Seeing how far he could go? Or how much she could take before she'd break? It felt like he was trying to use her up. Doing some of what he knew was a turn-on to get her started, then, knowing he'd succeeded, using the hell out of her until she had the feeling she was on the verge of the ultimate major freak-out, where she'd get pushed over the line and never find her way back. Winding up one of those whackos doing finger paintings in a state institution. Pushing, pushing. All the stuff she really couldn't handle, the hurtful stuff, the weird kinky stuff. In the ass. Because maybe he knew it was a guarantee to make her scream. Holding on to her hips like handlebars while she screamed—he didn't care, go ahead and scream!—and he did a lot of heavy grunting, keeping it going forever. Making her bleed, so that she stood in his rotten bathroom after, shaking

so hard she had to hold on to the towel rack so she wouldn't
fall over. Crying. Feeling sick, scared, wounded, afraid.

She wanted to split, get out. But she kept thinking if he'd
just give her a couple of days to get in some sacktime, get it
together, then she'd feel better, be able to think what to do. He
was never going to do it. She was just going to have to make
up her mind to split and try to get some rest someplace else.
Before she checked out for good. And Mom would have to
come down to the morgue to make an ID of the corpse on the
slab. She couldn't handle that particular picture. Couldn't
handle being this scared. Doing dumb numbers, being so
scared.

A big mistake, going to see Blake. Just to check what was
going down, because Blake was always on top of what was
happening. But Blake'd been too uptight, very antsy. As if she
was like on the wanted list or like that, and she could tell he
wanted her to split back to wherever it was she'd come from.
And that made her feel so fucking sad, brought her down so
hard. To have Blake do a number like that on her when Blake
had always been such a friend really, such a someone who
wouldn't dump on you with a load of bullshit semaphores,
body-language messages saying: You're making me uptight.
Nice to know you're still in the world. Now, go back to
whatever corner of it you're occupying these days. And don't
mess up mine. She shouldn't have dropped in on Blake. It was
like the end of something. The last day of school. Or the final page of a book you hadn't much grooved on reading but
had managed to get through anyway. Blake's treating her that
way. It just made her more scared. Like she was maybe coming down with something so bad, so contagious, you couldn't
have a friend when you had that kind of sickness.

Somewhere. She had to get out of this trap with Lane. She
had this really bad-vibes feeling Lane was into a death trip.
Her death trip. Death by fucking. She smiled grimly. Maybe
it could happen. She'd read this story one time by this Hu-
bert Selby. Was that the dude? Somebody like that. One of
those guys writing those spooky, too-real-type stories. Anyway, this one where this babe gets herself fucked to death by
seven zillion guys in some empty lot of something. And then,

just to ice it, this kid comes along and gives it to the corpse
with a fucking broom handle or something. Gross! But sick-
scary. Now it felt like Lane was into doing that kind of number on her, and she just couldn't believe how hard she'd
turned on for him way back. And how hard he turned her off
now. What was she *doing?* What did this whole thing prove,
anyhow? Something. No, nothing. Not a goddamned thing.
She closed her eyes and saw herself—again—climbing into her
bed at home, saw herself smiling at the feel of cool, clean-
smelling sheets; the heavily good feeling of being home.
Sighing, her eyes closing, turning on her side with her head
pressed into the pillow. Knowing Mom was downstairs cooking up something good. The pillowcase smooth, fresh under
her cheek, making her skin feel nice. Sighing. Home.

Fuck it!

She'd arrived at the point where she hated her clothes,
thought if she had to wear the same cruddy crapped-up jeans
and stinking T-shirt for one more goddamned day she'd go
totally bananas. Hated the fucking clothes. Wearing them
even made her hate her stinking skin. And walking around
with like maybe four dollars left. While Lane flashed that
obscene wad of bills in his flunkies' faces and the whole gang
of them leered at Lane's bread. Sick. Doing his hot little deals
on street corners with the most pathetic-looking gang of sadtimers she'd ever seen in her life. She'd even thought of
boosting maybe just a shirt from Hamilton's or somewhere.
But knew she'd get picked up the minute she even set her foot
inside the store. Because she looked like somebody who'd be
in there to rip off as much as she could stuff down the front
of her jeans. And she hated boosting anyway. It was sadtime
stuff.

Oh, shit! She felt a terrible kind of overheated achiness all
over all of a sudden. Thinking: Maybe those kids look at me,
and *I* look like some kind of sadtimer to them. Jesus! Is that
where I'm at?

She thought again about phoning home. Just to like check
in. But what if that shithead Marshall answered the phone?
The sound of his fucking whiny voice would send her nuts.
And Blake said Jude was staying there.

Maybe she'll get hung on Jude and forget the hell about me altogether. Jude's more like what she's after anyway. Jude's got it all together, with her little supermarket gig and her good-student number. Jude's gonna make out just fine, people! I wish to Christ I could get myself inside Jude's head, find out which button you're supposed to press to make it all come together. I could even understand it if Mom got off on Jude's staying there like forever. She'd probably think Jude was coconut cream pie after me. All sweet and delicious. Couldn't blame her, either.

I've got to get out of here.

Mom, come find me and bring me home! Shit, I'd go with you right now.

Another frightening thought occurred to her: What if Lane wouldn't let her go?

She hunched her shoulders as if tensed for a blow, and tried to think what to do.

Being at work every day seemed only to heighten her sense of unreality. Jerry was growing more openly hostile, purposely ignoring her when she attempted to speak to him, pretending he hadn't heard her. She'd feel her face and ears flushing with anger while she quietly repeated what it was she'd been trying to tell him. Her body suddenly wet with perspiration, the tension eating at her flesh like some slow-acting acid. He'd turn, having done his "Sorry, I didn't catch that act," and drape his arm heavily across her shoulders. And she'd want to strike him, shove him away from her. But bore it instead, forcing herself to be pleasant as her eyes clawed his smooth-shaven cheeks, as her mind drove the newly sharpened tip of her pencil through the charming dimple in his chin. She wanted to annihilate him, pour water over him, and hear him scream as he shriveled into vapor like the witch in Oz. She wished it could be that simple. Pour water on him and watch him die an agonized death. Her jaws ached after talking to him. She hated the smell of his cologne, the ostentatious diamond pinkie ring he wore; hated his Gucci loafers and hairy wrists; hated the sight of his tongue peeking from between his lips while he ogled Annette, the production assistant, passing a groping hand over the startled woman's bottom. She saw the flaring outrage in Annette's eyes and quickly crossed the studio to distract her, lure her into safer territory. If she had anything to do with it, everyone would ignore Jerry, drive him mad by refusing to respond to anything he said or did.

She was succeeding. Every time he saw her, Jerry's hackles rose. He wanted her off the show, out of the studio, away from the station, a million miles from him. He knew she was pissed by his stunts. But what killed him was the way she kept on smiling, nothing showing.

"One of these days," Annette hissed under her breath, "I'm going to take that son of a bitch out to the parking lot and run him over with my car."

"Forget it," Isabel advised. "Don't react!"

"I don't know how you put up with him," Annette said, her knuckles white where they clutched her clipboard. "You know he's out to get you."

"I know."

"What're you going to do about it?"

"Nothing. I don't know. Nothing."

"You've got to do *something*," Annette said. "How can you do nothing? If it was me. Christ! If it was me."

"I don't know," Isabel repeated, moving off to the Green Room to have a pre-show talk with her guest. *I don't know don't know don't know.*

Jerry watched the two women talking together, accurately guessing that the big bitch was telling that new twat to play it *her* way. He wanted to kill them both.

Marshall had gone off all regrets, promising to telephone first chance he could. But she knew that despite his protestations, he was just as glad to be leaving as she was to have him go. In a way, she wished she could simply fly away from her life for a while. In any case, they'd gone well past the peak of their involvement, and everything from this point on would be moving them downhill into a dissolution. She didn't care. He wanted Denny done with, disposed of, finished, so that— in his simpleminded way of thinking—the two of them could get back to where it was they'd been before. And that was never going to happen. Because she couldn't just dismiss Denny.

I alone am responsible for Denny. He never more than tolerated her, because she's mine. But how could he think I wouldn't notice, wouldn't care that he didn't like her? He's never once tried with any sincerity to communicate with her, never made an effort to see past the straggly hair and dirty feet. I've always known it was for effect. I've been aware she's been asking me for something. But he could only see her as a disruption, not as a person with needs as valid as his own.

The idea that she might have been remiss, neglectful of Denise because of her myopic involvement these past two years with Marshall haunted her. She hated the idea and tried not to succumb to the additional guilt and misery that accompanied the thought. Whether she had or had not been remiss, it was too late. All that was left for her to do was to continue to wait. With waning optimism.

The few tentative inquires made by Judy about Lane brought nothing. All the people who'd previously referred to him so casually—almost boastfully—were now suddenly totally ignorant of his existence. Lane. Lane who? Never heard of no Lane, man! The kids wouldn't even talk to Jude. Word was out she was staying at the house, and that moved her too close to a central source of parental authority, hassles. Jude returned from each session at her supermarket job feeling stymied, defeated. She wanted to offer Isabel something, but could only come back each time with empty hands.

"If people're talking and I happen along, they go dumb," she told Isabel. "I can't get *anywhere!* Six weeks ago, anybody wanted anything—uppers, downers, grass, speed, hash, H, *anything*—you could run Lane down in half an hour. All of a sudden, he's like the mysterious *Who?* Somebody's got to see him sooner or later, I mean, I just know if Den's anywhere, she's with him. Or he'd know where she is. She was very hung up on him."

Isabel felt she was slowly losing her reason. Nothing seemed to make sense. She clamped her jaws together and bore Jerry's constant digs, more determined than ever not to let him break her or penetrate her reserve.

He switched tactics with confounding regularity, one day bringing her coffee in the Green Room, innocently chatting away— all friendliness—prior to air time. The next day "accidentally" stepping down hard on her instep as he hurried across the studio to examine a display table of artifacts that had been set up by one of the guests, a curator from the museum. The day after that, he "accidentally" allowed the heavy steel door to the studio to close on her as she was coming through behind him. Then apologized profusely, claiming he hadn't known she was behind him.

He had a talent for inflicting bruises, causing pain, so that when she left the studio each afternoon she carried with her some still-stinging reminder of Jerry. She told herself not to think about it. She didn't. But her body bore the aftermarks of each confrontation: a raw scraped area across the top of her instep, a blue-purple bruise at the side of her breast, a coffee spill down the skirt of a beige wool dress. There seemed nothing he wouldn't try.

He rearranged the notes on her clipboard, unintentionally walked away with her pencil, brought his guests into the makeup room while she—in her slip, with a brief makeup cape around her neck—was being made up. She sat unmoving, feeling the heat of the hot rollers burning its way through the top of her head, her face turning red beneath the layer of Pan-Cake. Anything to shake her up, throw her off.

Ash took note, silently adding up the points against Jerry, wondering when the break would come. Unless she made an official complaint against him, there was little if anything Ash could do. But although he waited, hoping she'd come to him, Isabel said nothing, merely continuing on, working feverishly to stay on top of the incoming material, up-to-date with her guests.

On camera, she came across relaxed, noncompetitively intelligent, skillfully adept at incisive interviews. They were beginning to receive requests for guests to be directed specifically to Isabel. Knowing they'd get good exposure from her fifteen-minute segment. Ash was the recipient of a lot of back-patting, positive feedback. Everybody upstairs was happy. The grips in the studio were crazy about her. Annette adored her. The guests were enchanted by her. She was unassuming, possessed of enviable humility, a lovely sense of humor. Treated everyone equally, favoring none. Cracks were beginning to appear visibly in Jerry's charm. And Ash wondered what she was trying to prove with her stoicism. Half a dozen times in the course of a morning, Ash felt like pushing his foot down on Jerry's throat. He admired Isabel's grit, but worried about her. For a lot of reasons. There was a certain frailty about her, a positive delicacy—despite her height, her carriage—that hinted at a very real suceptibility to the pain Jerry loved to inflict.

There'd been one other woman once upon a time. Back in the days when Jerry was starting his upswing. Ash had been moonlighting as stage manager for a cabaret revue downtown on Old Street. Jerry had been starring in the three-person show. Backed up by a good solid all-round showman and a too-talented girl the producer believed promising. The director had given her half a dozen top-rate guaranteed show-stoppers. And Jerry had been scared, jealous. He'd tried to get most of her numbers cut. He didn't succeed. When that failed, he sat back and waited for his moment. It had come during the second week of the run. The girl had taken all the rave reviews Jerry had wanted. And he was tired of the show anyway. Complaining it wasn't doing him one goddamned bit of good appearing every night when the thing had turned into a one-way vehicle for that broad. He was walking through his numbers, drying on his lines, ad-libbing in the skits and blackouts, so that the punchlines got thrown away along with the timing, leaving the other two to carry the burden of the show. Trying to make Sandy look bad. It didn't work. The harder he tried to bring her down, the better she looked onstage.

He'd fixed her.

One of her big numbers had her standing atop a draped stool directly in front of the black velvet curtain that ran completely around the small stage. Jerry fiddled around with the curtains until he'd managed to work a small opening directly behind where she did this number. He'd thought he'd make her blow the number, get her a belly laugh from the audience she hadn't counted on.

During a silent moment, he slipped his hand through the hole in the curtain and up between her thighs. Her head had snapped around. Her face had frozen into a look of disbelieving shock as she lost her balance; the stool tipped and pitched her headlong to the stage floor.

Ash had seen it all. And in his memory, it seemed to take forever for her to hit. Sandy fell and fell, the stool turning. The cries form the audience, amused at first, thinking—as Jerry had intended—that this was part of the show. Then horrified as her neck snapped audibly. She was dead the instant her head connected with the stage.

Jerry had stood unmoving throughout, watching through the gap he'd made in the curtain. He was still standing there long after the ambulance had taken Sandy away, after the audience had departed and the worklights backstage cast an eerie too-bright light over the dusty flats and gaudy props.

Ash was the only one who knew what Jerry had done. And didn't know what to do with his knowledge. So did nothing. And had regretted it ever since. Because Jerry Brenner was a very dangerous man.

Ash was frightened now for Isabel. Pleased with his own good judgment in putting her into the spot. She was good. Better than good, and he'd known she would be. She more than justified his faith in her, his intuition. But he'd put her in the direct line of Jerry's virulent animosity. Believing she could handle it. But now not so certain. If only she'd say something, he thought. Speak up! Don't just go on taking it! I can't help you if you won't say you need it.

He kept his eyes open, slowly deciding that if Jerry kept up with his antics, he'd have to take the risk and intercede. Do something. One thing he could do was to keep Jerry the hell out of the makeup room while Isabel was in there. And so with a smile and a friendly arm around the shoulders, he asked Jerry if he wouldn't mind cooling it while the women were in the makeup room.

"She bitched, huh?" Jerry grinned, patently pleased with himself.

"No." Ash grinned back, thinking: Fuck you! "Lenny. He doesn't like interference when he's working. It distracts him."

Jerry shrugged off Ash's arm, his grin gone. "Fucking fag! Hate fucking fags!"

"Humor him," Ash said, still smiling. "He's one of the best makeup men around. We need him. And," he added, lying, "he speaks well of you."

"Yeah," Jerry muttered, and walked away.

Not much, Ash thought. But something.

With Marshall gone, there seemed more space, more freedom in the house for her thoughts, her movements. She could carry herself from room to room, talking aloud, feeling the knot of anxiety loosening somewhat as a result. Judy didn't inhibit her. On the contrary, she felt she could simply *be* with Judy, and when it occurred to her, she marveled at Jude's wisdom and intuition. A tiny eighteen-year-old sage who sat in a half-lotus for hours, deep-breathing, finding it not in the least extraordinary that Isabel should pace from room to room talking aloud.

"It's right," Jude said very seriously. "You have to do it, get it out. We all do. It feels right. It's good for you. It'd probably be even better if you could really cry and shout. Sometimes things're really hard to get out. I mean, was it me, and I had to put up with a sick dude like Brenner and still try to do my own gig and everything, I'd scream like a lot. And with Den doing this disappearing act on top of it, things're pretty heavy."

She'd looked at Jude, awed by her serenity, her magnanimous comprehension of Isabel's need to speculate aloud for hours on Denny's whereabouts. And that night that she and Marshall had argued, it hadn't even occurred to her to censor her thoughts or reactions in front of Judy. Now she wondered what it was about the girl that allowed such freedom for thought, for unchecked emotional responses. She'd never have risked speaking so openly before Denny. Denny's mannerisms and implied criticisms would never have permitted it. Yet, whatever she needed to do—be it walking back and forth like someone in a cell, or talking aloud like some street-corner fanatic—it was all right with Jude. And by making this comparison, Isabel came to see that Denny had always found it difficult, perhaps even impossible, to accept anything. Love was questionable. Displays of affection were questionable. Warmth and demonstrative people—and most specifically her own mother—were questionable. Why? She couldn't contain a need to discuss it, a need for some other viewpoint. She took her thoughts and questions to Jude.

"You've known her all these years. Be truthful. Tell me the truth. Were there things I should've done differently, that I did all wrong? Do you think I've failed her?"

Jude shook her head. "I don't think so," she said, on impulse drawing Isabel into her arms as she might have done with a small child, smoothing the older woman's hair comfortingly. "Nobody can get to where Denny's at. Because *Denny* doesn't know where she's at." Mentally adding: I'm starting to get scared for you. A kind of jittery, trembly sensation inside.

"Has she ever talked about her father, me? Does she confide in you?"

"Not much," Jude said, thinking about it; her hands smoothing, stroking, drawing the heat from Isabel's forehead with cool fingers. "She one time did this big number about your connecting up with Marshall. She really can't hack that guy. But you know, I think she'd come down hard on anybody. You know? If you were into a thing. She doesn't see you—I don't think—as a person so much, but more like her own personal property. And there are a lot of numbers she doesn't think you should be doing, because you're supposed to like get her permission or something first."

"How? I don't follow that."

"I've always had this feeling, even way back when we were like little, that Den gets mad at herself for loving you. As if she shouldn't have to care about other people, like it's a big downer that they have to matter. Like she can't handle *caring,* so she has to turn it into anger or put-downs. Like with Marshall. She called him an emotional ripoff artist and said he was just off on this big ego trip with you. She called him a 'biochemical jock.'"

Isabel laughed, sitting back from Jude. Her laughter had a decidedly hysterical edge to it, Jude thought.

"She said *that?*" she asked, amused.

Jude smiled. "She can be pretty funny sometimes. When she sort of forgets herself and just uses her brain, starts thinking. She's got such a good brain, you know?"

Isabel's laughter faded, and she asked herself if perhaps Denise hadn't been displaying more preception than anyone had given her credit for. Hadn't she been horribly accurate about other men Isabel had dated? The one who'd come to pick her up for an evening out. Denny had taken one look at him and beckoned Isabel out to the kitchen on some phony pretext to whisper, "Mom, he's creepy. I'll bet you anything he's into whips and chains and shit like that." Isabel had stared at her in astonishment, wondering how Denise could arrive at a conclusion like that about a good-looking, quietly intelligent businessman whom Isabel truthfully found very appealing. Only to accept his invitation up to his apartment for a drink to find the man was the proud possessor of a full wet suit, in which he proposed to make love to her. She fled home devastated. And there had been others, too.

"Do you think she was right, Judy? Is that how Marshall seems to you?"

"The truth?"

"Please!"

"I think she was. He's winding himself up to split now. I don't guess you'll be too sorry about that. But . . . I wish you hadn't asked me. I hate saying this stuff to you."

"No, no. Right now you're the only one who *talks* to me. Tell me!"

"Well, for one thing, he's been really down on me being here. Almost like the way Den's acting for him being here with you. I mean, the feeling is like I'm here and doing the shopping, cooking, you know. So that stopped him from getting into anything . . . practical. Right. That's the word. And for him to get heavily into feelings, laying it out about how he feels, is a bummer. He can't get off on that, you know. He's a right-now sort of dude. I don't know. It's like if he wanted to do something, he wouldn't know how to put it aside until later. You know what I mean? He'd have to do it right away this minute. And the sort of stuff he's into is the small-job number. Don't hassle yourself, sweetheart, I'll clean the john. That kind of thing. Into making people like him by being such a good guy, such a nice guy. Except that he's not really that good, that nice. I don't think. It's kind of unreasonable to be that *nice*. So, here I am, and I'm taking away the number he wants to be doing. Because if he can be the one doing that whole thing, maybe people will be like grateful to him for taking that mess of nasties off their hands, and they won't like notice he's not contributing all that much where it's *really* needed. Maybe I'm wrong. But that's the feeling, you know? Like, he'll dazzle you with all the niceness so maybe you won't notice how he's not too big on *responding.* I'm heavily into how things feel. And he's like, I don't know, jealous. Of how you're worried about Denny. And how when you're here, I'm here too. And when you're on the tube, you're like superstar time to him, and he can't hack that. Like it wasn't what he had in mind for you. Like he wanted you to do the school thing and get some nice quiet little gig and be his own personal private star. But you're doing the TV thing, and everybody gets to know you, sort of. So it's not just an exclusive number you do for him. And that leaves him outside, he thinks.''

''He loves me, Judy.''

''I know that. But that doesn't mean you've got to love him back just 'cause he does. It's not like an obligation, like you've *got* to love him. I mean, what would you do if somebody else came along now that maybe interested you?''

''I don't want to be interested. I've got too many other things on my mind.''

''But that's wrong, you know. I'm not saying you've got to go out first thing in the morning and try to get into a new thing with somebody else. But you've still got your life going. You can't shut off and just go on your job. You've got to think about these things. Especially now, when you'll keep meeting lots of new people. And something else I've really got to say. I mean, we're talking and you're asking me what I think, I figure I should *really* tell you what I think. It's like

Marshall's way into doing his nice number, really getting on everybody's nerves and like that. And you, you're the one being too nice. Putting up with it. That's kind of almost like as bad as his act. There's no rule that says you've got to put up with some dude just because he loves you and you're too respectful of his feelings and this big love trip he's on to tell him where to go. And it's the same kind of thing you do sort of with Denny. Taking it. You don't have to. Nobody has to *take* anything if they don't want to. I mean, d'you feel you've got these big obligations?''

"I don't know. This is a strange conversation."

"No, it isn't. It really isn't. It's a good conversation. And rapping's how you find out where your head's at. You've always been very straight with me. I'm just being straight with you now. So, project! Check out the feelings! How would you feel if somebody good happened along?"

"What *would* I do? As of right now, I don't want anyone, couldn't handle anyone or anything else." Is she right? Am I too much of a sponge, taking the injuries, just absorbing them without demanding my rights? My God! I think she's right.

"Come on," Jude urged. "Someone comes along who has words, interest. Would you go with it, see where the attraction would lead?"

"I suppose I would."

"Even into bed?"

"Oh, not *now*," Isabel said, fatigued. "Perhaps eventually. But right now, right now, *right now*. I can't even think about any of that."

"But you see where we've managed to get to?"

"Oh, I see it. I don't love Marshall. Judy, my daughter's out there somewhere doing heaven only knows what, and I'm sitting here with you projecting on how far I'd be willing to go if another man came along who interested me. It isn't real. I don't want any more men coming along. I don't even want to *think* about any more men. I only want some peace."

"It is real, though, you know. What it is," Jude said earnestly, "is, you've got choices. And saying to yourself that no matter what happens with Denny, you've got your own life."

"Judy, in ten years I'll be fifty. There's no market for fifty-year-old women. Not on television. Not with men."

"So you'd keep Marshall around for safety? You'll be a hot number on the tube for a couple of years. Then what? What's it all for?"

"No, no."

"What then?"

"I don't want to be married. Certainly not to Marshall. And as far as my job goes, I just want to do it. That's all. I don't know. What *do* I want?"

"To keep things as they are?" Jude suggested.

"As they are," Isabel said, considering it. Thinking seemed so difficult, such a complicated, enervating process. "No," she said. "I don't like the way things are. Not with Marshall. And not the way the job is right now. Not with Jerry plotting new accidents constantly. You're right," she said wearily. "You are right about me. I've been making excuses for Marsh, telling myself little stories. I'm glad he's gone. For two years, it's been three days here, four days there, with two or three weeks' separation in between. But this past month it was all day every day, and I've never felt more pressured, more compelled to direct my attention to someone when I felt he should understand that I simply wasn't able to give him that amount of attention. Concentrating on him made me feel I was depriving Denny in some way, made me resent him."

"Denny doesn't know what you think about."

"And the other thing," she said. "You're right about that, too. I think it was a half-serious gesture on his part, suggesting I go back, finish my degree. Something to keep my mind busy while he was away. But I did more than he thought I would. I took a job. And the job's become something much bigger than he ever imagined. He doesn't like it. Making little asides, snide-sounding references to the promotional material I bring home. My reading a book by someone I'm to interview. He paces up and down trying to draw my attention away. As if what I'm doing isn't serious, but some sort of playschool activity, and as soon as I finish, he and I will be able to get down to the *really* serious business of paying attention to him. Lord, I resent that! He hasn't the right to minimize what I'm doing or to try to forcibly redirect the feelings I have for Denise to him. He'd kill her off inside my head if he could. How can he think I'd stop caring about my child? I can't understand that. No matter what she does, I have to be here for her. Nothing else matters except that. But how did she *get* this way, Judy? How?''

"I don't know," Jude said softly. "Maybe you're after something that doesn't have an answer. Maybe Denny is, too."

"Going around in circles, you see? We're back to where we started. It's why nothing seems real to me."

When Marshall did telephone, their conversation consisted of stiff replies to stiffly posed questions, punctuated by long, uncomfortable pauses. She didn't know what to say to him. He couldn't reply to silence and felt she was further punishing him.

"This is a wasted call," he said coldly. "We're not saying anything."

"No, we're not." If you'd just ask about Denise, she thought; if you'd just demonstrate some concern, a little caring, I might be able to talk to you. But you won't, you can't. And Judy's right, I have to stop feeling obligated to you because you're still trying to love me.

"I'll call you again in a day or two. We'll talk then."

"Yes," she said, sounding vague. They exchanged goodbyes, and she hung up wondering why she hadn't told him not to bother calling, not to bother coming back.

Upstairs in her bathroom, preparing for bed, she stared at the row of prescription medicines, then reached for two Dramamine tablets to help her get to sleep. She swallowed the tablets and stood for several minutes staring at the plastic containers of pills. Then she closed the medicine cabinet, washed her face—her skin feeling stranger than ever beneath her hands—brushed her teeth, and got into bed. To lie in the dark all at once too awake, worrying about tomorrow's show, wondering what new trick Jerry would have up his sleeve; worrying about Denise, trying to guess where she might be.

She slept and dreamed Jerry held her captive on shore while Denise drowned before her eyes just a few feet away.

Jude lay across the bed with her chin resting on her folded hands, asking herself if she hadn't maybe done a really bad number by speaking the truth as she saw and felt it. She had this feeling she was seeing a breakdown happening, and hated it, hated having nothing to offer to stop its progress. And you couldn't go along doling out sugar-pill remarks to someone who was asking you point-blank for truth. That'd make you a walking cop-out, doing the all-things-bright-and-beautiful number.

Talking with Isabel, all of a sudden she'd felt so much older. As if Isabel was like just another kid, and she, Jude, was a whole lot older. This number Denny was pulling was making the lady crazy. And she'd never, just never understand where Den's head was at. Didn't she really care, after all?

If you said something nice to Den about her mother, she'd look at you like you were a mental incompetent and she was too totally bored by your sophomoric observations to stand them one more minute. God, Denny, why don't you try her on? She's a good fit, someone real. And you're going to wipe her out with this one. Runaway. You finally did it! Finally found the knife guaranteed to kill. Somebody's got to do something.

"You're here to stay, Jude." She'd said that. "It's very good for me having you here."

And she'd meant it. That was the thing about her. She didn't do any fancy shuffling, but always dealt right from the top of the deck. Couldn't Denny *see* that? Right from the very first time she'd ever come to this house to play with Denny, Mrs. Gary had always been so glad to see her, making a point to say so. "Hi, Judy. I'm glad to see you." Coming here to check out the new kid and her mother, to see how it was living in a house without a daddy. The big tall lady with the big tall kid.

How many hundreds of times had she said that? "I'm glad to see you." Things like that are so important. They give you an identity, a value to yourself. Almost more important than trying to get it on with Blake, say. Or with any guy. Having someone you really like a lot telling you the sight of you's a turn-on, that they get off on having you around. Blake used to be that way. But maybe that was only because it'd been his way of promoting me into a sexual number. It doesn't matter. Well, yeah, it does matter. I miss him.

Denny liked Blake. He was like big brother to her. Always looking out for her, always trying to clue her in on how to get her act together. Absolutely the only one she'd take any of that from, too. Anybody else ever tried coming on to her with some advice, she'd tell them to fuck off, and that'd be that. Blake.

She sat up and flipped the hair back from her face, thinking about Blake. Thinking hard about him. Trying to separate her feelings for him from something that was pinching at the edge of her brain, trying for her attention. Blake knows something. Has to. Of all the people, he's the only single one Denny would go to or call. Big Brother.

He'd saved her life that night. But wouldn't go to the hospital. Not wanting to be involved. But you're involved, whether you like it or not, Blake. For all the years you've put into looking out for Denny.

Tomorrow, first thing, before she went to the market, she'd make it over to Blake's place and try to get him to talk. It'd be nice to just see him, anyway.

She really wanted to stay straight. It felt better that way, even though she was really wiped, and walking around half the time feeling like she could fall asleep practically standing on her feet. It was okay the numbers Lane liked to pull making out. Snapping ammies, using coke. That stuff wasn't so bad, because you didn't *take* it and then wake up later all strung out needing to dive back in and get a whole fresh load of it buzzing in you again. Played pure hell with your nerves, though, and made you so crazy doing it that everything hurt like murder the next day, even your bones aching. Fucked stupid. Even with her period, he'd had to get into his thing. And she'd been counting on that kind of as a turnoff so maybe she'd get some sleep and wake up able to think. But no goddamned way. Another screaming session. More crying in the john. Blood everywhere. Scared scared.

She needed some money. Just something so she could get someplace quiet where she could crash and do some thinking. Think about getting some kind of job and someplace quiet to stay. Quiet. Half the time her head felt rotten from all that stinking hard-rock-acid shit Lane and his crew of cretins played so loud the whole fucking house vibrated. With the bass hiked up to there so you couldn't even hear whatever the hell the number was or figure out the group, but just wanted to toss from all that big boomboom rumbling all the time.

And now, on top of everything else, he was trying to get her on speed. "You're a fucking drag, you know!" he accused. "Laying around the fucking place all the fucking time. Take a coupla these and get it together!" Tossing a Baggie full of speed at her. She tossed it back.

But his brand of warning. And she was listening. She didn't want to be here anyway. Bad stuff happened in this house. Some she saw, some she didn't. Some she could hear in the middle of the night. What sounded like little kids crying, and a lot of heavy, dirty laughter from those sickies. Leo. The worst. She was scared of Leo. Leo was a maniac. He killed people, sadtimers, just for the hell of it.

It was when Lane said all very casual-like how Leo had these big eyes for her that she got really petrified and knew she had to get out before Lane started passing her around like *Playboy,* sharing her with the boys. Leo would kill her. He was a big SM freak, into those really sick magazines with animals and torture shit and stuff like that. A couple of times she'd gone into the ratty living room and seen blood. Once on the floor. And once there was this T-shirt, a really little-sized one, with blood splashed all over it. Sent her crazy, staring at this teeny-tiny little shirt, imagining the size of the kid that must've been in it. Made her shake all over, dropping the shirt and getting the hell out of that living room like she'd seen a real murder.

So, Lane said that, and she just played it very cool, and in the afternoon said she'd walk down to the store for some cigarettes and beer, she'd be back in a few minutes. Lane said yeah, yeah, and she made herself walk slowly, very slowly, through the house to the front door. She was really wobbly by the time she got to the porch and went down the steps, but kept it under control and walked slow slow up the street until she got to the corner. Then she started to run like hell, not knowing why, but running so hard she was panting and her side was starting to hurt. Kept running and caught a bus, sat in the very last seat and counted her money. Two dollars and twelve cents. And chewed on her finger, trying to think where to go, what to do.

Thought of turning a trick but knew she couldn't, never had, just couldn't. Thought of robbing a bank, and laughed inside her head. Sure. Thought of why in hell she'd ever started with Lane in the first place, and knew it was because he was so fucking *old* and went with him that first time thinking how Mom would freak finding out she was balling a guy that old. But shit! Nobody knew. It was nuts. Doing that kind of stuff when nobody even knew she was doing it. Wound up giving him a dose. He'd pounded her in the gut until she passed right out cold. Then woke her up, threw her out, and told her she was goddamned lucky she wasn't dead. And gave her a good-bye present of a Baggie full of all kinds of mixed shit.

A safe place, that's what she needed.

She rode the bus all the way out to the Indian Hill zoo. Walking up and down the pathways, not seeing the animals or the people, trying to think. Feeling a funny kind of relieved feeling, as if she'd just escaped jail. Sat on one of the benches and remembered the kids who'd been going to set up the commune. Somewhere outside the city, on the lake. Right. Near Oakbridge. It was still light. She could hitch a ride.

She closed her eyes for a minute, shivering, feeling the wind whipping up her sleeves, down the back of her neck; thinking about the living room at home, the fireplace. Thinking about going over with Jude on a Sunday morning. Lying on the rug staring into the fire, the newspaper spread out all over the place. Seeing her mother sitting at the end of the sofa with her feet tucked under her, in that green velour robe, the one that made her skin look so white, like paper. Her hair all over the place, longer, nicer hair than Cher's even. Because Mom's hair was thick, it curled. And was a trip to touch. Why didn't you come find me?

Terrific, Den! Really got your brain screwed on nice and tight. Come find me. Sure. Like how?

Too late anyway.

She got up to make her way to the southernmost park entrance. Only about a mile from there to the Old Shore Highway. It wouldn't be hard to thumb a ride.

Five

For days afterward, Isabel thought about her conversation with Judy, about the quality of their statements, the depth. And saw more clearly than ever how truly distant she and Denny had been for such a long time. Their conversations at best had been like throwing pebbles into a pond, never seeing the pebbles strike bottom, but seeing only the disturbed surface of the water.

She brooded. Trying to see the point of her existence. Because she seemed to have evolved into some new form of herself, someone whose thoughts and actions were carefully measured, like doses of highly toxic medicine; someone whose motives required more meticulous scrutiny. She questioned the validity of her needs, applying them against her desires. Questioning constantly.

She felt that what she did was distinctly separate from what she was. The one who worked at the station, who daily appeared on camera, was the one who *did*. And the one who grappled silently with Jerry, contending with his continuing animosity, was the one who *was*. It seemed as if she was spending the majority of her time coping with one thing or another for the daily reward of fifteen minutes' air time. Being what she was in order to continue doing what she did. It was beginning not to make sense. Why go through all that just to be on television for a quarter of an hour? What was it proving? The people tuned in to see the guests, not her. They turned on their sets to hear what the latest author or the newest celebrity had to say, how they looked. It hadn't anything to do with her. She was a sort of sieve through which her guests were strained, emerging smooth, palatable.

She had most of her life fought the stigma of her looks, preferring to believe the person inside her was important, not what other people saw. And now it seemed the only one who hadn't been overly impressed by her physical attributes had been Howard. He'd been attracted to her intelligence, her arguments, her determination not to merely accept facts because they'd been stated but rather to consider the origins of concepts and follow them logically toward the facts.

He'd been drawn, he'd once told her, to her "rampaging disinterest."

Howard! Again the pain, remembering.

She'd traveled through many of the stages Denny had. Not unwashed hair and dirty bare feet. But going sockless, wearing penny loafers—minus the pennies—and rolled-up Levi's, an old high-school-letter jacket she'd found abandoned near the playing field one afternoon in her senior year of high school. Defiantly, she'd worn rings of almost black eye shadow and thick red lipstick, her hair in a long ponytail that had danced disrespectfully as she'd turned her back on her parents and the boys who'd asked her to proms.

She'd been high-school valedictorian. Made an antiestablishment speech and got herself hissed and booed off the stage. But she'd done it fervently believing, not for pure effect. And twenty years later, here was the world and the kids doing and saying all the things she'd been saying and doing then. The newly established norm.

She'd been just as miserably critical of her parents as Denny was of her. Maybe more so. It had seemed so pathetic and shattering to wake up one morning and hear those two people talking so emphatically about such ordinary, boring, inconsequential things; to hear them talking and realize they weren't *thinking*. They were just getting through time, killing time, never stopping to ask themselves what it was all about or why. They might've been working to make changes, even small ones, using their time alive sensibly, productively. But they'd concerned themselves with cocktail parties and what sort of impression the new couple at the country club had made on the big Saturday-night dinner-dance crowd.

Upon entering the university, she'd installed herself in more appropriate clothes, because she didn't want her prior anger and disappointment to prejudice her new classmates against her before she'd had a chance to know whether or not she was going to care to know them. And with her altered style of dress, her view of her parents seemed to mellow accordingly, and she was able to see them as forgivable, gentle people trying to do the best they could with what they had, harming no one. And doing, she thought, a far more successful job with her younger brother, Gerard, than they'd managed to do with her. Maybe they're learning, she'd thought, looking forward to a time when Gerard might discuss with her his impressions of these two people, their parents. And a time when those two people might be able and willing to discuss themselves.

The time never came, though. And it was only a quirk of fate that had her back out at the last minute from a Sunday-afternoon drive to the country, because she'd just met Howard and had wanted to spend the afternoon with him. They'd talked and talked throughout the afternoon, and had still been talking—in her living room by then—when the police telephoned to say there'd been an accident. Her parents had died at once. Gerard held on for three days before slipping away while on the operating table undergoing a second surgical round.

Howard had made her talk it out, cry it out, express her sorrow and anger. All of it. He'd put her to bed and watched over her sleep and held her hand through the horrific funeral. Like Jude now, he'd helped her examine her past actions and announced her relatively innocent of serious misdeeds and omissions. And unlike Marshall, he'd made no sexual demands upon her. He'd wanted her intact. Not sexually, which she wasn't, having given herself to an intriguing junior she'd met her second month at the university. But intact emotionally. And she wasn't. Not for months. There were parts of her self dangling in the air above her head or off to one side, and it took a long time for her to pull those pieces of her fragmented self together. He'd waited, holding her for hours while she drew strength and certainty and love from the contact. He'd been there when she most needed him, and he'd displayed great foresight in anticipating her needs. There'd been no pressure. Because he'd loved her, he'd given her all the room she'd needed.

Howard. He'd had a good healthy ego and a marvelous inquiring mind. He was going to be an exceptional doctor. Researching cell factors. His doctorate meaningless except as a key to open laboratory doors. All this. And he'd encouraged her to grow.

He'd have interested himself in my work. He wouldn't have been competitive about it, but would have seen it as something worthwhile, worthy of his interest simply because it interested me. We would have discussed the guests, the show itself, Jerry Brenner. And with Howard beside me, I would have been able to handle all of it. Because he'd have offered the support I need. The support I'm receiving from Judy. The support I'd like to receive from Denny, offer to Denny. Marshall. You've done nothing for me.

Who am I to you? Why do you claim to need me? For physical comfort, for sex, for reassurance, because *she*—you can't even speak her name—you say she went after you with a verbal ax and frigid responses and tried to castrate you. I wonder what she'd have to say about you. Your conversations all dealing with abstracts, obscure points of reference. I thought I needed that. Two years ago, it may have been what I needed. But not today. I don't need someone who makes me feel as negative as you do. Because what you need has to do with what you can penetrate, what you can feel through your skin or sense through "auras" and bubbles of bright light.

The dilemma. How was she going to extricate herself? Too much pressure from too many directions. Marshall in love without knowing how to give love. Denise out there somewhere, running away. Jerry Brenner on the constant lookout for some new spot at which to aim his blows. She closed her eyes—dry, dry achingly dry—and covered them with her hand.

Howard. Why did you have to die? Why did they have to keep Denise away from you? I've lost you, I'm losing her. This feeling that I'm clinging to the side of a mountain, hanging on by my fingernails. The temptation to just open my hand and let go, take the fall.

Howard, that first time. I remember so clearly, so well. The certainty, the profound knowledge of the rightness. Sitting eating hamburgers in that coffee shop downtown after classes one day, when you put down your hamburger, leaned on your elbow on the counter, and said, "It's going to be the two of us for good. Do you know that, Isabel?" And I nodded, thunderstruck. "No one else would ever be as right, isn't that true?" I nodded again. "I love you, Isabel. I want to be where you are."

Howard! I need you to be here now.

Blake was immovable. Nothing Jude said would change his stance. He wasn't talking.

"But you know something," she persisted, overcome by a sudden desire to wallop him, whack that unyielding look of stubbornness off his face. "Can't you *understand,* man? Denny's killing her this time. I can *see* it. She'll do this, then come around to check out the damage, only to find she's lost her audience. Don't you care, Blake? Doesn't any of this matter to you? Where's your head, for God's sake? People are in *trouble.*"

"I'm staying out of it. And I don't need you coming around here laying a guilt trip on me. You go be the conscience kid. That's your gig. Fine. Dynamite! You do it. You're all hung up on Denny and her mother, this big loyalty kick. There's nothing that says I've got to jump in there with you. Shit! We're not a thing anymore. I don't owe you."

"How about Denny?" she argued. "What about your Big Brother number? Isn't that your trip, Blake? *Blake!* What *happened* to you?"

"I saved her life," he defended himself. "I was the one. Me. Everybody else split when things started happening. Don't dump on me, Jude! I did what I could. It gets nobody nowhere if I start shooting off my mouth. What Den does is *her* business. Why don't you climb down off it?"

"You're going to have a beautiful life," she said. "Really beautiful. You don't give a shit for anything or anyone any-

more. I can't believe this is still you. Just worrying about your
own skin. Well, maybe if you're lucky, you'll make a couple of
million and you can be the next Howard Hughes, maybe
hire a bunch of flunkies to really keep you out of the action.
Let me just lay this on you, Blake; your skin isn't worth anything! Denny, wherever she is, whatever she's doing, is worth
more than you. At least she's trying. At least she's tried to
make some kind of effort to get her head straight. Maybe not
the right way or the best way, but she's *trying*. But you, you're
so hung up all of a sudden, you can't even try. What're you
living for? Where are you going? Eh? What? Where?''

''I don't need this,'' he said, his expression beginning to
crack. ''Why d'you want to lay this kind of head trip on me,
Jude? I wouldn't do it to you. People have a right to be where
they want to be, do what they want to do. It's not up to you
to interfere.''

''Blake, you're being so childish. I wouldn't do it to you,
don't do it to me. Open your eyes! This is the big grown-up
world. This is it! Accidents happen. People get hurt. People
I care about are getting hurt right now. Are you planning to
walk away from the scene of the accident every time and leave
people to bleed to death because you can't risk getting involved, you can't risk having to answer for yourself? I mean,
do you know what that *makes* you?''

''It's what *you're* trying to make me out to be!''

''No.'' She shook her head. ''You're doing it to yourself.
You're twenty years old, for Pete's sake. You plan to spend
the rest of your life being an adolescent, never taking responsibility for anything or anyone? Always making a fast get-
away or going dumb when things start happening? That's one
truly beautiful picture you're lining up for yourself! I can really get off on that.''

''Back off, Jude!''

''I was really into you, you know that? I thought we had
something so good happening. Now I don't know how I
could've been so dumb. I don't know. Maybe I was hung up
on your face or something. Because right now there doesn't
seem to be all that much inside of you. Except a lot of defense strategies and a heavy flight pattern. I came over think-

ing we could get down to some truth, you know? I came because we used to be something. I thought. Now, I feel so brought down. Really down. Because I loved you. The past month, I've really been missing you. How could I be so dumb? Forget I was here. Okay? I'll split, leave you to get on with your beautiful future."

She stubbed out her cigarette and got to her feet.

"You make me sound so bad," he said, his expression one of acute distress. "You come here and lay a heavy load of guilt and parental-type responsibility on my head, say a lot of hard words, and expect me to take it."

"Nobody says you have to take anything. I'm only trying to find *you* in here somewhere. You didn't used to be a coward. It makes me so mad. That's the thing, you know. It's so damned *demoralizing* to think I spent almost a whole year of my life believing I was in love with a stinking coward. It makes *me* look so bad. Like as if maybe my head's in the wrong place or I've just absolutely no goddamned judgment at all. I can't hang around here. I might start believing some of the weird stuff you're into."

"What's your trip?" he challenged. "Goodness and light. Laying down the truth like girl-scout cookies."

"It's a whole lot better than turning into some kind of vampire or something that only comes out at night. Blake"— she softened her voice—"how can you *be* this way? Denny's important to you. I know that! I was important to you. And I know that too. The only thing you're into is an occasional joint. You're an A student, for Pete's sake. You haven't even got long hair! And you dress like one of those dudes in an old Mickey Rooney movie. I *like* all that stuff about you. You've always come across like you've got a brain of your own and you wouldn't buy anybody else's trip. I *still* care about you. And if you cared about me the way you used to like to tell me you did, you'd see I'm hurting for these people because when you love someone it means their grief is yours. Why won't you help?"

"Don't say I was the one who told you, Jude."

"You know I'd never do that."

"It's not much."

"Anything. A place to start."

"Okay," he said at last, reaching for paper and a pencil, writing down an address, and then handing it to her.

"What's this?"

"Den dropped over a while back. She said she was staying with Lane."

"Has he got her turned on to anything, or anything?" she asked, stifling an intense desire to ask him why he'd sat on this information for so long.

"I don't know. Ask her yourself, you want to know."

"But you know. I know you know. What's happening to her, Blake?"

"Who knows?" he said tiredly. "She doesn't know herself."

"Why did you bother, Blake? Really, why? Why did you go to all the trouble of breathing into her mouth, keeping her alive, if you don't care?"

"Because. Because she's never been all that great at breathing on her own."

Jude's head snapped back as if he'd slapped her.

"You're a born survivor, Jude. Most of us can't make it without some help. Think about that the next time you do a dump on one of us lesser mortals. All that heavy self-righteousness gets a little hard to take sometimes. We weakies like to stick together. Like me and Denny."

"You're not weak," she said quietly. "What did happen?"

"I don't want anybody dying on me," he said, looking disconcerted. "I don't need that."

"You were scared. It's not a weakness to be scared, Blake. I've had a couple of people die on me, you know. I was *very* scared. But you pick up your cards and keep playing. That's what you're here for." She paused for a moment, looking again at the slip of paper. "Anyway, thanks for this."

"It probably won't take you anywhere," he said, sleepy now. "She was talking about cutting out. Just make sure you watch out where you go walking, babe. There's heavy action coming down around Lane and those guys. You want to make sure you don't go knocking at any doors without some backup.''

"Meaning?"

"Don't go alone. I wouldn't get off on finding out something had happened to you. You can put me down, call me all kinds of names, the whole sheet. But you're just as important to me as Denny ever was. More. And you know it. Because what we were into was a whole other thing. Den's always been a kid sister. Just remember, you're the one who walked. I never asked you to go."

"Why couldn't you just talk to me about all this instead of playing it like some kind of paranoid?"

"What's the difference? You're off. You've done your move. That's all there is to it."

"You give up too easily," she said. "Wouldn't you fight for what you want?"

"Are you telling me to get out there and start killing dragons?"

"That depends on your priorities, Blake. I never said goodbye for good. Anyway, listen, I've got to go. I'll be late to my gig."

"I'll see you, huh?"

"You know where to find me. And I'll see you in philosophy, Monday afternoon."

"Okay, Jude." He smiled a small smile. "Later."

Jude arrived back at the house that evening a few minutes after Marshall got in from the airport. Isabel, looking strained, was sitting in the living room, her fingers curled around a glass of whiskey she was holding on the sofa beside her. On the coffee table was a stack of books and stuff she'd brought home from the station.

"Listen," Jude said, pulling the paper from the pocket of her jeans. "I think I found out something."

Isabel turned her head questioningly. Marshall glanced over. At once, Jude knew she should've waited, shouldn't have blabbed it out while he was here.

"What is it, Judy?" Isabel asked.

She looks so tired, Jude thought. So tired and uptight. Why do you have to come here, man? Why don't you just split, leave her alone? She doesn't need this.

"It'll hold until later."

"No, that's all right. What is it?"

Marshall was obviously annoyed, Jude saw. She'd interrupted them. She hoped he wasn't laying another heavy pressure trip on Isabel.

"Lane's address," Jude said. "I got it out of Blake."

Isabel's heart leaped. "Did he know all this time?"

"I honestly don't think he did. He said Denny dropped in to see him. Listen, I've got this stuff put together for dinner, so why don't I get into that now, okay?"

Isabel didn't say anything for several seconds, then nodded. She felt suddenly very close to Denny, within touching distance. "I'll help," she offered.

"No, that's cool. I did it all up before I left this morning. You just relax."

"Judy, thank you."

"I know."

In the kitchen, Jude leaned against the counter, feeling the tension. She didn't like what was coming down. It felt bad, wrong. She wanted to go back to the living room, stay beside Isabel. She had that older-sister feeling again, that protective feeling. It wasn't fair for him to come charging in, laying down a lot of emotional garbage right now. Not fair. Didn't he know that, couldn't he see?

"How is it," Marshall asked carefully, "you don't mind her doing a little private finding out on her own, but you very much mind my even suggesting it?"

"She's part of all this," she said, her fingers tight around her glass. She didn't feel like talking, wished he hadn't presumed upon a welcome and simply shown up at the house. She wanted to sit very quietly and think about Denny, about seeing her, being close enough to touch, talk. "She's involved with these kids, they know her. None of this is personal, Marsh. Why do you insist on taking it as if it is?"

"Six weeks," he said. "How long do you suppose things are going to go on this way?"

"Six months. Six years. The rest of my life or Denny's. I don't know. Is there some specified length of time you have in mind? Have you set up time limits, Marsh? Two more weeks, and Denny time's up? What're you trying to say?"

"This . . . all this—it's going on too long. That's all."

"Oh, yes," she said with a sigh, "far too long. And every bone in my body keeps reminding me it's nowhere near finished. I would like it finished, my life settled. And I think if Denise had her way in this conversation, she'd tell you she'd like it finished, too. She's not any happier with all this than I am. But it's up to the two of us to work it out. What do you *want* from me, Marshall?"

"This is the first time I've arrived back, and there's been no . . . Things have changed."

"Everything has changed," she concurred.

"And how long is *she* going to stay?" he asked.

God! she thought. Now you're doing it to her. Unable to speak her name. "Judy?"

"That's right."

"Just as long as she likes." ·

"I see."

This is the last time you're ever going to come to this house, Marshall. You don't belong here. I don't want you here. You're too filled with petty jealousies, envy. "Say what you're thinking," she invited, taking a sip of the whiskey, feeling its fire the length of her throat.

"I'm . . . It's just jet lag," he alibied. "It's rough getting back into being on the go."

She didn't hear his answer. She was, for a moment, experiencing an inner lifting, a resurgence of optimism. Just to know Denny's whereabouts, the state of her being. That's all. No answers or promises. Just to know.

He looked at her, at her legs and the way she had them crossed, at her arms and the way her breasts pressed roundly against the front of her dress. In his thoughts of her, from a distance, she was small, fragile, in need of sheltering. Her reality always surprised him. Because she was anything but small. And not at all delicate. Thinner now than she'd been when he'd left. He noticed that, and the dark smudges beneath her eyes, the deepening lines either side of her mouth, the two—a furrow—between her eyes. Making herself sick with worry over a kid who isn't worth it. You don't need me, he thought. You really don't need me. The thought flattened him. This tall, black-haired, white-skinned woman with arching cheekbones and deep-set eyes. With her hair knotted this way, she looked like a flemenco dancer. But she wasn't Spanish, not small or especially graceful—except in bed—and definitely not in need of sheltering. Not by him, anyway. So why was he here? She wasn't the same as she'd been. How could she be? Appearing on television five mornings a week. Meeting celebrities. A free wardrobe. Money. She was now earning considerably more than he was.

"How hungry is everybody?" Jude asked, appearing in the doorway, a paring knife in her hand. "Big, medium, or little?"

"Medium," Isabel lied, really not at all hungry.

"The same, I guess," Marshall said without looking up.

"Okay." Jude returned to the kitchen. To bludgeon a tomato to death.

"Why don't you like her, Marsh?" Isabel asked.

"I haven't said I don't like her."

You make me think, she thought, of that time when I was maybe twelve and this friend of my mother's came over wearing a terribly shabby coat. A terrible coat. An embarrassing coat. And after she'd gone, I asked my mother, "How can she *wear* that coat? It's so terrible." And my mother said, "She *knows* it's terrible, Isabel. She hasn't the money for a new one." That hadn't occurred to me: that she knew how awful her coat was. I thought I was the only one who knew. You're the same about your likes and dislikes, Marshall. You think you're the only one who is aware of them.

"You don't have to say it," she said. "You show it in the way you speak to her."

"You're attacking me again," he said. "Why?"

"Come sit beside me. Let's not shout at each other across the room."

Looking as if she'd asked him to lift the side of the house, he got up and crossed the room to drop down heavily beside her on the sofa.

"Look at me," she said, setting her glass down. "Look at me, Marsh." *See* me! See how things are for me, and stop inflicting more pain on top of pain on top of fear, worry, pain.

Reluctantly he turned his head. And at once the sight of her face this close to his melted him down. Her eyes at this range were deep, dark; her mouth wide and soft, mesmerizing. His arm went around her, drawing her closer.

"I don't understand," he whispered.

She hadn't expected this, was caught off her guard. And found his body's warmth comforting. To be held, secured. For the first time since the night of Denny's near-death, she actually wanted him. Suddenly, without any warning, she felt herself thawing. And searched his eyes for some communication, some message. See me, know me! Don't be petulant and self-important now! Help me! You could help me if you'd just risk extending yourself. Offer empathy, support, closeness. Sympathy, too. I'm paying a monstrous price for a very small success you see as a major one.

His eyes closed, and his mouth opened over hers. His hand slipped up over her ribs to cover her breast, and she responded, her entire body untensing, her insides softening, loosening. She put her arm around his neck, returning the kiss, very stimulated by his lips and tongue, the contact. Pure physical comfort. If you'll offer me only that, simply that, without anything else, I'll accept it, Marshall. I have a need, an awful need to hold on for a little while.

They broke apart, and he held her hard against his chest, his mouth moving over her ear. He wanted to say: I love you. But for the first time, he couldn't get the words out. They were stuck in his throat. As if he'd just swallowed a peach pit and it was lodged midway down his windpipe, choking him. For these few seconds while she remained motionless inside his arms, her eyes closed, her lips slightly parted, her breathing erratic, he felt unequal to her needs, her unstated demands. I can't, he thought. I can't handle this. Not with that kid out there who won't come home, forcing you into deeper-than-ever responsibility for her. And not with yet another kid out in the kitchen insisting her way into our privacy. Too many distractions. Problems. You belong to too many people.

She sat thinking about how in the two years they'd known each other they'd never once done what they'd planned to do. Every single time they'd arranged to go out for an evening and she'd dressed and made up in accordance with those plans, he'd arrived at the front door in a state of immediate lusting need, and invariably her clothes had gone unseen by anyone but him, her makeup had become heedlessly smeared about by his kisses and their activities in bed. She could effortlessly enumerate the number of times they'd actually gone out through the front door together as intended. Always, always he hurried her upstairs to bed. And later on they'd eat whatever was left over in the refrigerator.

It had to do with a certain disrespect she'd allowed him to develop. For her and for the plans they made. A certain disrespect she'd allowed to arise within herself. Always it had been that rush to her bedroom, where he'd revealed himself already at the bursting point, hard and impatient for the feel of her flesh, the acquiescing accessibility of her body. There was never any time, never the slow-building anticipation generated by an evening spent over dinner, with conversation. He arrived in heat, and she inevitably was forced to react to his need. Her own need invariably inspired by the evidence of his. Because there was something very heady in being responsible for creating such a powerful desire in someone. Power knowing she might, if she wished, control this man because of his desire for her. Knowing, but incapable of doing. Because that seemed too dishonest, too manipulative. Yet, wasn't it what he'd done all this time to her: manipulating her with his desire?

All she'd shared with Marshall was her body and certain censored thoughts. Not her interior life. Not her most private hopes and fears. I'm not willing to sacrifice genuine communication for the sake of mainly broken promises and a substantial number of regularly received orgasms. It isn't enough, she thought, her body beginning to cool rapidly. If I can't have both—the words and the physical contact—I'd prefer to do without. Having my body satisfied and my brain ignored doesn't work. I wind up dissatisfied in every area.

She drew away gently, trying to find words with which to convey her decision to him, when Jude announced, "We can eat now, if you're ready."

All the way out to Oakbridge, having had to thumb rides three different times, only to get there and find the kids had split. Nobody left. And the house that had held the commune all freshly painted and occupied by this young couple with two little kids. The girl was nice enough and said Denise could use the telephone if she wanted. But there wasn't anybody to call, and she felt really scared all at once, standing there at the front door. Scared. There was nowhere left to run to.

"Hey, are you okay?" the girl asked, with a little kid clutching at her knees, a baby in her arms.

Denise looked at her. Two dollars and some pennies, and it was already dark outside. She couldn't, no way she could go back to Lane. He'd hand her over to Leo. Leo would destroy her. She was hungry. And so goddamned tired. She looked down at the little kid and automatically reached into her back pocket for some Kleenex, bent down, and wiped the kid's nose. The kid just stared at her and let her do it.

"Why don't you come on in?" the girl suggested, backing away from the door, watching Denise shove the soiled tissue back into her pocket. She saw Denise straighten, hesitating. "Come on." The girl smiled. "It's cool."

Denise stepped over the threshold, wondering what in hell she was doing.

"Listen," she said, looking at the girl's face, the cleanness of her skin and hair. "I hiked out here, you know, 'cause I thought like my friends would still be here. But they're not. I mean . . ."

"You need a place to crash," the girl said.

Denise nodded.

"You can stay until morning if you want. There's a cot upstairs in the baby's room. Okay? Eat with us, too, if you're hungry. It's not much. Just spaghetti."

"Why?" Denny asked, suspicious.

"Larry works at night," the girl said, closing the door and moving down the narrow hallway to the kitchen. "I get kind of lonely way out here all by myself at night. You can keep me company. Hungry?" she asked, looking around over her shoulder. "We were just going to sit down to eat. Come on," she urged gently. "Come meet Larry. He's righteous."

What was happening? She couldn't understand it. But maybe, she thought, maybe it's just the way it seems. Just friendly people. They probably think I'm a sadtimer. She looked down at herself, then walked into the kitchen. It was warm, smelled good. Food. Her stomach growled. The girl and this Larry dude looked at her. Her stomach growled again. Feeling like a total moron, Denny smiled.

Six

An embarrassing silence throughout dinner interrupted only by pass-me's. Jude took off to her room as soon as she could, upset by the negative waves emanating from Marshall. It felt as if the dining room—the whole house, in fact—was filled with undulating curves and streamers of bad vibes. And she thought if she maybe stayed out of the way, the atmosphere might possibly lighten a little.

She got into this old book of poetry she'd found for a quarter at a garage sale and came out of it only when she heard the sound of Marshall's car starting up the driveway outside. And had a really bad moment, hoping they weren't going to go out looking for Denny now. Because she hadn't had a chance to talk to Isabel or warn her, tell her the rest of what Blake had said.

Then, thinking about Blake, she thought she'd go downstairs and phone him, say hi, let him know she felt good about what they'd managed to get straight between them that morning.

Isabel sat trying to keep a realistic lid on her optimism. She was so excited after all these weeks of disturbed, restless sleep and constant worrying. The prospect of seeing Denise. Just seeing her alive and well. Most likely with her defiance unaltered in any perceptible way. And thinking of that, she suddenly wondered just what she thought she'd accomplish by going to this place. If she did find Denny. What would she say? I just wanted to see you, know you were all right. That. And Denny would stand, hands on hips, all impatience, saying something like: Well, now you've seen me. Not bothering to add: So you can go. Because it was implied. Didn't need saying. But despite all that, it would be such a relief, so restorative, and such a relief just seeing her.

It did no good trying to reason with herself this way, because every instinct in her said this trip, this effort to find Denny, had to be made. Justified, unjustified. It didn't matter. For my peace of mind, she thought. So I can sleep tonight and perhaps tomorrow night too. And go to the station, do my job without being preoccupied, without speculating constantly on your whereabouts, the state of your being. This is for me, Denise. I wonder if you could understand that. I wonder. Lord, Denny, what did I do to you? Day and night for weeks, I've gone over and over your life and mine. Minutely, like an archaeologist, scratching gingerly at the layers of time coating our relationship, trying to locate clues, artifacts. Something to show me where or how or when the schism occurred. If you'd only *tell* me. It's your attitude of calculating uncaring that defeats me so completely. My head aches from these nonending attempts to piece it all together. Just be there and alive, and I'll gladly go away and leave you to get on with whatever it is you're doing.

The last time she'd come to the house, she'd been so restless, so agitated. Her skin blotchy, broken out for the first time in years. Her long, usually gleaming hair had hung around her face like a ragged black curtain through which Isabel had had occasional glimpses of her dark-circled, evasive eyes.

"Denise," she'd asked, risking the usual sarcastic, biting response, "would you like to come home?"

"I don't know," Denny had answered unpredictably, studying her bitten fingernails. "I would, sort of, like to. Sort of. You know? But maybe in a couple of weeks or something. I don't know. Not right away. I've got a lot of stuff, things to do."

"Did you quit your job?" she asked, trying not to come across too nosy, too motherly.

"They let me go. About a month ago, I guess."

"The apartment is for you, you know," she'd said gently. "You could do your own cooking up there, use the outside entrance. It's awfully quiet without you around."

"I guess it is." Denny had lit a cigarette, then used two fingers to lift the hair back from her face. "I'd better get going. I've got to meet some people."

"Do you need any money, Denny?"

Looking away, she'd said, "I guess I could use a little. If you can handle it."

Isabel had given her thirty dollars. As she was leaving, Denny had stopped and put out her hand to touch Isabel's hair.

"Remember when you were thinking about cutting your hair? I'm glad you didn't. I like it this way. It makes you look really pretty."

It was such an atypical gesture—actually venturing to touch her mother; such a rare compliment, Isabel had been suddenly, dangerously close to tears. Denny had hugged her abruptly, whispering, "Oh, Mom, I've fucked everything so totally. Blown the whole thing." Before Isabel had had a chance to say or do anything, Denny had freed herself and rushed away. Isabel had watched her go off down the street in her patched, baggy jeans, her scuffed clogs, heading for the bus stop. She'd stayed at the front door watching until Denny was out of sight. Then she'd gone back inside, to slump down on the sofa, staring into the haze of smoke left by Denny's cigarette. Like the formless plasm of a ghost.

If only you could tell me, talk to me. I want so much to help you. Every time you say or do the unexpected, it's like holding out a diamond on the palm of your hand for me to look at, then snatching it away before I've had any sort of chance to see. VD. I wouldn't have condemned you, made you feel worse than you already did.

Oh, Denny. What happened to the little girl who loved taking sips of her father's morning coffee while she sat on the edge of the bathtub entranced, watching her father shave? That little girl who'd appear wearing such a smile—oh, the loveliness of those smiles!—a dab of shaving cream gracing the tip of her nose? Where did she go? What became of that little girl who'd call me back upstairs for third and fourth good-night kisses? The little girl who was so beautifully fussy about which outfit she'd wear to school, displaying outrageous signs of femininity that made you an all-the-more-lovable, too-tall ten-year old. What happened to that little girl, Denise?

By fourteen, you were saying things like, "Your clothes are so old-fashioned!" You couldn't stand the way I dressed. "I hate this guck. Why can't we just have hamburgers?" You couldn't stand the way I cooked. "How can you go out with creeps like that?" You couldn't stand my men friends. There hasn't been very much you could stand, it seems. The only defense I've had has been silence.

Bitchy. Constantly, unrelievedly bitchy. You've seemed to me to be trudging around, bent double under this monstrous load of complaints you have against me and the rest of the world, airing your opinions and your criticisms with a beleaguered attitude meant to convey just how trying your life has been, having to cope with a mother so hopelessly inept in every area.

I've tried to match the phases through which you've traveled against comparable ones of my own teenage years. And found that although I remember with painful clarity how despicably phony my own parents seemed to me for a time, I was still respectful, still angrily obedient. It was love for them that made me so distressed at their failings.

Now I wonder if motherhood isn't some long-term time bomb set at birth and destined to detonate in adolescence. I think of opening the door to your room late at night, to stand beside the bed looking down at your sleeping face, wishing you could wake up retaining that same sweet expression that overtook your features in sleep. It made me feel like the worst sort of fool, getting up every morning hoping this would be the morning we'd be able to greet each other with open affection. Or even just greet each other. But you'd stumble into the kitchen holding a shifting mass of books to your chest, ignore the breakfast I'd prepared, drink half a glass of juice while grumbling about one thing and another, and then take off for school. Defeated, deflated, I'd sit down at the table with the morning paper and a pot of coffee and drink and read my way through half the morning, trying to pick myself up out of the low brought about by another unsuccessful beginning to what would be another noncommunicative, hostile day.

I love you. And loving you, have become gradually filled with desperation, because love is not enough. Trying to be understanding doesn't help. Nothing helps. Nothing works.

Yet, for all that, I'm still so hopeful for you, so sure you'll find something or someone who'll make sense to you, so that you can begin to make sense to yourself and start finding your way out of your discontent. I felt so positive it was beginning when you finished school, had a place of your own, a job. Those months when you and Jude came Sunday mornings with your gifts of coffee and doughnuts. Good times. They were. Beginning to approach each other. Occasional embraces that meant so much, moved and shook me so deeply I could think of nothing else for days after but the tremendous gratification of having you volunteer yourself into my arms. I am hopeful of you, Denny. But all my hopefulness, all my thinking, cannot bring you any closer to me any more quickly. And part of me is dying every day with you gone.

"I'm really kind of tired, Isabel." Marshall said, hearing at once how feeble the excuse sounded. But he really didn't want to be out at nearly nine o'clock tracking down that pain-in-the-ass kid, that mouthy obnoxious kid.

"Please, this is very important to me."

"Okay." Resigned, he took the slip from her to look once more at the address.

She sat back, looking out the side window, seeing lights passing in a blur, noticing a dog trotting along the sidewalk, two men strolling along, chatting animatedly. At a stoplight, her eyes were arrested by the face of a small black boy with an exquisite mouth, huge sad eyes. And wondered what a small boy of perhaps eight, or nine at most, was doing out all alone at night. And wondered what a young girl of eighteen was doing out in the world all alone. Wondered what she herself hoped to find. And wondered too why she always managed to find something, some little thing to hope for. Am I a fool?

Am I someone who deludes herself, diverts herself by fixing on things? Is that realistic? Am I realistic? What's real?

Six months ago I wouldn't have believed it possible I could become accustomed to appearing daily on television. But now, here it is the secondary focal point of my daily existence. Getting up early every morning to collect up my notes, my materials, to drive through the still-empty streets in the company of delivery trucks and stray animals on my way to the close-to-deserted studio. Saying good morning to the guard on the gate, parking the car behind the building, walking in through the sound-stage door, because the front of the building is not yet open; greeting the grips who've already prepared the first pot of coffee of the day, pausing to pour myself a cup before continuing on out of the studio, down the stairs and along the corridor to Lenny's little domain. To strip down to my underwear, be wrapped in what feels very much like a hospital gown, and climb into the makeup chair in front of the wall of mirrors, to sit sipping my coffee, watching Lenny's reflection as he brushes out my hair, puts in the heated rollers, and then begins the process of applying layers of glamour to my skin, my eyes, my cheekbones, my mouth. And while he does all that, I go over my notes—holding them at arm's length in front of me—or perhaps finish the last chapter of the book written by the guest I'm to interview. With Lenny patting and brushing and sighing softly over me, relishing the length of my hair as he rather mindlessly gossips about this and that; a monologue I do not hear, am not expected to respond to. It's Lenny's world, his control. I belong to Lenny for fifty-five minutes while he works his transformation. The room is pleasantly warm, the chair is comfortable, and I find myself succumbing to a kind of animal pleasure at his attentions.

But then, just when I've been lulled into a state of tranquillity, Lenny's done for the moment and I've got to climb down from the chair and hurry back along the cold corridor, up through the control room, and on in to the miniscule changing room. Get into the clothes I was fitted for one afternoon last week, taking care not to get any of the makeup on the clothes; then—time counting down now—hurry back out through the control room, glancing at the panel of screens and the half-awake engineer, on my way back to Lenny to have the rollers removed from my hair and watch the hair get brushed out, brushed up, coiled, pinned, and patted. Done. On to the Green Room for a few minutes with my guest—if Jerry hasn't ferreted him or her away on some pretext—offering coffee, offering ease if there's a slight case of nervousness, then off again for a hasty production conference with Ash and the detestable Jerry. And, finally, it's air time. Every day, Monday to Friday, I live for it. Praying Jerry won't step on my insteps or elbow me in the breasts, won't hook his cufflinks accidentally into my clothes or my hair in an effort to disarrange me; praying Jerry will just once leave me alone. The eternal optimist. I probably am a fool. It doesn't matter, though. Nothing matters. Except trying to find Denise and trying to find out how it all came to be this way.

Stop for a minute. To think about the interview she'd taped that morning. Because this particular woman was on such a tightly scheduled tour she wasn't going to be available for tomorrow's live show and there hadn't been an opening on this morning's show.

Isabel had for years loved the writing, looked forward to meeting the author. The biographical and promotional advance material had had a peculiar slant to it, a slant that seemed unrelated to the author's work. As if whoever'd written about this woman either hadn't read her work or was trying to market her like some new laundry product. Isabel had agreed to do the interview solely because of the exceptional quality of the woman's most recent novel; almost in spite of the accompanying material.

She'd found her sitting in the Green Room smoking a cigarette, drinking black coffee, watching the *Today* show. A publisher's rep with her. She'd looked up and smiled when Isabel introduced herself, offering a firm, solid handshake and a mouth curved into a splendid smile. A small woman with light brown hair and magnificent, old-soul eyes, dressed very tastefully in a cream-colored crepe-de-chine shirt and chocolate-brown trousers belted around a tiny waist. A small woman radiating tremendous energy and intelligence, warmth. Isabel was captivated by her, knowing at once it would be a very good interview. Which wasn't always the way, regardless of the quality of the writing. So many inarticulate, uncertain people who could, on paper, become positive, articulate, and insightful.

A very good interview. An opportunity to ask a number of probing questions and receive well-thought-out, incisive replies. She'd been genuinely sorry to have the interview end. Fifteen minutes hadn't been long enough. An hour wouldn't have been long enough. After the show, Isabel had asked, "Do you have children?"

"A daughter," the woman answered.

"So do I," Isabel had told her.

"Terrible, isn't it?" The woman had given Isabel another of her brilliant smiles. "The ultimate agony. Trying to be objective, failing; having yourself turned sideways and upside down by someone you thought would be such a friend and ally, such a great comfort to you in your old age. I think our mothers all told us to get married, have children so we'd know what hell we put *them* through. A sort of quiet, generational revenge."

"But you love her." Isabel had smiled back.

"Of course. How can you not? I will love her and have moments when I wonder why I ever had her, moments when I actually hate her. But whatever the season, we'll belong to one another. I think they must all come home in their hearts at the end. Because we're all women together, finally. And the pain of a lifetime's experience makes us into old friends. I feel that coming."

"How old is she?"

"Fifteen. And yours?"

"Almost nineteen."

Not enough time to talk. The publisher's rep came to hurry the woman away, leaving the thoughts, the talk, incomplete.

"Can you see the number of that house?" Marshall asked, peering through the windshield.

"That's the right number," she said, looking at Blake's writing. They were here. At the place Denise might be. Please be here. I need you to be here.

Marshall parked the car. They got out and walked back down the street toward the house.

Sometimes Brian wondered what in hell he was trying to prove. It was a little hard to keep sight of his original motives. Playing lawman like some bad movie. Sitting for nights on end in the car because he'd managed to hear or see something that might lead somewhere. But rarely did. Occasionally, the hours of waiting, the silence, were rewarded. And then it all made sense. It did, too, give him a place to be, a definite purpose. Or perhaps the illusion of a purpose. His thinking frequently became nonconclusive. Possibly affected by the stillness, the darkness, the lack of definitive action.

But after Geoff, the whole of Brian's private world had disintegrated so totally, so quickly. And grief, anger, were dangerous when they turned inward. So, he'd had to redirect these negative energies into a positive area. In a way, this was how he said to Geoff: I'm sorry. This was how he filled a considerable number of his night hours. Sitting in the car, watching and listening, waiting, thinking. Thinking about all sorts of things. Free mentally to roam here and there, to rewrite his life and play it out again so it came down better the second time around.

This watch was going to get results. He'd sensed that from the beginning. Instinct had a lot to do with it. And he knew this one was going to work. There was a kind of shaky, anticipatory stirring in his belly, and he was watching with more than usual alertness, attention; taking care not to let his mind wander too far afield. Which it did sometimes. Conjuring up images of everything from miraculously restored family units to the enticement of pale, sinuous female bodies offering themselves with murmured promises of love, warmth.

He saw the car pull over to the curb, saw the couple emerge from the car and come down the street to climb the rickety front steps of the house. And felt the hair on his arms rise, the skin at the back of his neck tighten. The stirring in his belly turning to a quivering tension.

"Dammit!" he whispered to himself, reaching for the mike hooked under the dash. What the hell is this? he wondered, watching the man knock at the door.

In the darkness of the porch, it wasn't possible to make out the woman's features. But he could tell she wasn't a kid. And she wasn't in the right place.

"Better send in a couple of units," he said in a soft undertone into the mike. "On the quiet. Something's happening, and I don't like the feel of it."

"What does Larry do?" Denny asked, standing by the sink helping dry the dishes.

"Larry? He works at the radio station."

"Which one?"

"Oakbridge."

"What does he do there?"

"He's a DJ," Cathy said, smiling. "A kind of poor people's Wolfman."

"Really?" Denise smiled too. "He has a handle and like that?"

"Oh, sure!" Cathy laughed, putting on an announcer-type voice, "This is the sound of Oakbridge coming to you, good people, and this is your man, Larry the Lover Glover. Isn't that too much?"

"You're kidding! That's for real?"

"Believe it!" Cathy said. "He's got a big audience. The station has a very strong signal."

"I know it. You from here?"

"California," she said, passing Denny the last of the dishes. "La Jolla. Ever been to California?"

Denise shook her head.

"San Diego's kind of the pits, but La Jolla's really okay. Anyway, Larry's from Sunnyvale, and he got this gig in La Jolla, which is how we met. I was a typist like at the station. Anyway, we were there two years. We had Christy in La Jolla. Then we moved to Minneapolis 'cause Larry had an offer. But he couldn't hack the station politics, you know? And it was too much of a middle-of-the-road station. So he started checking around, and he got this gig here. We've been here four months, and he's really high on this gig. He has guests and like that. The hours are kind of a bummer, twelve till six every night except the weekends. But he comes home, sleeps till like noon, and then we have the rest of the whole day together. I'm starting to get used to it. But nights alone're kind of spooky. I like having company. What about you?"

"Oh"—Denny draped the dish towel over the rack—"I'm from the city here. That's all."

"You want some coffee?"

"Okay, sure." She still couldn't figure any of this out. The easy atmosphere, the no-sweat way they'd rapped over dinner, inviting her to crash for the night. There had to be a catch. Something. People didn't do for nothing.

"Runaway?" Cathy asked casually, setting the percolator on the stove.

"Are you *kidding?*" Denise turned wide-eyed to look at her. "I'm almost nineteen, man!"

"Really?" Cathy said. "Well"—she shrugged lightly—"age doesn't have all that much to do with it. I mean, if you're running, you're running. You know how old I am?"

"How old?"

"We got married when I was eighteen." Cathy laughed. "I'll be twenty-two next month."

"Shit!" Denny smiled. "You're my age, for chrissake!"

"Old married lady with two kids."

"You like it?" Denny asked seriously.

"A lot," Cathy said, just as seriously. "Really! Before Larry, I guess I was kind of a groupie. Into a whole lot of nothing stuff, weird shit. Larry kind of made it all come together. You know?"

"Like how?"

"Like just believing. That's part of it. And part of it's knowing the whole thing fits together. With Christy and Tink. *My* people, you know?"

Denny nodded. But she couldn't shake off the feeling she was being handed a con. All the nicey-nice sincerity, the sweetness. There were pieces of broken glass somewhere, concealed hooks. Had to be. Didn't there? Why should these people do something for nothing? Nobody else did. Except Mom. But Mom had to. Obligations, duty. All that shit.

Runaway. Is that what I am, for chrissake? I'm no goddamned runaway.

No? What d'you call it, then, cookie? What name do you put on it? You split with the no-name, no-address number. So what d'you call it?

Bug off! I'm trying to think.

These two. With their kids. Maybe they were into a group thing, looking for a threesome. No. Too straight for that. She could tell. She'd be out the goddamned door so fast if they tried any of that shit on her, they wouldn't see her goddamned dust!

But, man, it felt so good to know she was going to be able to sleep. No Lane around to shove ammies under her nose so she'd go off sixty thousand times while he rode her out like she was some goddamned Harley-Davidson or something. Man, she was going to be okay. She'd escaped. Handle whatever came up around here when it happened.

"I don't like the look of this place," Marshall said under his breath.

"Neither do I," she said, experiencing a chill of apprehension. She couldn't, didn't want to imagine Denny living in a place like this. But if she was here . . .

The door was opened by a huge man whose age was almost impossible to determine. He might have been twenty or forty. With long, greasy-looking hair in a ponytail. A lot of overgrown facial hair. And a particularly red, particularly unattractive thick-lipped smirk. The sight of his mouth brought to Isabel's mind those magazines Jerry favored. With full-color photographs of nude girls whose bodies were contorted in such a way as to present themselves totally open to the camera's eye. Their vaginas so red they seemed like fresh-made wounds. She'd picked up one of the magazines Jerry had left behind—intentionally, to upset her?—in the makeup room, opened it, stared at the photographs, feeling faintly sickened, and at once put the magazine down again. This man's mouth had almost precisely the same effect upon her now. That and his daggerish fingernails. He was wearing a startlingly clean white T-shirt and filthy blue jeans, heavy black leather boots with thick soles and heels. Gigantic muscular arms. And an increasingly loose, increasingly lascivious smirk that overtook his face as he looked at Isabel, letting his eyes meander meaningfully down the entire length of her body and up again.

"Hey, mama!" he said in a soft voice that was somehow as startling as his immaculate shirt. "What's happening?"

"We're looking for Denise. Or Lane," she said, her voice emerging clotted, heavy with the fear that had shot through her system as he'd taken his eyes on their bold tour of her face and body. Irrational fear, she told herself.

"Oh, yeah?" he said, looking over at Marshall, his expression changing to one of mild disgust. As if he was thinking how easily he could dispose physically of Marshall.

"That's right," Marshall chimed in, sounding equally glue-voiced. "Is either one here?"

"Well, come in, come in!" Leo invited, taking a step to one side, swinging the door open wide. "We'll just have us a little look-see."

Marshall didn't want to go inside, but followed Isabel as she stepped into the dimly lit hallway and stood waiting to be shown where to go.

"Come on," they were told, following this frightening man down the hallway. He threw open another door, and in a grotesque mockery of courtesy, bent low over his outstretched arm, indicating they were to precede him inside. Isabel took a step into the room, with Marshall close behind her, instantly gripped by the feeling that they shouldn't have come here, shouldn't have accepted the invitation to enter this house. Denise couldn't possibly be here. Isabel could tell by the feel of the place that Denise wasn't here.

There were four other men in the room, all of them terrifyingly similar in looks and dress to the one who'd opened the front door. At the sight of Isabel and Marshall, the four got to their feet—one had been leaning against the wall smoking a roach that he now let drop to the floor, two had been sitting on the floor, and the fourth had been bent over looking out a rear window—and stood, hands on hips, smiling expectantly, looking at Leo.

"Is one of you Lane?" she asked, her heart racing. This was beginning to feel like a bad dream, something bizarre and overfull of negative airwaves.

"Is one of us Lane?" Leo echoed from the doorway.

The four in the room laughed.

Marshall said, "Come on, Isabel. I think we'd better go."

He moved to take her arm, and one of the four, in a lazy gesture, dropping his arm between Marshall and Isabel, causing Marshall to angrily swipe at the imposed barrier.

"Don't!" Isabel warned Marshall softly, sensing how readily these five men would shift from mimicry to violence.

"Hey, man!" Leo drawled from the doorway. "Take it easy, baby. *Easy!*"

Marshall didn't like it, didn't like feeling as afraid as he did. Nothing had actually happened, yet the air was charged, threatening. The two who'd been on the floor were casually moving around in back of Marshall now. He could somehow feel their breathing, sense their smiles. Isabel looked over at the one blocking the door, asking, "Is Lane here? Are you Lane?"

"Well, now, mama, that depends," he said, smiling at her. "It depends on like who's looking for him."

"I'd like to talk to him," she said, forcing herself to remain calm. "I understand he knows my daughter. Or she's staying here. I'm looking for her."

"This is an absolute waste of time!" Marshall declared loudly, his face brilliant with color. "Let's *go*, Isabel!"

"Isabel wants to talk to Lane, man," Leo said to Marshall in that damnably soft voice. "Just re-lax!" He pushed away from the door and moved closer to Isabel, his smile flourishing. "Who's your daughter, mama?"

"Denny," she said. "Denise Gary." She was drenched with perspiration, her underarms soggily cold. She'd never met people who frightened her more. But she told herself it had to be possible to reason with them, deal with them calmly. They were only people, after all.

"Uh-huh," Leo nodded. "Denny."

"Do you know her?" Isabel asked hopefully.

"Do we know her?" Leo asked the other four. "Do we know Denny?"

Isabel turned to see each of the four moving slowly closer to her and Marshall. The air in the room was hot, clouded with sweetish-smelling smoke, perspiration. The smell of damp male bodies. Mildew. Water-stained ancient wallpaper, filthy scarred floorboards, and raglike curtains half-hanging over the window.

"She looks like you, mama, I got eyes to know the chick," Leo said, taking another step that placed him directly in front of her. "I got big eyes to see any little chickie looks like you." He pressed his long-nailed thumb against her chin, his body inches from hers.

Marshall's arm shot out, knocking Leo's hand away. "Don't *touch* her!" he said loudly, his voice unsteady. "Keep your hands off her!"

"Marshall, *please!*" she said, just barely above a whisper.

"You're a hard case, eh, man?" Leo said softly, menacingly, the smile gone. "What's the matter with you, man? You need some tranquilizing? Don't *interrupt* when I'm rapping with Isabel, Marshall! It's *impolite*. He has bad manners," he said to the two who were now standing directly behind Marshall. "Didn't nobody ever tell you it's not nice to come knocking at people's doors, then coming on all impolite? That's not nice, is it, Sheffie? What d'ya say, Big Time?"

"That's right, Leo," the one called Sheffie agreed. Isabel looked around. Sheffie had large, hyperthyroid eyes that glittered wetly.

"Riiight!" Big Time drawled. Big Time was the smallest of the group, with massive shoulders and overlapping tattoos running the length of both forearms. Isabel's eyes were caught by the blending shades of blue, the scrolls and loops.

"You are im-*po*-lite," Leo repeated. "You gotta learn yourself some manners, baby."

"This is ... Get out of our way!" Marshall insisted indignantly, his indignation ludicrous. "We're leaving!"

"Marshall, you're not helping," Isabel cautioned quietly. "Please, just stop it!"

"*You* don't know what you're *doing!*" he snapped at her, his eyes filled with fear and anger and accusations.

"You're getting on my nerves, man!" Leo said. "Your friend's like getting on my nerves, you know," he said to Isabel. "Why's he so fuckin' uptight? How can you hack such an uptight dude, a nice mama like you?"

She looked again at Marshall, trying to warn him visually to control himself. He was irritating these men. Couldn't he see you didn't act this way with this sort of people? "He's tired," she said apologetically. "*Is* Lane here?" she asked Leo again. "Or Denny? If neither of them is, we'll get out of here and stop bothering you."

Leo laughed. "Hey, mama, you don't bother me." He once more pressed his thumb against her chin. His proximity repelled her, as did his obscenely overthick lips and too-long fingernails.

Marshall, seeing this disgusting creature taking what he felt were considerable and outrageous liberties, leaped across the room and whacked Leo's hand away from Isabel's face.

With effortless strength, like an affronted disdainful gorilla, Leo flung Marshall halfway across the room, right into the arms of Sheffie and Big Time, who took hold of him and, with what felt like iron hands, held him immobilized.

"Take it *easy* man!" Sheffie said softly, his bulging eyes glossily earnest. As if he too was trying to warn Marshall. "Trouble with all you civilian dudes, you just don't know how to cool it."

"You are one very nice-looking mama," Leo said, returning his attention to Isabel, smiling down at her. He was enormous, at least six and a half feet tall, perhaps two hundred and fifty pounds. She was so stunned by the way they'd tossed Marshall around, she couldn't speak. They'd handled him like a weightless puppet.

"One *very* nice-looking mama," Leo went on. "You wanna rap with Lane, see, you gotta be very nice to Leo. And me, I'm Leo. Dig it? You wanna make a little nice with me, mama?"

"We'd like to go," she said, her voice faded down to a thick whisper. "We've obviously made a mistake." A terrible mistake. Disappointment like a blood clot in her throat. And fear impairing her breathing, sending sweat into the palms of her hands.

'No mistake, baby! Now, these guys''—he nodded at the other four—"they like teenies. Nice unbusted little teenies, all fresh and sweetlike. But me, now, I like a big, good-looking mama knows where it's at, glad to get it, has the moves down right.''

She shook her head and stepped back, colliding with another body. The third of the men was standing directly behind her. Like a wall.

"Take off your coat, Isabel mama," Leo invited. "We'll sit us down like, do a little conversation-making."

"Please," she said, glancing over at Marshall's panic-stricken face. "Just let us leave."

For some reason, her saying this made Leo angry. She could see it in his eyes and felt even more frightened. She and Marshall weren't going to leave this place undamaged. Bad things were about to happen. Nightmarish things. And her stomach was churning, the perspiration streaming down her sides now, her lungs struggling as if she wasn't receiving sufficient oxygen, as the one behind her inserted his hand down inside the back of her coat collar. She felt his knuckles on the nape of her neck. Leo, smiling differently all at once, reaching behind him, extended his hand, pressed something and a knife blade materialized in the air in front of her. She gasped and again collided with the man behind her, the hand hard, unyielding against the nape of her neck.

"Don't!" she whispered, convinced she and Marshall were about to be tortured, murdered. For no reason. Except that they'd come here. Unreasoning, abstract violence. She wanted not to believe it was happening.

"I said to you to take off your coat," Leo said, as he slid the knife inside the overlap of her coat. She felt as if she'd stop breathing altogether as she watched. There was a horrible pounding in her ears, as in one violent upsweeping motion the knife sliced all the buttons from the front of her coat and sent them flying through the air. They fell clattering to the floor in various parts of the room. The hand inside the back of her collar yanked down hard, and the coat was gone. The whole thing lasted no longer than five seconds. She gasped at Leo, speechless, turned to stone with fear.

"Oh, *yeah!*" Leo said. The voice soft, soft. Licking his lips, his eyes traveling hungrily, greedily over her. "I do like what I see. I like, I *like!*" He seemed to be dancing inside his skin without moving. Something childlike, giddily eager about his eyes. His hand lifted like a magician's, and he made the switchblade flash and dance before her eyes. Unblinking, paralyzed, she watched him point the tip of the knife at her belly, saw the knife come closer, felt the tip pressing into her. She was holding her breath, her abdominal muscles tight as knots, trying to pull herself away from the blade. Leo changed the angle, pointing the handle down, the blade up; then his arm came flying upward, the blade ripping its way up the length of her dress. At the same moment, the hand behind her tore down the zipper. The dress fell apart like tissue paper, cascading down her arms as laughter roared in the room.

Marshall, stunned into silence now, was watching to see what would happen. He was so terrified, he failed to realize he'd wet himself.

Leo's eyes grew large, moist. His tongue darted out to wet his overfull lips, and Isabel's stomach felt as if it was turning over completely. She was panting, her chest heaving with her efforts to breathe. Her arms trapped by the one standing behind her, she was compelled to remain where she was, her eyes round with terror as Leo slipped the knife blade between the cups of her brassiere and with a tiny *snick* snapped the elastic.

No, she prayed. Nonononono. *No!* A little click, a swift hand gesture, and the knife vanished. Then, with an oddly delicate gesture, Leo lifted aside the two halves of the brassiere and again wet his lips. The destroyed lace bra slithered down her arms like strange damp animals. Marshall cried out, and Sheffie, looking apologetic, backhanded Marshall across the mouth. A string of blood broke the dreadful whiteness of his face, trickled down from the corner of his mouth to his chin.

She felt she was dying, wished she could, prayed for everything to dissolve, disappear into blackness, so she could be removed, saved from what was happening. Her wrists were trapped, held tightly behind her. Leo smiled broadly at each of his four friends, then at Isabel, his huge hands fastened to her breasts, squeezing so that his long fingernails sank deep into her flesh. Then, showmanlike, he opened his hands, held them palms outward in the air at his sides, opened his mouth wide, ducked his head, and fastened his lips and teeth to her nipple. She screamed, her eyes closing tightly, revulsed as those thick red lips sucked painfully at her, teeth biting down. She felt degraded, sick, tried to twist away. But Leo shifted his head and laughed into her face before sticking out his tongue like some demented, monstrously overgrown schoolboy playing the clown, lapping at her nipple. She cried out again, trying to shrink away. The one behind her wedged his knee between her thighs, wrapping his arm around her bare middle. Leo, on top of her now, shoved his hand down inside her tights—the tights ripping, shredding—down between her thighs, fingering her, his nails tearing at her. She was sobbing without tears, her eyes straining from their sockets. Rape. It was happening. Leo was forcing his fingers up inside her, and she was afraid to move, to resist; afraid if she did move, those fingers, burning, ripping their way up inside her, would do even more damage than they were doing. Marshall was whimpering. She hung impaled on Leo's hand, unable to remove her eyes from his face. Pain, the pain. Her mouth was trembling uncontrollably, her shoulders and belly quivering.

"I like your cunt, mama," Leo whispered, his mouth over hers, his hand wedged inside her like a brick. "I'm gonna eat you first. Then I'll fuck you good. I bet you come, baby. I'll make you beg for it." He withdrew his hand, and she stood trembling, her mouth open in shock, her body shaking, shaking as he unzipped his jeans. One of the others said, "*Yeah!*" in a hungry voice as Leo put out his hand and wound his fingers into her hair, scattering the pins. Several dropped onto her shoulders, then tinkled to the floor.

"Gimme a little head, mama," he said, dragging her down to her knees by her hair. "You do a good job, now, I'll eat you out so good you'll ask Leo for more."

He yanked savagely at her hair, wrenching her head toward him, and she shook her head back and forth, trying to speak, trying to say: No!

The one in back of her still held her wrists captive, and she could feel him behind her, feel the hard stubs of his knees digging into the base of her spine as a disembodied hand reached around in front of her to squeeze her breast. She shuddered and struggled to rise up out of this, away, but Leo's hand wound into her hair kept her on her knees on the floor, pulling the hair out of her scalp as he tried to force her to open her mouth. He was getting very angry, his temple visibly pulsing. She wanted to scream again, could feel the scream rising but wouldn't open her mouth, kept her face averted, wouldn't.

The door exploded open with a crash, revealing two uniformed policemen brandishing revolvers.

"That's it!" one of the policemen said evenly, quietly.

Leo and the other one released her, and she folded over until her head touched her knees. Her hair fell forward, covering her face. She stayed bent double on the floor, her scalp throbbing, her stomach heaving. Concentrating on not vomiting, calming her stomach. Pain. The fingernails, filthy fingernails. He'd torn her apart. Burning pain. She heard the five men being put into handcuffs, their soft-voiced, easy bantering.

"Hey, baby, don't get rough! No need for the old rough stuff. Nice mama's okay. Right, mama?"

She heard them being taken out. The sound of sober, authoritative voices. Heavy footsteps. The sound of the front door closing. The slam of four car doors. Then four more. Slam slam. Engines accelerating.

Marshall, quivering with rage, stood with his fists clenched at his sides, watching the policemen herd those five pigs out of the house. Then, finding his voice, looking down at Isabel, near-naked, curled over on the floor, it all broke inside him, and he screamed at her.

"You asked for this!" His voice thinned to a hysterical shriek. "You asked for it! I've had enough! *Enough!*"

"Take it easy, now," a voice said from the doorway.

Marshall looked over, to see a tall redheaded man on the threshold. Something about the expression on the man's face brought Marshall back to reality.

"Get out of my way!" Marshall snapped, pushing past him, running out of the house.

Brian stood for a moment looking at Isabel, then picked up her coat and draped it around her, dropping down beside her, speaking quietly.

"Are you all right?" he asked, trying to get her to lift her head so he could see her face. He felt peculiar, anxious, an agitated desire to hold her, soothe her, ease her. There was something too terrible about the silent shaking of her shoulders, the naked, vulnerable curve of her bent spine.

She couldn't answer. Nor could she get up off her knees. Her dry sobbing was going on and on, and she couldn't bring herself under control. All she could see, feel, think of was that hideous mouth fastened to her, the teeth biting. Those fingers, that hand pushing up into her. The searing, burned interior. Worse, far worse than rape. She shuddered convulsively, and Brian sat down beside her on the floor and wrapped his arm around her, bringing her over against him awkwardly.

"I really ought to be mad as hell at you," he said gently, frightened for her. "Seven months' work right out of the window."

The voice reached her. Deep and sympathetic, caring. She raised her head to look at the man sitting beside her, his arm around her.

"I'm Brian Connors." He smiled, displaying a mouthful of white teeth that reminded her of the author she'd interviewed that morning. The small woman with the wonderful smile. "What are you doing here?" he asked. Her face was so white her eyes so stark with shock, he felt a tremor of fear ripple down the length of his spine.

"I . . . c-ca-came . . ." I can't talk, she thought. Why can't I talk? She opened and then closed her mouth, still shivering.

"What's your name?" He kept his voice down to just above a whisper, gentling her.

"Is...Isabel. Gary."

"Your husband—was that your husband?—split on you. That was kind of a stupid thing to do."

"He..." She shook her head, her unblinking eyes fixed on his. "Not...my...He's...not."

"Did they hurt you, Isabel?" he asked solicitously.

She shook her head again, unable to take her eyes from his. He seemed so sane, so profoundly sane. I am hurt, yes, she thought. Terribly, horribly hurt. But she couldn't say it. I am hurt. *Hurt.*

"Scared," he said, his hand warm on her arm, his arm solid around her. He couldn't believe the performance Marshall had put on. This wasn't someone you screamed at. This was someone...special. Her face. The hair. "You've got good reason to be scared," he said. "Gang bangs are a big number around here. You almost got yourself worked over by five of the worst freaks, deviates in this city. For what?"

"My...dau...dau..." She couldn't get it out.

"Your daughter," he said. "I see." He glanced at her arms folded over her breasts, seeing the fingernail impressions rimming the tops of her breasts. The sight of those marks making his stomach muscles tighten. She was such a lovely-looking woman. Her skin so white, so pure, it seemed pore-less. "Let's get you out of here for a start," he said, smiling encouragingly. "We can talk someplace else."

He removed his arm and got to his feet, put a hand under her elbow to help her up. She straightened slowly, then lurched, throwing out her hands, clutching at his forearms to steady herself. They stood that way for a moment, her eyes still fastened to his. You are seeing me, she thought, but I can't let go...if I let go I will fall...I don't want to fall, but the pain...oh, God, it hurts...I want to be away from here...get me away from here, *please.*

"You'll be fine," he said at last, bending to pick up her coat, holding it up for her. She shoved her arms into the sleeves, then frantically wrapped the buttonless sides around her, the lining cold, shocking against her naked skin.

"He's going to go back, get his things, and leave," she said, suddenly able to speak, as if his eyes were transfusing her with coherency. She could speak, knowing that was precisely what Marshall would do. He'd be gone by the time she got home.

"A very nice fellow," Brian observed, his initial distaste for the man compounded by this insight. "Will you press charges against those five?"

"Should I do that?" she asked, pushing the hair out of her eyes, accepting the transfusion. She couldn't understand how she could be talking, answering questions, but knew it was important to stay in touch.

"You should do that, yes."

"Will they go to jail if I do?" Their voices quiet, familiar-sounding. As if they'd talked thousands of times before and could speak an intimate sort of shorthand. Strange. How strange.

"Maybe."

"If they don't they'll come after me?"

"Doubtful. Do you want some coffee, Isabel?"

Her teeth were chattering as she watched him pick up her handbag, then examine her ruined dress, discarding it with a shake of his head, leaving it on the floor.

"Yes. I do, yes."

"All right," he said, putting a steadying arm around her. "Come on. I'll buy you a gallon or two of coffee, get you thawed out. They didn't hurt you?"

"They planned more." Why couldn't she stop staring at him?

"Some, then," he said, guessing at what they'd done, appalled by the mental images. "Do you want a doctor?" he asked, stopping with her at the doorway, continuing to examine her eyes.

"No." What was it in his expression? she wondered. "You seem amused," she said as they started for the door. "Do you find this funny?"

"Funny?" You're a very injured lady, he thought. More than just tonight. "Nothing's funny," he said. "On the other hand," he continued, taking her slowly down the rotting front steps, "everything's funny. You're hurt some. But you'd have

been hurt a great deal if I hadn't happened to be around tonight. So, if you want to have a breakdown, you'll let this eat
away at your brain for months to come, until it finally sends
you over the edge. But if you want to get on with your life,
you'll try to think of yourself as lucky you weren't cut up or
mutilated in some way, put it way back in the darkest corner
of your mind, and keep on going.''

She looked at him but said nothing. She'd once again lost
her ability to speak.

He took her to an all-night coffee shop downtown and installed her in a booth at the back, ordering a pot of coffee
from a very pretty young waitress whose youth and freshness
reminded Isabel so strongly of Denise that she wanted to take
the girl into her arms and just hold her, hold her. She was reacting so strangely to everything that was happening, she
couldn't be sure she hadn't already gone mad.

The girl went away; then Brian lifted a package of cigarettes out of his shirt pocket, offered Isabel one, which she
refused, and lit one for himself, all the while continuing his
close examination of her face.

''Who's your daughter, Isabel?'' he asked at last, dropping his match into the crowded ashtray.

''How do you know about my daughter?'' she asked, her
powers of speech restored. Would it be this way for the rest of
her life: sometimes able to speak, sometimes not?

''You told me,'' he said patiently. *What did they do to you?*
he asked her silently. *And why did I bring you here instead of
taking you home? I know why,* he realized. *I want to give that
bastard a chance to get well away if he's going. And I think
you're right about that. He's the kind who'll run. As far and
as fast as he can. I don't want to deliver you back into that!
I'm trying to spare you something. Further anguish. I don't
know. But there's been enough ugliness for one evening. And
you're someone,* he decided, finding something distin-
guished, almost aristocratic about her features. *Someone.*

''I don't remember,'' she said, trying to recall when she'd
told him about Denny. ''Denise,'' she told him now. ''My
daughter,'' she added unnecessarily. *Marshall, please be gone
when I get home! Please be gathering your things together*

now. I never want to have to see your face again, never want to have to hear you or see you or speak to you.

"Runaway?" Brian asked.

"Not really," she said exhaustedly. "She's almost nineteen. Too old to be a runaway." She thought about that for a moment, then amended her view. "Yes," she said.

"What were you trying to accomplish tonight?" he asked, having already guessed.

"Trying to find her," she said, the shivering growing worse. "Looking for her."

Brian leaned forward across the table.

"Let me tell you something," he said. "Wherever your daughter is, she's going to come home when *she* decides to. *If* she decides. That's a damned hard piece of truth to hand out to you, but there it is. What you did tonight was *dangerous*."

"If it was your child, wouldn't you want to know, wouldn't you try?"

He leaned back in the booth—Geoff's face flashing before him, grinning, a happy-young-boy image—and took a deep drag on his cigarette. "It *was* my child, Isabel. And it was terminal. That's why I am where I am right now."

"I don't understand." Was he not a policeman, after all? Did he have a runaway too?

The waitress plonked down two cups without saucers, and a carafe of coffee.

"Hungry?" Brian asked Isabel, detaining the waitress.

Isabel didn't answer.

"Two BLT's on whole-wheat toast," he ordered. "Better bring my friend a cup of good hot soup, and throw in a couple of sides of french fries, too."

Isabel stared at him dumbly. His hair was brilliant orange-red, cut just below the ears, thick-looking. His eyes green. Light green, shot with black speckles. His skin splashed with freckles. He was very pleasant-looking; a prepossessing man of such calm and control it seemed to glow on the surface of his skin. Strands of white hair. She could see them. He was no longer young. But not yet old. Only his eyes. They seemed elderly.

"It means," he said, effortlessly picking up from where they'd been before the waitress had interrupted, "that I know all about trying to find hows and whys. And I know what happens to your life when it's your kid who's gone sour. Whatever way. Everything falls apart. *You* fall apart. You can't seem to get answers anywhere, and it's suddenly impossible to get your life moving again. My son was fifteen. They found him in the boiler room at the high school, with the needle still in his arm. His mind was a runaway. Anyway"—he sighed—"my wife hung on for about eight months, then packed up, took our twelve-year-old daughter, and went back home to her parents in Scotland. That was almost five years ago. I got into what I do now because it was too late for Geoff but maybe not too late for a lot of other kids."

"How very noble," she said.

"Don't take it out on me, Isabel." He looked hurt. "I'm here to help you."

"I'm sorry," she said, feeling a terrible misery. Like the aftermath of a funeral. "I don't know what I'm doing, saying."

"I think I know what you're doing," he said without smugness. "You're trying to get it all out from inside. That's good. But know what you're doing. Know!"

He poured coffee into both cups, and pushed one across the table to her. "Drink some," he said. "Then we'll talk about it. I've got as much time as you need."

She lifted the cup with both hands, shaking so much that the coffee sloshed over the rim and down her fingers. She set down the cup. He put it back into her hands and urged it up to her mouth.

"Drink. Are you divorced, a widow?" he asked.

"Widow," she whispered, managing to swallow a mouthful of the coffee. It burned going down. As if her interior was frozen.

"Any other children?"

She shook her head, more coffee spilling over her fingers. Seeing Howard's face after the test results. The shock. His saying Why? over and over. Neither of them understanding. And the awful emptiness she'd felt in her womb, in their embraces for a time. Until it was accepted. *Howard!* Like a child, a small, lost voice inside her crying out: They *hurt* me!

"And your friend's so in control, he starts screaming, then runs out on you. That's very nice. We all need lots of friends like that."

"It's not his problem," she said, trying to be fair. But finding it difficult. If he hadn't provoked them. If he hadn't... "You can't blame him."

"That's true. I don't have to like him, either. How old are you, Isabel?"

"Is that a routine question?"

"Personal one," he admitted.

"Forty."

"Keep drinking." He smiled. Forty. It suddenly seemed the perfect age to him. "It's more effective than booze. Never mind what old wives tell you about the restorative powers of brandy."

She drank some more.

"What?" she asked, noticing the way his eyes changed all at once.

"I want you to press charges," he said, looking deeply into her eyes, feeling more angered, more hurt by the minute at what had happened to her. *"Do it!"*

"It doesn't matter," she said, too drained to try to think.

"It matters!"

"All right. I don't care."

"Care, Isabel! Don't give up because of tonight. You haven't lost yet."

"You don't think so?" She looked up at him, something inside her lifting slightly.

"I know so. And I'm an authority. Now, come on," he coaxed. "Talk to me."

The baby started crying around seven, waking her up. Without thinking, she climbed quickly out of the cot and lifted the baby from his crib. Wet. Holding him, she switched on the light and looked around for a diaper. Found a box of disposables over in the corner, dropped the side of the crib, laid Tink down, stripped off the soaking diaper, and inexpertly fastened on a new one. Tink watched her, round-eyed, interested in this new person.

"Bet you're hungry, right?" she said to the baby. "Bet your mom would groove on sleeping in, too. Right?"

Tink gave her a big toothless smile, and she laughed.

"Just stay there for a sec and let me get some clothes on," she said, retreating to the other side of the room, keeping her eyes on the baby while she pulled on her jeans and T-shirt. "Okay," she said, going back for the baby. "Let's see what we can find for you."

On tiptoe, she carried the baby downstairs to the kitchen.

When Cathy came in a while later, she had to laugh at the sight of Denny sitting drinking coffee with one hand, holding the bottle to the baby's mouth with the other.

"I can see you've done a whole lot of that." Cathy laughed, plonking Christy down in the high chair. "Better get your practice in now. It'll make it a lot easier if you ever have any of your own."

A sharp negative response leaped into Denny's mouth, but she looked at Tink, then at Cathy and Christy, and said nothing.

"I'll just finish my coffee and split," Denny said, watching Cathy removing eggs from the refrigerator. "Get out of your way."

"Larry and I were talking when he came in," Cathy said, setting a frying pan on the stove. "And we thought if you're like really strapped and have to have a place to crash for a while, maybe you could swap some baby-sitting. You know?"

"You mean stay?"

"Up to you," Cathy said, dropping a lump of butter into the frying pan. "I know there's a gig going at the vegetable stall about half a mile up the Old Shore Road. I mean, if you're all hung up on receiving charity and like that, you could go check it out, see if you're interested."

"How come?" Denny asked, her suspicions on the rampage.

"I like you," Cathy said openly. "Why not?"

"That's all?"

"Sure," Cathy said easily. "You want a whole lot of reasons?"

"I don't know."

"It's up to you," Cathy repeated, watching the butter melt. "Better than hacking around out in the cold."

Denise didn't respond. She was thinking.

"Oh, wow! I almost forgot," Cath said, glancing at the clock.

She dashed out of the room, and returned carrying a small portable TV set, which she plugged in and set on the counter.

"They've got this chick on who's really too much," she said, changing stations.

Denny watched the picture take shape, saw Jerry's face, and groaned inside. Jesus Christ! she thought. Don't tell me you're going to do a number on my goddamned mother!

Cathy dished up an egg, all cut up, to Christy, put a spoon into the little girl's hand, poured herself a cup of coffee, and sat down at the table, her eyes on the screen.

"She really knocks me out," Cathy said when Isabel's segment started.

"Why?" Denny asked, dry-throated, mystified.

"I don't know. I mean, I really groove on just looking at her, because she's so outright beautiful. And she gives you the feeling, listening to her, that she wouldn't make you feel like a dog, being with her. She's so sort of quiet and intelligent. Not proving anything by trying to down the guests like to make herself look good or anything like that. Just a someone who happens to be beautiful. Not like being beautful's the whole trip for her. I'd love to meet her."

Denny stared at her for several seconds, dumbfounded, then turned to look at the screen, making an effort to blank her mind and see her mother the way Cathy did. Trying hard.

Seven

She couldn't talk about herself, her feelings, her reactions to what had happened this evening. But she could, she found, talk about Denise, the way she did so often with Judy. About the reasons possibly responsible for her absence and her frame of mind. How strange that she should feel this way, she thought. But it wasn't the sort of receptivity she'd been accustomed to lately. Talking to Brian gave her the feeling she was conversing with yet another specialist in a world of such precise and far-ranging specialization that here was someone applying his expertise to the exotic area of drug-overdose aftermath, the psyche of the runaway.

"What about *you?*" Brian asked after a time, wanting to get deeper into the woman, know more about her. "How do you *feel?*" He couldn't understand the absence of tears. And while he didn't particularly believe tears to be strictly within the female domain, he thought that had he undergone an experience of a comparable nature, he most likely would have cried. In private, well away from the house, he'd cried for hours at a stretch after Geoff's death. Perhaps that's it, he thought. Perhaps she'll go home and let it all surface there.

"I'm very uncomfortable," she said. The stinging pains were becoming worse. She was finding it difficult to remain seated. "I would like to go home."

"Sure," he said, understanding. "Let me just give you this." He removed a card from his wallet, turned it over, and wrote his name and number on the back. "You can always reach me at this number. If you do feel like talking to someone, or something comes up and you need a hand, give me a call."

"What about the charges?" she asked, frowning with the pain. Inside her was a red-hot column of liquid fire.

"You go down to the precinct tomorrow or the next day. The forms will be ready. All you'll have to do is make a brief statement, sign it and some other papers, and that'll be that."

"You can't guarantee they're not going to try to find some way to retaliate if I go ahead with this."

"You only get guarantees with new cars, Isabel. And it's pretty damned hard getting anyone to honor those."

In the car, as they drove toward her house, he glanced across at her. Her eyes were closed, her arms wrapped around herself. The long mass of hair lay spilled over her shoulders and down her back in tangled disarray. She was no longer shivering.

"Do you work?" he asked, looking forward again.

"I work," she said, her eyes still closed.

"What do you do?" he asked, taking another look at her. Her lips were completely bloodless. White.

"A talk show. On the local station. *Mid-Morning.*" She didn't want to talk now. She wanted to sit very still until this ride ended.

"I'll have to tune in," he said. "You're *on* the show?"

"I'm on the show." She opened her eyes and turned her head.

He read the expression in her eyes and said nothing further. He had the ominous feeling, an almost psychic knowledge, that she was bleeding. Stopped for a light, he looked down at her knees, seeing dirt smears, holes in her tights. And remembered she was naked under the coat. Fingernail impressions rimming her breasts. His breath caught in his throat, and he battled down a surging emotional response to her, what had been done to her. Jesus! he thought, noticing the buttons were all missing from her coat. "I'm sorry," he said softly.

"For what?" she asked, her eyes once more closed.

"For tonight. What happened."

She nodded but said nothing more.

* * *

Jude, in a long flannel granny gown, was sitting at the kitchen table with a glass of milk and a sandwich, waiting for Isabel to come home.

Having heard Marshall come in earlier and go tearing through the house like a whirlwind, then go driving off with screeching tires, she knew something big had come down. She'd stayed up in her room, afraid to ask Marshall. But after he'd gone, she wandered through the house, nervously waiting for Isabel to get home. And the longer she waited, the more scared she became, thinking that something awful had happened to Isabel. As she sat imagining the worst, she grew more and more upset at the prospect of Isabel's being hurt in some way. Because Isabel was important. And Jude didn't know how she'd handle a bad scene like that. All she could think of was this one time talking to Denny, trying to get her to climb down off her hate trip and appreciate her mother.

"She's really *for* you, Den. And all you ever do is talk about her like she's some kind of conspiracy against you or something."

"You've never had to *live* with her," Denny had said with a superior, knowing look. "It's a whole other bag, living with her."

"Like how?"

"Like all that cleanliness and motherly shit. All that 'I'm-your-mother' jazz, 'I'm trying to understand you.'"

"You hold it against her that she's clean and she loves you?"

"Not just that," Denny had said impatiently. "It's where her head's at."

"Tell me about that!" Jude had challenged. "Where's her head at? Lay it on me!"

"Shit! I don't know. That uptight Marshall creep getting her into that back-to-graduate-school number and the big important production job."

"So what's wrong with that?"

"He's a walking con, and she doesn't even see it!"

"What difference does it make if he is conning her? I mean, the thing is, she's getting off on her gig, having something to

do with her time. Don't you think it's like her right to make
decisions and do something if she wants to? Or are you maybe
mad at her for not sitting around spending the rest of her life
doing a heavy black number over your dad? Or maybe like
waiting for you to decide to come around?''

"She doesn't even *talk* about him anymore," Denny had
said bitterly. "Like he never was, or something."

"Man, I don't hear *you* talking about him!"

"That's different."

"Different! Are you ever selfish! Where does it say she's got
to spend forever rapping and grieving over somebody who's
been dead all these years? People who do that are unreal. Real
is getting on with it, you know. Real isn't doing a big number
about what *used* to be. Real is accepting the way things are
and getting on."

"Okay, okay. But why the hell does she have to take up with
a zero like Marshall? Man, she can't even see he's just off on
this big ego trip, being seen with her. I mean, like they're
playing this whole cute domestic number when he's around.
And d'you see the way he won't even *talk*, can't hardly open
his mouth to get a word out if we happen over? Like we're shit
and he'll just maybe tolerate us because he doesn't want to
mess up what he's getting into with her. I wish somebody'd
off that prick, man. I really do."

"Maybe she's happy," Jude had offered.

"Shit she's happy! I'll bet if she ever got a shot at a halfway decent dude, she'd freak. Marshall's fucking *nowhere!*"

"But you wouldn't tell her you think that."

"No way! She wants to eat up that act, that's her problem.
It's none of my business if she wants to get it off with a dumb
jock like that who's just playing her because he's hung up on
the fact that she'll do stuff he like suggests. Probably the only
time in his whole weird life anybody halfway decent-looking
ever gave him the time of goddamned day, for chrissake."

"She's not stupid, Den. You know she's not. Why're you
so down on her?"

"I'm not down on her. I . . . I don't know. I just get this
feeling like if I really laid it on her, all the stuff I've been into

and like that, she'd try to *handle* it. You know? And I'm sick of that whole number."

"You don't want her to love you?"

"Love sucks."

"Den, your head's really fucked up. You know that? It really is. What d'you want her to do? You want her to do that typical mother number where she downs everything you're into and lays out a lot of bullshit rules about how it's to be when you're in *her* house? I mean, come *on*, Denny! She did that big garage thing for you because you said you wanted some privacy. Then you tell her: Sorry—you're going to move out. You're so ungrateful!"

"Why should I be grateful?" Denny had been furious. "For what?"

"How about like for the fact that she's letting you do your thing? Like how she lets you come and go whenever you fucking well please. And she trusts you. She's *supportive*. Whatever you want, it's what she wants for you. Like how she's always so damned happy to see you whenever you take the time to bother to drop over and let her know you're still alive. Like how she's always slipping you ten or twenty. She knows you need bread, but she doesn't make you crawl for it, doesn't make you say how much. And you don't even have the manners to say thank you. Like it's all coming to you, like she's got to pay you off for the rest of her life because your dad died on you. Why're you blaming that on her anyway? It's not like it was her fault he died."

"Who said it was? She's okay," Denny had conceded grudgingly. "I wish . . . If she marries that moron, I'm never going over there again. I swear it! If she's that fucking blind she'll marry that biochemical jock, I'll . . . Shit! She can't be that stupid she can't see he's a nerd. He's just out to *fuck* her!"

"It's her life, Den."

"It's *my* business."

"Why don't you just admit you care what she does, that you love her?"

"Love sucks."

You stink, Denny! Jude thought now, sitting at the kitchen table, waiting. You don't even have the goddamned decency to call your mother. You don't even care she's going crazy worrying about you. I ever get my hands on you, Den, I'll... What can *I* do?

Hearing the key in the front door, she gripped the kitchen table and waited, so relieved to see Isabel appear through the front door she could hardly catch her breath. Then, seeing her come closer, seeing her hair all over the place and her legs all dirty, her tights torn, Jude was scared again.

Isabel walked slowly, stiffly down the hall to the kitchen, and stood looking at Judy—her sweetness and youth, the baby-powder-scented smell of her like some sort of fairy tale after the events of the past several hours.

"What happened?" Jude asked shakily.

Isabel didn't seem to hear. "Did Marshall come back?"

"He went roaring through here, then took off. He split for good?"

"I knew he would," Isabel said, looking dazed as she sat down opposite Jude, keeping her arms folded across her chest. "Well," she said, her eyes fixed on Jude's, "that's that."

"What happened?" Jude asked again.

"What happened? I'm too tired to talk about it."

"You went to that place," Jude guessed.

"We went."

"Oh, God! I should've warned you, but there wasn't any chance. Blake said it was bad action, that it wasn't good to go there without a lot of backup muscle."

"You can tell Blake he was right," Isabel said, her voice unintentionally laden with irony. "However"—she sighed, getting to her feet—"I'm still alive. And I have to go to work in the morning."

"I don't think you should," Jude said softly. "I really don't think so."

"I'm all right."

"I could make you a cup of tea or a sandwich or something."

"No, thank you." Isabel turned to go.

"You're really okay?" Jude didn't believe that.

"I'm fine. Good night."

"Good night," Jude murmured, distressed.

She pulled on a shower cap and was about to climb under the shower when she noticed the streaks of dried blood at the tops of her thighs. She stared down at herself, starting to tremble again. Those obscene filthy fingernails. She closed her eyes for several seconds, then went ahead under the shower, somewhat soothed by the flowing heat. But when she began to wash between her legs, pain shot through her entire body, and she moaned, putting her hand out to brace herself on the wall, afraid she'd faint. Biting her lip, waiting for the pain to pass, feeling that huge hand forcing its way inside her. A huge, dirty hand with black-rimmed fingernails. Four fingers wedged inside her. She wanted never to be touched again, hated having even to clean herself.

The pain ebbed into a pulsing interior aching, and she righted herself to finish scrubbing her skin. Her breasts discolored here and there. Bruises by morning. She was so exhausted, she nearly fell asleep in the shower. But once in bed, she couldn't get to sleep. And got up to go into the bathroom, open the medicine cabinet, and take two Dramamine tablets. As she swallowed the tablets, her eyes moved over the row of plastic prescription vials. She turned the containers so all the labels were facing forward. A row of varicolored pills of interesting potential. She stood a moment longer, then closed the cabinet and returned to bed.

In the dark, the incident played itself again and again. The most shameful, loathsome experience of her life. And Marshall was gone. Having blamed her. *Blamed me when it was not my fault. I did not ask for any of that. If you had said nothing, done nothing, we might simply have walked away from there. Denny, where* are *you?*

The restaurant and that strange, calm man insisting she talk it out. *We're all mad,* she thought. *All of us. Sanity's an illusion. Reason too. It doesn't matter. Nothing matters. Denise is gone. She'll come back when* she *wants to. If she wants to. Why don't I have the right to bring her back? What rights* do I have as a mother? None. No rights. No privileges. Nothing. Say good-bye to Denise.

Finally, the Dramamine taking effect, she sank into sleep.

To dream she was in Ash's office, waiting for him, with something important to talk about. But her jaw, her whole mouth, hurt horribly. Her tongue probed the interior of her mouth, and a tooth—as brown and weathered as an ancient legacy from some long-gone civilization—dropped into her palm. She stared at the tooth, fascinated, turning it around and around, anxious to study it, but more teeth were coming. And she held her hand up to her mouth as a second and then a third tooth dropped out. Ash came into the office, and she wanted to talk to him but couldn't because the teeth were falling out more quickly now, and in moments she had an entire handful of those brown, pebblelike teeth. Her mouth ached. Ash turned, finally, saw her, and said something.

Then, suddenly, she was in a hospital, and they were telling her: You have a week left. And she understood. Cancer of the mouth, the jaw, the skull. Something. She couldn't talk. Her hands scrambled frantically, constantly for paper and pencil. She sat in her pristine hospital bed scribbling messages. A week. She felt so frustrated, trying to make people read her eyes, understand what she was trying to tell them. Denny. I have to see my daughter, tell her I love her. Only a week.

There was no fear. None. One week left to her life, and she was glad, relieved. It didn't matter that the interior of her mouth was brown, empty, her tongue rotted to a shriveled brown stump. Mute, in pain, she kept on scribbling messages on small pieces of paper. Come to me come to me come to me. I have to say good-bye I love you. Come to me.

During the week that followed, she found it very difficult to get from one place to another, one thought to the next. She seemed to be standing still while everything around her was moving, so that she was dizzy most of the time, and apathetic. She drove herself to perform with some measure of animation while on the air, motivated solely by the knowledge that if she didn't, Jerry would use her present weakness against her to have her removed from the show. Mercifully, he left her alone for that week. She didn't know why and didn't care, was simply grateful not to be the recipient of further accidental bumps and bruises, the victim of petty thievery and rearranged program notes. Had she not had this determination to outlast Jerry's planned accidents, she wouldn't have gone to work. She longed to lie down on her bed and simply stay there undisturbed, uninterrupted. She felt her life outside the station was slipping away from her, was already sliding beyond her control. Marshall was gone. She was very glad of that. She could attend to her spurious thoughts, her minimal needs, without having to fret about Marshall's frame of mind, his ego, his sexual demands, his pending visits.

The mere idea of making love—to anyone—was utterly repugnant. She cringed at the thought of being touched. What she wanted now was what Denny had always claimed as her prerogative: to be left alone. When Ash or one of the engineers approached her with something needing discussion or clarification, it was all she could do not to shout at him to leave her alone. How could she think, straighten her thoughts, know what she felt, if people wouldn't leave her alone?

She was in perpetual pain. And felt she was going mad. And thought perhaps that wouldn't be so awful. Other people would then have to take care of matters. She'd just be crazy and do whatever crazy people did while others took over solving the problems. Not that there were any great problems. Denny had gone away and didn't appear to have any desire to come back. She couldn't accept this. So she thought of going mad as the perfect panacea. Something to remove her from the necessity of waiting, hoping, from the tiresome chore of attempting to separate emotional pain from the physical pain.

In an aside to Ash, Annette, the production assistant, said, "Something's wrong with Isabel. She's like a zombie. It's as if she wakes up five minutes before air time, stays awake long enough to get the segment done, then goes back into her coma."

"I've noticed," he said, very concerned. He had plans for Isabel, big plans, some already in the works. He couldn't stand the idea that she might be starting to break under the pressure of Jerry's nonstop attacks.

When he got a chance, he invited Isabel to come up to his office.

"We need to talk," he said, sitting down with her on the oversprung sofa.

She looked at him, fascinated by his face, by the silver streaking his hair. She didn't think she'd ever actually looked at Ash before. He had really quite wonderful eyes. Like a cat's. She wondered if they'd glow in the dark.

"Isabel," he said, touching her arm in an attempt to break her stare, "what's wrong?"

She blinked, refocused, and looked at his mouth. "Something's wrong," she said, confounding him. "I'll have to take care of it."

He had no idea what she was talking about, and was more than a little alarmed by her distracted state. "I want you to take a few days off," he said on impulse. "We've got enough tapes to cover. A week," he amended. "You're working too hard."

"I dreamed about you," she said, remembering.

"Snap out of it," he said softly. "We need you around here."

"Do you?" she asked, a puzzled expression furrowing her forehead. "Really, do you, Ash?"

"Just hold on," he said. "Stay with it a little while longer, and I promise you good things will start happening. Don't give in now."

"Am I an example?" she asked. "Or a nice diversion for Jerry's anger? I have the feeling the only one here who sees or values what I'm doing is me. Do you care about *me?* Or is it that you only care about what I'm accomplishing for you?"

"Both," he said, without hesitation. "Both. Now, go home and stay away for a week, get yourself taken care of, whatever it is."

He stood up, and she sat a moment longer looking up at him, then got to her feet and held her left hand out to him.

"Care about me," she said tonelessly, her hand like ice in his. "I can't."

He stared at her as she withdrew her hand, turned, and walked out of the office. His heart was pounding, his hands trembling as he lit a cigarette and sat down heavily behind his desk.

If it was Jerry, he thought, he'd kill him.

She knew something had to be done. The pain was growing worse. She couldn't even bear thinking about going to the toilet, knowing in advance the searing, gasp-provoking pain would become even more activated and start clawing her inside. So, after leaving Ash, she telephoned and got an emergency appointment, went directly from the office to her gynecologist.

In her paper smock, she lay on the examining table and stared fixedly at the ceiling as the doctor probed and prodded and looked, turning the pain into an enraged beast.

"What happened?" he asked her.

She told him the bare details.

He shook his head, his mouth a tight line. "You've got half a dozen nasty infections. Suppurating. They should be drained, cleaned. I'm worried about septicemia."

"Do it," she said, her eyes still on the ceiling. "Do whatever you have to do."

He did it. She wished she could cry. But she couldn't. So she stared at the ceiling, her face contorted, agonized. Then at last was assisted off the table and into the changing cubicle. She managed to dress herself—her legs and belly trembling with shock and pain—then sat down in the doctor's office and accepted the prescriptions he wrote out for antibiotics, ointment, and listened as he told her what to do, how to do it, and under what circumstances she should call him at once. She listened, nodding, tucked the prescriptions into her bag, and—her entire focus turned inward to the mutilated interior of her body, thinking Brian had been mistaken, she had been mutilated after all—thanked him and went on her way, walking with legs that had no substance. Her head a great distance above her body. Her feet moving independently.

She had the prescriptions filled on her way home, standing staring at the rows of bottled vitamins, her eyes moving from the end of one shelf to the end of the next. Then, looking at the containers of prescription medicines behind the counter. Bottles and boxes. Pills and liquids. Her mind matching the neatly arranged rows with that small column of vials she'd lined up in the medicine cabinet. Her name was called, she paid, and drove home, had dinner with Jude, then went upstairs to shower, applied the ointment, and sighed shudderingly as the cool cream at once began calming the pain.

At the end of her week at home, the antibiotics and ointment had done away with the pain, the infections were healing. She could walk, function. As she lay on her bed each night, she began running over all the details of the studio—the cameras, lights, props. Testing her memory, she'd go over each item. And became impatient if she missed anything. This exercise enabled her to get to sleep. She would sleep and be assaulted again and again by enormous hands that forced themselves into her. She'd awaken in the night and again silently recite the list of studio accoutrements. She knew she was going mad.

She did, because of the surprisingly passionate way in which Brian had insisted upon it, make a trip to the police station. To give her statement and sign the complaint. She did it, and continued on her way still caught in the peculiar detached state. Her hand could hold a pen, sign her name. Her mind, throughout all her daily activities, was elsewhere, idly, dully reminding herself of clothes needing to be taken to the cleaners, linen needing to be collected from the laundry, the fact that there were no paper towels or napkins left for the kitchen.

She'd go off planning to do these errands, get into her car, and forget where she was supposed to be going. So she'd drive around for hours at night, listening to the car radio, obediently stopping for lights and stop signs, braking for the occasional small animal that shot into the road, and sometimes, with a shock of recognition, see a familiar figure walking along the sidewalk. Only to come up alongside and see with a sick sinking feeling that she'd been mistaken again. She drove. Then, having done none of the things she'd started out to do, she'd go home. To find Judy in the flesh busily preparing a meal. Or a meal Jude had fixed earlier and left warming in the oven. Notes from Jude. Dinner's in the oven. I've got to work late. Love. Dinner's in the refrigerator. I'll see you later. Love. I changed your sheets. Love. I took your stuff to the cleaners. Love. I picked up the laundry. Love. No calls. I'll be over at Blake's place. Love.

Dinners. She talked to Jude. At least, she thought she did. Jude seemed satisfied with whatever answers Isabel gave. And glad not to have to think about cooking, Isabel ate whatever Judy prepared, then wandered away, either upstairs to bed or into the living room, to sit watching television, staring at the color images, feeling herself turning one-dimensional, flat.

Time. Time had become a tow rope, slowly, steadily pulling her from one day to the next, one week to another. She wondered disinterestedly where Marshall had gone. It didn't matter. She wondered where Denny had gone and if she'd ever call or come back; doubted she would, prayed to hear her voice. Wondered about that strange Brian Connors and his dead son with the needle in his arm.

She yearned for something to smash the glass, break her out of the apathetic lethargy in which she was encased. Time. It was meaningless. She'd waste the evening sitting staring at the TV set, then go upstairs and spend the better part of the night working over her notes and material for the next morning's show. She no longer seemed to require sleep. Spent quite a bit of time in her bed, but little of it sleeping.

She'd lie gazing at the ceiling, thinking: Please come home and let me live. Too many things happening. My life, my reason going. My child, my little girl, the teenager, the people you've been through all the stages of your life. All the things you are that you're withholding from me. Yes, it's your right to a private life, to private thoughts and actions. But I don't know how to stop caring about you. Just telephone, let me hear your voice. Something. Anything. A postcard. Just to know.

He hoped she'd call, found himself staring at the telephone from time to time as if willing her to call. But why should she? There was no reason for her to call him. But he wanted it. And found himself thinking of her constantly. He took an entire morning off just to watch *Mid-Morning* and see her. He thought he could detect fatigue and hints of anxiety in the corners of her mouth, around her deep-set eyes. Then forgot all that and simply watched, seeing how good she was, how exceptionally perceptive and bright, with what intuitive purity she drew forth the best from her guest. She was a wonderful interviewer, able to make even a bakery owner seem witty and charming, interesting. Brian was disappointed to have the show end, to see her smile into the camera saying, "Thank you for joining me this morning. I hope you'll tune in again tomorrow morning, when my guest will be . . ."

A surprise to find someone of her caliber on a local show. Definitely good enough for a network show or syndication. He stopped himself. He didn't want to waste time and energy projecting on her potential. He wanted to be *with* her. And couldn't find one legitimate reason for staying away. Nor one for pursuing her, either. Except that he wanted to, was eager to know how she was and if her daughter had come home. Had to see her. To find out if the feeling, the response inside himself, would be the same. He disliked the idea of interrupting the routines of her life. But couldn't stay away any longer.

So he changed his clothes and headed downtown, preparing opening lines like some half-assed schoolboy; abandoning preparations, telling himself he'd say whatever seemed to need saying when he saw her.

He lied blithely to the receptionist, said he was her brother, and got himself admitted to the interior of the building with a little tag clipped to his lapel. VISITOR. His name in Magic Marker underneath. Found his way along the corridors to the studio and went in through the heavy door on the heels of a young woman with a clipboard and an officious air. Learned that Isabel was in a production meeting with the producer, received a new set of directions, and retraced his steps back along the corridors and up a flight of stairs to the proper office, positioned himself against the wall, lit a cigarette, and waited for her to come out.

He stood thinking about her, recalling every detail of her being. Her hair, when he'd chanced to touch it. Soft, thick. The shape of her mouth and the lift of her chin, the delicacy of her ears. Stood thinking, becoming doubtful. Wondering if he hadn't been too presumptuous, too pushy in doing this— coming here.

The office door opened after about fifteen minutes, and half a dozen people came hurrying out. Brenner he recognized and disliked on sight. For no real reason except that the small man cast a dismissing up-and-down glance in Brian's direction, then went sauntering off down the corridor like a small, large-headed boy dressed in his father's clothes. His arms too long too, Brian saw.

At last Isabel emerged. And looking at her, seeing her eyes, he felt suddenly weak, totally sobered. Wondering what he'd thought he'd achieve when he'd set out on this drop-in surprise visit.

Why did I come here? he asked himself in the second or two it took her to come through the doorway. I came because she has a beautiful face and I have this need to... What? I came because I had the silly idea we could go someplace to talk, find out more about each other. I came out of curiosity and appetite. It isn't enough. Not good enough.

Her eyes looked glazed, uncomprehending, lifeless. Her eyes frightened him. She didn't look in the least surprised to see him. She simply stood waiting for him to say something. He smiled and pushed himself away from the wall, saying, "I came to take you out to lunch."

"All right," she said.

Strange. It was like visiting an art gallery, commenting in that quiet fashion used in libraries or museums, exhibitions of the rare or antique. She didn't move. Behind her, inside the office, a salt-and-pepper-haired man got up, walked around his desk, and quietly closed the office door.

Brian put his hand on her arm. Her head moved. She looked down at his hand. "Come on, Isabel," he said, working at keeping his smile. "You must be starved. Are you finished here for the day?"

"My car's downstairs," she said senselessly.

"I'll take you in your car, then, if you like. Let's go get your coat."

Like a sleepwalker, she led him downstairs, located her coat and bag, allowed him to help her on with the coat. They left the building and went out into the cold air, where she suddenly seemed to emerge from her trance.

"You don't have to bother with this," she said, looking at his determined profile as he propelled her along, noticing he was wearing a suit, a tie.

"I do have to bother," he corrected. "Someone's got to be around when you need it. We all need someone to be around for that."

"But it doesn't matter. It really doesn't."

"It matters!" he said, pulling her to a stop. "*You* matter! And you're giving up. I care about that. I want to know why. Wake up, Isabel! Come out of it!" He felt a great sense of urgency, of caring. Wished he was in a position to take hold of her, hold her in his arms and transmit his urgency, his caring.

He was talking to her as if he thought she was sleeping, and she blinked, trying to make sense of this. What was happening? Had he come to warn her? Had he been wrong about those five? Were they going to come after her?

"Look at you," he said softly, sounding sad. "You're worn out. You can't go on this way. You've got to get it out, talk about it, do something. Which one's your car?"

Bewildered, she turned to look at the rows of cars in the lot. "I don't see it," she said, suddenly unreasonably alarmed. "I can't remember where I parked it."

"Think!" he said gently. "Just take your time and think."

"I can't!" she said wildly. "I can't!"

He put his hand under her chin and turned her head, saying, "Take it easy, now, Isabel. Slow, easy. Now, turn around and pick out your car."

Her eyes clung to his for a moment; then she blinked, her eyes shifted, and she looked slowly up and down the parking lot. With enormous relief, she saw her car and began walking to it.

"Why don't you give me the keys?" he suggested. "I'll drive."

Marshall again. She held onto the keys, stubbornly shaking her head. "I'm not crippled. I can drive."

"Isabel, I'm trying to help you. I want to. Let somebody take some of the load off you. Let somebody help. Me. I want to help you."

"No! All of you. Men. You think you can handle everything. But you can't. You can't handle anything. I'm fine. I can drive. Don't order me ... telling me what to do. Do this, do that, as if I've become incompetent. I'm not... I'm—" She couldn't remember all at once what they were arguing about. She looked at him and allowed the words in her mind to be spoken. "I want to know if she's dead," she said. "I have to know." Then she lowered her eyes, handed him the keys, opened the passenger door, and got in.

He started the car, then turned, took hold of her hand, and said, "I'd want to know, too. You're all right. Everything's going to be all right. It's not unreasonable to want to know."

Her spine felt as if it'd finally given way altogether, and she sagged against the door with her eyes still on him.

"I'm all right," she repeated in a whisper, her hand still enclosed by his.

It was colder than hell working the stall. Even with the little heater inside, it was almost too cold to breathe. But by the end of the second week, she had it figured out and spent every free minute crouched in front of the tiny space heater, cupping a cigarette between her palms, doing a lot of heavy thinking.

She was really getting off on the baby, having a ball in the mornings with Tink. She could do those diapers in about two seconds flat now, and got a charge out of whipping off the crapped-up one and slapping a clean one under the baby's bottom.

Cathy and Larry left her pretty much alone and didn't want to take the bread she tried to give them. But they finally took it, and everything was cool. Before he went off at night, they'd sit around and she'd listen to them rap about his gig.

He was into some pretty good stuff, talked about some of the people he had on the show and some of the weird-shit calls he got in the middle of the night from sadtimers out in the boonies.

"A lot of very lonely people out there," Larry had said the night before. "But nobody's into admitting to being lonely. It's like the all-time, ultimate dirty word, man. You can be anything, but lonely's a no-no. Say you're lonely and the world's going to down you 'cause you're not supposed to suffer from that kind of sickness. *Lonely?* Man, you must be some kinda sickie, you're lonely. What's the matter with you, baby? You gotta get your shit together. No way it's cool getting into this lonely gig. Everybody's into it, but nobody's saying. You know?" He lit a cigarette, passed it to Cathy, who took a drag and passed it to Denny. "So," he went on, "they have to play it cool. Call me up at four A.M. to rap about some spaced-out crap like the Devil's Triangle or exorcism, do I groove on Satanism? When what they're really calling to say is: Hey, I'm lonely and I'd really groove on talking for a few minutes, breaking the mothering silence here that's cracking my skull. I keep wishing just one time somebody'll call in and say: Just rap with me about some real stuff. Because I've been getting into your show and I thought maybe you'd like to hear that. I don't know. Nobody wants to admit there's this need we've all got to have people around. About the only one I know who's not scared to say it is Cath, here."

"It doesn't cost me anything," Cathy said. "If I tell you I'm lonely, we'll spend some time together."

Larry laughed. "Some time. Like four years."

"Bragging or complaining?" Cathy smiled.

"No complaints." They exchanged a very meaningful smile.

It hurt. Denny didn't know why. But it just hurt rotten. She passed back the cigarette and went upstairs to bed. She hated weekends. Too much time to spend watching those two do their happy-family bit, listening to Larry's philosophy lessons. It was all shit. But it still hurt. And she wished she hadn't told them anything, not even that she had a mother in the city. They didn't even know her name. Just Denny. And that was too much.

She curled up on the narrow cot, goddamned tears fucking up her breathing. Thinking about that time she'd caught the two of them doing it. About seven years old she was then. Woke up in the middle of the night with this bad dream, and got out of bed, went down the hall to open their bedroom door, and there they were. His big naked ass in the air, and her legs wrapped around his goodamned neck. Groaning away, the two of them. Until *she* moved her head and saw. Shit! The look on her fucking face. But cool. So cool, the two of them. He just pulled the blankets up over them and got off, saying, 'Come on, honey. It's all right.' She'd listened to them talking away, explaining. But she'd known. She'd *known*. They always left her out of everything. Like at the hospital, making her stay in the goddamned play center in the lobby. Not letting her go upstairs.

No. Not true. Man, how you fucking lie to yourself! They never left you out of one goddamned thing. And *they* wouldn't let you inside that shiteating hospital. Not her. And after he died, she tried so stinking *hard*. It was seeing, knowing how hard she was trying. I wanted to tell her to stop trying. But she kept on working away at it, trying, trying. Tell me what you want, Denny. Tell me how you feel. Tell me, Denny. I love you. I want to help you. You mean everything to me. Your happiness is all I want. Why don't you stop *trying?* I'm not worth it. I can't even get inside my own goddamned life.

But, Jesus, I've got such eyes to see you. Why can't I *stop?*

About two o'clock Tuesday morning, the studio phone rang.

Larry picked up and heard a voice he knew say, "I'm really lonely, Larry."

"I know it," he said gently. "Why don't you go home, babe? Maybe she's lonely too."

"I've got to think about it."

"That's cool, Den. Take all the time you need."

Eight

Lunch was a wasted effort. She ate almost none of the salad she ordered, but sat gazing at him as if taking stock of the minutest details about him. He tried to eat, managed several mouthfuls, then set down his knife and fork and gazed back at her. She seemed not at all bothered.

This was a breakdown happening right in front of him. She was willing it to happen. There had to be something he could do to stop her before she reached the end. Then, self-consciously, thought about how he must appear to her—a big, beaming buffoon with neon hair and awkward hands. A fool out in the world thinking he could save lives. But it didn't matter if she saw him that way. It was only important that she was worth saving. So eminently worthwhile a person. With talent and a future.

"You think I'm going mad, too, don't you?" she said at length, surprisingly. "I can see it in the way you're looking at me."

Her saying this served to ease his apprehensiveness, and he picked up his fork and ate another mouthful before answering, their eyes still on each other.

"I think you *want* to," he said thoughtfully, buttering a roll. "You're trying awfully damned hard to get there."

"That's the funny thing," she said, as if speaking to him from another world. "I'm honestly not trying. It's the first time in my life I haven't tried. It's just happening all by itself."

"You're not fighting it, though," he said.

"I don't seem to be able to."

Her eyes searched his, and he wished he could know what it was she expected of him. Or if she expected anything at all. He waited for her to elaborate, but she lapsed back into silence, and he once more lost his appetite.

"What would you like?" he asked, after the waiter had removed the barely touched plates.

"I'm tired. I'd like to sleep."

"I'll take you home," he said, putting some money down on the table.

He didn't know what to do, couldn't get her to talk, felt it would be the wrongest thing possible to apply any pressure to make her talk. But looking at her as they walked out to the car, studying the pale perfection of her profile, he was overcome by a yearning to bring her out, stop her before it was too late. Maybe he could find the daughter. But what would that solve, what good would it do? If the girl didn't want to come home of her own volition, it would help nothing, forcing a confrontation between mother and daughter. Yet, finding out whether she was alive or dead would be valuable. Although, were he to return to Isabel as the bearer of bad news, he'd be intentionally eliminating himself from her life. Because from that point on, she'd be bound to associate him with tragedy. He'd do nothing.

He drove her home and walked with her to the front door.

"Try to get some sleep," he said, taking hold of her hand. "You haven't been sleeping, have you?"

"No," she said inaudibly, wondering how he knew. "I don't sleep."

"Is it just Denise?" he asked.

"No. It's everything." She withdrew her hand, opened the door, and went in, leaving him standing there. He turned and went down the steps, heading back to the main road and a taxi. Lighting a cigarette, his collar pulled high, he walked along glad of the gusting wind, the penetrating cold. It seemed to help him think.

There was a taxi cruising past the corner. He whistled it down, hopped in, and they were off, back to the station to collect his car. Sitting in the back of the cab, he thought about money. What good did it do you having it when there was so little it could do for you when you needed help with people? Sure, he put it here and there to help in a kind of institutional way. Funding drug rehabilitation programs. Funding shelters, halfway houses. Funding this, that, and any other damned thing. But how the hell did you fund someone's life, set it moving again?

The company just chugged along on its own now, producing more and more money. If he showed up two or three times a week for a couple of hours, that was enough. There were people he paid to ensure production levels. And he couldn't back out altogether. He still cared about the place, the business. But since Geoff, he just couldn't involve himself as he had. Couldn't help but wonder if his concentrated involvement in the company hadn't in some way blinkered him to Geoff's problems. He'd spent months afterward looking for someone or something to blame before at last admitting nothing he might have changed would've appreciably altered the course of events. Because there was, in retrospect, something curiously final about all of Geoff's life. And if he took it further and questioned that sense of finality, he felt he'd be getting into areas of mysticism and religiosity that struck him as fanciful, dangerous. Straw-grasping at its zenith. No, he'd found it better to make sensible efforts in the areas where he could. Funding, funding. Giving his money, his time. Spending most of his free hours sitting in the dark in the car in some rundown neighborhood, waiting for something to break.

He'd spent the majority of his adult years trying to rescue the business his father had almost succeeded in running into the ground. His father using the company money to finance his jaunts here and there, his somehow dreary women and his hunting lodge that was no more used for hunting than his dark-paneled office had been used for business. It was all so damned classic. Yet the man had been so lovable, so damned lovable. A lovable waste of a lifetime, of talent and intelligence. Brian had, since Geoff's death, been having third, fourth, and fifth thoughts about the quality of his late father's life. And the more he examined it, the more convinced he became it wasn't his father who'd been wasteful.

But Brian the young man had heard the call of duty, felt the flush of ambition, and gone out like some light-headed crusader to save the floundering business. Gone public, issued stock, merged half a dozen times in as many years, and ended up with an autonomous money-making monster in which he now kept a hand, partly out of waning pride and mainly out of a profound desire to keep on funding the various programs. Each time he wrote a check, silently saying: This one's for you, Pop. And this one's for you, Brian. And this one's for you, Geoff. Save a kid a day. Keep guilt from your door. Repay emotional debts with dollars.

Volunteering himself to the police department like some comic-strip character, spending most of his nights on stakeout; doing boring sit-around work the force was delighted to have him take off their hands. You want to sit on your ass in a car half the night freezing your balls off, Connors, be our guest. Here's your radio, your ID. Have a hot time. He didn't mind. It gave him the feeling he was helping. Just a little.

Now, this woman. The first woman he'd encountered in years who moved him in any way at all. Going down for the third time without calling for help or making any effort to save herself. Just sinking down, down.

It made him sadder than almost anything ever had, casting a pale purple haze over all his outward perspectives. The interior ones, too. Like the lights Geoff had affected in his bedroom. The ones that made everything glow eerily. He couldn't sit by and let it happen again. Put any title to it you like, he told himself. Call it self-gratification or an acute case of heroics. But even if he ended up looking like the halfwit of all time, he was going to haul her back into the boat.

What for, Connors? So she'll be grateful and lie down for you? No, not that. This woman never would. I like the image, but it isn't real. Why? Because I meant what I said to her. That was truthful. Comes a time when we all need someone to be around. Just to be there. Maybe do a little hand-holding to help you get through a bad time. I'll hold your hand. And help you. Whether you want me to or not. I can't just walk away.

* * *

She spent the remainder of the afternoon sitting in the living room staring at an old photograph album, her fingers tracing the edges of the snapshots she'd so lovingly put into the corners, labeled, dated. Feeling the ache in her dried-out eyes, fatigue rattling against her ribs. Returned the album to the sideboard when Jude arrived home, and sat in the too-bright kitchen with Jude for dinner.

She fell asleep early, to the murmur of Judy's radio. Slept and dreamed, as she did on those nights when the attack wasn't running a replay, that she was back in the hospital bed, desperately scratching out notes to anyone who'd read them. And woke up screaming. It was too real this time, too close, too terminal. She woke up, her scream dying in the air, and sat gaping into the darkness, hearing the sound of bare feet running—the sound so like the echo of her own heartbeat thudding in her ears; saw the door fly open and the light go on. And Jude, in her granny gown, her hair looking electrified, her face looking scared, asking, "Are you okay?"

It could have been Denny standing there, might have been. Isabel shook her head and put her hands to her face, shielding her eyes from the light; then pushed her hair away, pressing her palms against her temples, trying to hold her head together. It felt as if it was about to split open.

"You had another nightmare," Jude said, coming to sit on the end of the bed. "You want me to get you something? Tea, or some aspirin? Something cold to drink?"

"Nothing," Isabel whispered.

"Would you like me to stay with you for a little while until you go back to sleep?"

She looked at Jude's small earnest face and said, "Yes. Stay for a while."

"Okay." Jude jumped up to turn on the far bedside lamp, then switched off the overhead light. She climbed into bed and settled herself, reaching to turn off the bedside lamp.

"When I was little," she said, moving closer to Isabel, her voice very unchildlike in the dark, "the best trip of my life was getting into bed with my mom and dad."

Isabel lay rigid, listening to Jude's husky voice, then felt the girl insinuating herself closer, an arm reaching out to encircle her, a small body radiating warmth.

"It makes everything so much better," Jude said, "having someone to put your arms around. Could I hold you?"

Isabel opened her arms and closed them around Jude, holding on for her life; torn in too many different directions by the act of once more holding someone. So easy to pretend it was Denny. So good to allow the terror to recede. Jude sighed contentedly, and Isabel closed her eyes.

"I want you to stay," Isabel whispered. "I'm so afraid. Everyone's going away. Everything's falling apart. Like trying to hold a handful of sand. No matter what I do, it all keeps slipping through my fingers. I don't know what to do anymore. I can't seem to think."

"I know," Jude whispered back, wondering how she was going to tell her about moving back to Blake's.

"Don't go yet!" Isabel whispered feverishly, as if reading Jude's mind. "Please stay with me."

"Go to sleep now," Jude crooned. "You're so tired. Sleep, I'll be here." She'd have to work something out with Blake, delay it a little. How could she go now, when she was needed? She lined her body up against Isabel's, feeling the good way she used to as a little kid, being held against Isabel's breasts, secure in her arms, breathing in the warm sleepy smell of her. She thought about what could have happened that night a few weeks ago. The way Isabel had looked. She tried to imagine what had taken place. Jude was sure they'd raped her. And probably forced Marshall to watch, or something awful like that. It scared Jude crazy just thinking about it.

Isabel thought: This child for my child. Could that be possible? One who needs, one who has a need to be needed. But which of us is which? She stroked the long, silken hair, her hand recalling the motions, her body recalling Sunday mornings when another small body had burrowed its way between her and Howard, nestling with a satisfied sigh within the circle of her mother's arms. Circles.

Once upon a time, I lay within my mother's arms and knew it to be the safest place on earth. My daughter lay, once upon a time, within my arms. But I couldn't keep her. This child rests her head on my breast, entrusts her arms to mine, and we make a circle. She gives me back for a few moments what has gone away. I return to her what she has lost. To help each other survive the night.

Her eyes fluttered closed, and she slept once more.

I'm becoming fixated, Brian told himself. Like some rare kind of junkie. Hooked on this woman. But he couldn't stop thinking about her, couldn't stay away. And went to the studio every day to take her to lunch. Each time a replay of the first time. She accepted his presence as a matter of course, went with him wherever he chose to go, picked at her food, then sat staring at him until it was time to leave.

She's doing this on purpose, he thought—allowing herself to be carried away into the center of the stream, where the current's strongest. Letting herself drift effortlessly into a quiet madness. Watching it happen gave him a feeling of desperation, of helplessness. There had to be some way to stop her.

By the end of a week of these fruitless encounters, he insisted on following her home. "To talk," he said. "We've got to talk." She shrugged her shoulders, thinking: It doesn't matter.

She unlocked the door, and he followed her inside, helping her out of her coat, removing his own. He noticed she'd disposed of the coat she'd been wearing that night, the one minus its buttons. What had she done with it? he wondered. Probably thrown it away.

She walked through to the kitchen, thinking she'd make some coffee, then forgot why she'd come to the kitchen and sat down at the table, watching him travel the length of the hallway.

"Why do you keep coming back?" she asked, studying him as he lit a cigarette. "Why do you smoke?"

"I don't know why I smoke," he answered, looking at the cigarette between his fingers before meeting her eyes. "And I keep coming back because I'm a nice guy. I want to help out."

"There's nothing to help with."

"What happened to your boyfriend?"

"He went. Took himself off to save someone else."

"Would you care to run that one through again for me?" he asked.

"Forget it," she said. "It didn't mean anything. How is it you talk one language to me and another when you talk to young people? You did it with Judy when she was here. And the waitress today. Are you some sort of unofficial interpreter?"

He laughed and took a drag on his cigarette. "Maybe so," he said. "There just happens to be another language for the young. And if you can speak it, it doesn't matter how old you happen to be or how you dress."

"Is that what's wrong with me? I don't know the language?"

"There's nothing wrong with you, Isabel. You're fine. You've got some problems right now you're having kind of a hard time handling."

"I don't want to talk."

"Then tell me what you do want," he said reasonably, asking her for perhaps the tenth time.

"Denise was constantly telling me to leave her alone. 'Just leave me alone!' She would say it over and over. 'Leave me alone!' I couldn't ever understand what she wanted to be left alone to do. Now, I think I'm beginning to know."

"And?" he prompted, feeling they were beginning to get somewhere. It was the most she'd said to him since the night they'd met.

"There's no room to think, not enough time. You need to be left alone with yourself so you can find out what you think. But even when I'm alone, I can't seem to think anymore. I spent two years with Marshall. I thought I loved him. He's gone, and I don't miss him, don't even think about him. That night Judy called me from the hospital, he wanted us to get married at once. Like some sort of bizarre celebration of what had happened to Denny. I thought he was mad. He thought *I* was mad, at the last. I think we're all mad. And I still don't know why you keep coming back. What does that mean, you're a 'nice guy'?"

"Hell, I don't know. What am I supposed to say to you? I'm a boy scout? I'm working on merit badges? I've got eyes for your body, and I'm only here hoping to wear you down? What do you *want* me to say?"

"Is that true? Is that why you're here, because you've 'got eyes for my body'?"

"Some. Do you think people do things from strictly pure motives, Isabel? Of course I'm interested in you. In all the ways. But it's not what I'm pushing, you'll notice. I'm not some sort of self-serving ghoul. I don't have a need to cash in on someone's vulnerability. It doesn't mean I don't think about it. Because I do." He smiled. "I get off on you."

"You get off on me," she repeated. "You're right. It is another language entirely. You've proven your point. But it doesn't mean anything. You get off on me. I don't want you. I don't want anyone. Except Judy. I need her right now. But that's all. Why do men always say these things? As if saying you want me is going to turn some sort of key in my head and automatically make me respond to you because you've risked stating your desires. I don't *want* you. I don't want any man."

"I haven't approached you."

"You don't have to. None of you feel you have to do that sort of thing anymore. You all speak right up, and I'm supposed to be so honored, so flattered, I'll take you upstairs to bed, because it's such an enormous compliment to be wanted, to be chosen to receive you. My brain isn't dead yet, and I resent your assumptions. I resent myself for going along with Marshall's assumptions for two years. I don't want you. I'm doing what I want to do. My job. I'm very good at what I do. Very good."

"You are. That's true," he said, putting out his cigarette. "But I didn't say what I did because it was supposed to make you respond positively. I'm not challenging your right to say no. I'm only trying to be a friend, trying to help."

"Help by going away," she said, feeling uncertain, but compelled somehow to say it. "I have too many things to think about. You can help by leaving me alone. You block my view."

"You're giving up," he said. "Do you know that? You're just sitting back waiting for it all to happen. You *want* to go under. Play crazy, and soon enough you'll be there."

"Stop it!" Her voice rose. "Why do I have to keep *telling* you? Go away. Please? Will you go away? You upset me. Coming around upsetting me. I can't take it. I don't want the traffic, people coming, people going. You'd only wind up being another Marshall. Someone whose body feels a little differently, someone who has another set of words to say, someone whose hands aren't quite the same. Different. But the same in the end. I want to be left alone. That's my choice. I don't want to go through any more 'love' affairs. You'd be the last, and you'd kill me."

So there is something there, he thought, his hope renewed. Feeling beneath the words.

"All right," he said softly. "If anything comes up and you need a hand, you've got my number?"

"I can handle whatever comes up," she said stiffly.

"All right, Isabel. All right." He stopped to kiss the top of her head, then walked through to the front of the house, picked up his coat, shrugged it on, and let himself out.

Touched in spite of herself by his gesture, she pounded her fist on the table, wishing she had something she could smash. Or that she could cry. Something. Instead, she got up from the table, went upstairs and through to her bathroom, to stand studying the row of medicine vials for quite some time before finally closing the cabinet door, switching off the bathroom light, and spreading out the work she'd brought home.

Jude didn't come home that night. She telephoned to say she'd be at Blake's if Isabel needed her for anything. Isabel lay alone in her bed feeling rejected. Trying to reason with herself, yet still feeling abandoned. Near dawn, she slept, only to awaken with her heart pounding and perspiration streaming down the back of her neck, her hair saturated. The hospital dream again.

Perversely, she felt strengthened by sending Brian away. After all, she told herself, wasn't it better to end something of her own volition before it was ended for her? The idea of another involvement, destined to end, as they all sooner or later did, with the man in question moving elsewhere, was too defeating to be considered. She couldn't tolerate any more planchanging, comings and goings. So that what she'd anticipate would never be what she received. No. Better to be alone. She was too old to believe in perfect people, and a fool for allowing herself to be persuaded into believing in Marshall in the first place.

A fool, yes. But for a time it had been so good. And she'd relied upon his piercing embraces as much as he'd relied on her availability. That was it, of course: the need for sharing. And there was an attraction to Brian. It was there undeniably. The look of him did please her, it was true. His light, nonaggressive way. The shape of his mouth and eyes, the appealing length of his finely molded hands. It was all there. He'd kissed the top of her head, and her treacherous body had gone moist in response. No. She wouldn't be tricked by her body. Not again.

Two days. Her eyes raked the busy corridors, questioning his absence. She felt a little frightened at how literally he'd taken her words. I didn't mean it, she thought, something childlike inside her alarmed by his failure to be there. I didn't mean it. But what *did* I mean?

He couldn't have said why, but he couldn't stay away. He'd think about it, tell himself he wouldn't go that day. He wouldn't. And then suffered through the afternoon and evening, haunted by thoughts of her. He made it through a second day, no less agitated. And on the third day, he had to go, get in his car and drive downtown to the station. To be there waiting for her. He told himself he was being ridiculous. But he kept seeing her as she'd been that night, with her head on her knees. He'd seen the naked curve of her spine and the abject hanging of her head, and now he no longer possessed the objectivity, the distance to remain uninvolved. Fear mixed with longing and sympathy.

Her eyes flickered at seeing him. Something so small it might have gone unnoticed had he not been anxiously searching for it. But a response to his return. It was enough.

* * *

Two or three nights a week now, Jude slipped into bed with Isabel, to hold her, to try to talk to her, to sleep in her arms. Isabel remained silent. She spoke less and less. And the less she said, the more concerned Jude became. Isabel seemed no longer to hear her when Jude talked to her.

Blake began dropping by the house in the evenings to study with Jude or just to rap, and he also noticed how strangely remote Isabel was becoming. She'd greet him pleasantly at the door, absentmindedly offer him things to eat and drink, say she was glad he and Jude were friends again—sounding as if she was referring to small children—and then drift off to her room or drive away in the car.

Sometimes, Blake and Jude would follow after her. To make sure she was all right. But she just drove for miles; then she'd turn around and drive home again. Occasionally slowing.

After the fourth night of this, it suddenly registered in Jude's mind.

"She's cruising the streets, looking for Denny," she told Blake. "Oh, *God!*" she exclaimed, feeling heartbroken. "God, Blake, this is so bad! If you know where Denny is and you're not telling, I'll never forgive you. Never!"

"Man, if I knew where she was," he said, equally disturbed, "I'd haul her ass back here in a sling if I had to. What the fuck's she *doing?*"

"See why I have to stay?" Jude said. "I can't leave her alone. It'd be like . . . I don't know. Running off and leaving a little baby all by itself."

"She's no baby," Blake said.

"I know that," Jude said. "It's just...all this. It's so *sad.*"

They turned when Isabel did, and followed her lengthy, circuitous route home, watching the car slow several more times. Jude felt as if she was slowly being squeezed flat.

By the end of the third month of Denny's absence, Isabel realized she'd passed into a new phase. She'd ceased praying for Denny to come home, having arrived at the conclusion it would never happen. She accepted her own death as her immediate future. And began casually deliberating over ways and means.

Jude, sensing a negative change in the atmosphere, said, "Try to hang in. I've got a feeling Denny can't last much longer. She'll give in and call you."

"*I* can't last much longer," Isabel said tonelessly, heading for the refuge of her bathroom.

Jude didn't know what to say or do. Isabel's words made her more scared than ever.

After more than a month of daily visits to the studio, Brian decided it would be a good idea to give it a rest. So he kept away for a week this time, put in more hours at the office, and in a state of preoccupation, maintained his most recent nightwatch. Sitting in the car staring at the mock-brick facade of a rundown house in the worst section of the city, thinking about Isabel. Yearning like a kid for Isabel. Scared half crazy for Isabel. He thought of sending her flowers, gifts; writing to her. Thought of every way possible he might get past the blockade of her self-imposed defenses. Nothing. A life going down the drain, and there wasn't one damned thing he could do to stop it happening. Because she wouldn't let him.

In his hours at home, he worked out in the basement, pounding away at the bag until he was exhausted, then braving the gelid air in the bubble to dive into the heated pool and swim laps. Trying to take himself so far into physical exhaustion that his mind would get off Isabel. But it didn't work. He'd swim up and down, then lie on his back floating on the surface of the water, seeing his breath smoking upward in the cold air, gazing up at the top of the bubble and beyond, seeing the dark outlines of denuded branches overhanging the area.

Come the summer, he'd have to have the trees trimmed back. By the time the leaves came in, the entire pool would be in shadow. And he liked to swim in the full light of day with the water cool and the sun hot on his back.

Every day he watched the show, holding his breath until she appeared on camera. Once she was on, he could let out his breath and enjoy watching her, listening to the tone of her voice, noting the changes. She seemed to be shrinking, her cheekbones almost daily more prominent. Her shoulders becoming bony beneath the softly draped outfits they dressed her in. A certain hesitancy around her mouth. But the fluidity was still there, the appeal. He'd sit and watch her and know simply from the look of her that the daughter hadn't yet come home. He'd know when that happened. It would show all over her face.

He caught the offhandedly cute-snide references Jerry Brenner made to her. Calling her "the station's Playmate of '52," prefacing her segment by saying, "Here's our very own sex idol." One after another, little caustic jabs at her. So absurd, too. Because her quiet subtlety made his remarks seem as preposterous as the man himself. It angered Brian, because he saw Brenner as one more pain-in-the-ass problem she was having to cope with. One more something to add to the "everything" that was driving her under. He wondered how she managed to pull herself sufficiently together to do the show each day. And decided there was a strength there, a determination he admired, an ambition he understood all too well. In the face of adversity, never admit to the odds. Just keep going.

He'd go into the house, take a hot shower, get dressed in heavy old clothes, and go out tramping through the snow to the perimeters of his property. Trying to work it off, swim it off, walk it off. No good. None of it.

I'm in love with you. Don't go under. If you and I never come to anything at all, at least let me see you get up off your knees and keep walking. I love you. I wish I knew what to do for you. Wish there was something you'd *let* me do for you. Love you.

She telephoned, but nobody answered. Let it ring six times, then hung up fast, her heart drumming crazily, as if she'd just tried to boost something in a store or'd been on the verge of popping a fistful of uppers, speed. For chrissake! she thought, backing away from the phone. Now I'm scared. Like if I call she'll maybe yell and scream at me or something, do a big number. Something.

Come off it, Den! She never in her whole life yelled or screamed at you. And anytime she got mad, it was 'cause you did it to her.

Well, maybe she should've. Maybe it's like unnatural to be that goddamned *good*.

Man, are you ever weird! No matter what way she is, you can't hack it! Maybe she just doesn't give a good goddamn that you split. Maybe she's busy getting it off with good old Marshall, happy as Larry, not giving one goddamn about you, kid.

Yeah. And maybe she's going bananas, thinking I'm like dead or maybe somebody offed me.

Boy, you're one stupid chick, know that? How would *you* feel if you got home and somebody'd offed *her*? Or she'd split on you and the house was all locked up, empty. No note. Nothing. Just gone.

Mom, I want to come home. So bad. I've got such eyes to flop on the floor in front of the fire and get warm. I feel like I'll freeze to death doing this gig. Next week. One more week, and I'll have enough bread so I don't have to take any of yours. Another week. Then that's it.

She felt better. She'd decided.

Nine

Isabel sensed something amiss as soon as she entered the studio the following Monday morning. Jerry was around somewhere, she could tell. His presence somehow disturbed the air in the building. It was too quiet. The grips mechanical in their good mornings. She went through the sound stage and on out the other side, glancing into the empty Green Room as she went past on her way to makeup.

Jerry was in the chair. Lenny looked up at her, his eyes revealing his upset. Lenny hated scenes, and Jerry was angling for one. Jerry's eyes met hers in the mirror. He smiled, raising his coffeecup to his mouth. She backed away, went along through the engineer's booth to hang up her dress, then poured herself a cup of coffee inside the studio. Stood drinking it while she watched the grips get the sets arranged, adjusting the lights, maneuver the cameras here and there, the huge cords snaking their way soundlessly across the floor.

Her stomach was unsettled, fluttery. Nervous. Jerry was up to no good. Was he just going to sit in the chair until air time and prevent her from getting into makeup? Yes, he'd do that. But why? It was so stupid. Yet, everything he'd done for months was childishly stupid. Bumping into her, taking off with her clipboard and notes, stepping on her feet, making audible comments while she and her guests were on the air. All sorts of things. Anything and everything he could think of. Five minutes. She left the studio and went back down to the makeup room. Jerry was still in the chair.

Lenny, red-faced, was standing with a fine makeup brush in his hand, obviously trying to control his anger—his tears? Isabel wondered—as Jerry complained, ''This is the wrong fucking color! You know that, for shit's sake! Get this garbage off and put on the lighter Pan-Cake!''

Unsteadily, Lenny put down the brush, reached for the cold cream, and began removing the makeup. He didn't dare look at Isabel, didn't dare trust himself to speak. Isabel turned and went up to the Green Room. She'd have to do her own makeup. But she didn't have any. Nothing in her bag but a lipstick, a compact of pressed powder, a Tampax, and a hairbrush. Some perfume. She closed her bag, retrieved her cup of coffee, and sat very still, trying to think.

Annette popped into the room, saw Isabel, and stopped. ''You're supposed to be in makeup, aren't you?'' Annette said.

''I want you to do something for me. Please,'' Isabel said quietly, opening her handbag. ''I want you to take my car and drive to the all-night drugstore up the road. Get me some foundation—guess at the color, some dark eyeshadow, the darkest you can get, some mascara, any kind, some coverstick, and some heated rollers.'' She pulled out two twenty-dollar bills and pushed them into Annette's hand. ''Please? And hurry!''

Annette took the money, Isabel's keys, and without another word dashed out. On her way down the corridor, she looked into the makeup room, saw Jerry in the chair, and knew. She ran faster. In the parking lot, she ran smack into Ash.

''Where the hell are you going?'' Ash asked, half-smiling.

''Check the makeup room!'' she yelled, sliding into Isabel's car, jamming the key into the ignition.

Check makeup? Ash greeted the guard and went inside. He walked down the corridor to the makeup room. Saw Jerry sitting in the chair, saw Lenny—his lips sucked tight—and continued on upstairs to his office. Wondering where Isabel was. Probably Annette knew. Going too goddamned far this time, Jerry, Ash thought, glancing at his watch. There was just enough time to make a couple of quick calls. Dragged the phone across his desk and lifted the receiver. Asking himself how far Jerry might go.

Annette got back twenty minutes before air time.

"I'll have to use the women's lounge upstairs," Isabel said, taking the package from her, flying out of the Green Room, down the corridors, up the stairs, and into the lounge. The light was so bad. And her hands were shaking so much she could scarcely function. Plugged in the rollers, then grabbed the makeup sponge, wet it in the john, and returned to start applying the base, telling herself to stay calm, be calm. You can get it done. Just take your time. *Why* does he do these things? First the base, then the powder. Thank God the compact was invisible powder. Using the lipstick for blusher. Thick—it wouldn't blend easily. I despise that man! Hands shaking so badly she could scarcely open the eye-shadow container. Took a deep breath, telling herself to go slow. There's enough time. You'll do it. Began stroking on the eye shadow, seeing her television face starting to appear. Good. I can't keep on with this. This is the end. The mascara. Carefully, holding her right wrist with her left hand for steadiness. The rollers. She brushed out her hair, rolled it up quickly. Just the top. She'd have to wear it down; there wouldn't be time—no pins anyway—to put it up. She was going to look like a clown. Just what he wanted. Spiteful childish pranks. But not childish. Upsetting Lenny. Me, of course. What he had in mind, Lenny being purely incidental. A writeoff. The rollers in, she picked up the lipstick, did her mouth, added a little more color to her cheeks. Looked at her watch and felt panic bursting in her chest. There wasn't going to be time enough to change clothes. She'd have to go on in what she was wearing. An old black skirt and white blouse. Her Aran cardigan. A gift from Marshall. She smoothed the blouse, tucked it more evenly into the waistband. She wanted to cry. I look crazy, she thought, removing the rollers. Crazy. Wildly tugging the brush through her hair, wishing she'd cut it when she'd thought about it years ago. How can I go on with hair hanging all over the place, like a schoolgirl? No choice, no choice. *Why* is he doing this to me? She brushed out her hair, parted it in the middle, pushed it back over her shoulders, snatched up her bag and clipboard, and tore out of the lounge, nearly falling on her way down the stairs. Her heartbeat gone crazy too as she ran down the main corridor, around the corner, back up the four steps and into the Green Room, to find the place empty. Where's my guest? Looked at her watch again as she pulled open the heavy, heavy inside door. Air time. And there was Jerry on the set with her guest. The red lights on.

Ash started forward to speak to her, but she didn't stop. She pushed her handbag at Annette, and carrying her clipboard, walked right past the cameras up onto the set, seated herself in the vacant chair, clipped on her mike, reached over to shake hands with her guest and say, "Good morning. I'm Isabel Gary, and my guest this morning . . ."

Ash darted through the studio and into the booth to talk to the cameramen through their headsets.

"Keep Jerry off camera," he told them. "Stay in close on Isabel and Mrs. Pearson . . . Don't mike him," he told the engineer. Then, back to the cameramen: "Keep two on the guest, three on Isabel, and one back for a cutoff full shot."

Then, lighting a cigarette, he nervously eyed the monitors. For the first minute or two, Jerry tried to include himself in the interview. But the guest, an elderly woman who was in town with an exhibit of antique watercolors, responded to the pressure of Isabel's hand and the oddly urgent light in her eyes and directed her attention solely to Isabel. Irate, Jerry glanced at the studio monitor, saw he wasn't in the picture, got up, and stalked noisily off the set. Isabel kept talking. Her heart skipping erratically, her voice slowly steadying. Just keep going, stay calm. *But it isn't over yet! He won't leave it at this.*

Standing just beyond the cameras, Annette was watching, her eyes moving back and forth between her program notes and the set. Jerry shoved her out of the way as he went slamming out of the studio and into the engineer's booth.

"What the fuck's going on?" he demanded of Ash. "You can't cut me off that way!"

"I'll talk to you *later!*" Ash said sharply, firmly. "Stay out of there! You're not going on camera today. Now, get out of here!"

"You can't do that—"

"I'm *doing* it! Wait in the Green Room. Or in makeup. You seem to enjoy Lenny's company. Get out of *here!* I've got a show to get out."

"You can't . . ." Jerry spluttered. This wasn't the way he'd planned it.

"Out!"

He went out, to pace up and down the corridor, enraged. That bitch. That fucking bitch, he'd fix her. Curiosity grabbing him by the throat, he ducked into the Green Room to see the interview being wrapped.

Annette hastily picked her way over the cables, while one of the grips escorted the elderly woman out of the studio.

"Fast!" she whispered to Isabel. "Here's the news. Get over to the lectern! You're doing the whole show!"

"I can't!"

"You've got to! Ash said you're doing it. After the news, you've got a commercial, then a seven-minute segment with a guy from the Lion's Club. Then another commercial. Then fourteen minutes with some puppeteers. It'll be an easy one. They're doing nine minutes of a skit. Five with you. Just keep going. You can do it. After the station break, one more live interview, and then we go to tape. You come back for the sign-off, and that's it." Annette pulled a strand of hair out of Isabel's eyes, shoved the yellow news printouts into her hand, got her around back of the lectern, and moved quickly out of the way.

The camera's red light winked on. Isabel looked into the camera's eyes, smiled, looked down at the pages of large type, and began reading. She had no idea what she was doing, just kept looking up into the camera every so often, forcing herself to read slowly, steadily, until she got to the end.

A two-hour marathon session of being directed here and there in the studio, with Annette pulling her this way, that way, presenting her with people to be interviewed, pages of notes to put on her clipboard; taking notes away, giving her more. By the time the sign-off music was being miked into the studio and she was saying, "Have a good day. Thank you for being with us, and tune in again tomorrow to *Mid-Morning*," she was completely drained. Her blouse saturated, the Aran sweater smelling woolly with wetness. Her hair heavy as a lead helmet. The overheads went off, the cameras were parked out of the way, Annette was showing the last of the guests out of the studio, and Isabel sat on in the captain's chair on the set trying to catch her breath. She'd never worked so hard in her life. Her mouth felt misshapen from smiling, talking.

The sound stage emptied as she sat blankly watching from the vantage point of the raised platform. The air-conditioning—never on during a show because of the noise—came on now, and she felt the first cooling draft catch her in the spine, along her arms. She sat feeling she'd run a very long race over plotted obstacles. She'd managed to make it. But couldn't shake the feeling that there was more to come. More and worse. Tiredly, she got up at last and walked slowly across the studio.

The temporary lull and silence until they'd begin setting up for the next show to be aired from this studio. Her footsteps echoed in the vast room. She took a deep breath and headed for the inside door. As she was passing the draperies that separated the stage into sections, a hand shot out from behind the draperies and savagely took hold of her upper arm.

Aside from the suddenness, she wasn't surprised.

"Hope you enjoyed yourself." Jerry smiled grotesquely. "Because that's your first solo and your last."

She stepped closer to him in order to ease the pain of his grip on her arm.

"Why do you do these things?" she asked softly. *"Why?"*

"You've been working your way up from the minute you first came here," he said, the awful smile still plastered to his face, the majority of his body hidden by the bulk of the draperies. "But you're not going anywhere. And you know why? Because I'm the one. Me. And you're nothing. Decoration. Set dressing. That's all. I've handled broads like you before. You're nothing new to me. I think of you"—he laughed, stepping slightly away from the curtains—"about the same way dogs think about fire hydrants." He laughed again. "What're you on, Is? All spaced out like a fucking zombie. Wouldn't notice shit if you had it all over you." She felt something wet hitting the front of her skirt, felt it hitting her legs. And looked down, seeing what he was doing, something went CLICK very loudly inside her head. She clenched her fist, swung her arm, and hit him on the side of the head as hard as she could. Jerry released her and hit her back. A blow that landed openhanded across her eyes, so that for several seconds she couldn't see. Saw dancing white stars. Her mouth opened, and a scream tore open the silence.

Ash shouted, horror-stricken, from the doorway. Annette dropped her clipboard and Isabel's handbag and streaked across the studio to throw herself between the two, knocking Isabel out of the way. Suddenly the place was alive with people. Isabel had regained her balance, easily plucked Annette out of the way, and closed her hands around Jerry's throat. He clawed at her hands, but her hold simply tightened.

She wanted to kill him. All the things he'd done to her. Her hands squeezing. A thunderous roaring in her ears. People were shouting, voices crashing against her ears. But all she could see was Jerry's despicable face slowly turning red, then redder. Her own voice hissing, "I'll kill you, kill you, kill you!" Her eyes seeing Ash and Annette, their faces distorted, unreal. She saw them, captivated by the way Annette's hair seemed to be floating slow-motion in the air around her as her body moved emphatically in time with the senseless sounds emerging from her mouth. Looked again at Jerry, who was gaping at her wide-eyed, his mouth open wide, strangling. Good. "Kill you, kill you." Peripherally, she saw motion, and turned her head slightly, to see Ash approaching from the far end of the studio, his jacket billowing like tweed wings. Motion, everything spinning. She felt herself rising, being lifted, caught up in a spinning, eddying motion. Distant noises, echoing. She was rising, going higher; the faces and voices diminishing, losing volume; the people shrinking, shrieking; dwindling as she rose above them, ascending weightlessly.

Ash saw her eyes, saw something there that sent a violent tremor of fear spiraling through him. He reached out and tore her hands away from Jerry's throat, crying, "Isabel, enough! *Enough!*"

She was jolted, grounded by the impact of his voice. She let her arms drop to her sides.

"Zip up and get out," Ash told Jerry quietly. "You've violated every union and contract agreement in existence. You don't *do* these things, Jerry. Sane people don't go on and on provoking, damaging, until there's nothing left for the other person to do but strike back in self-defense. You're finished here, Jerry. Get out while you can still walk."

He turned to look at Isabel. Her eyes were still vacant.

"Come with me, Isabel," he said. "Come on."

She couldn't seem to move.

"Come *on*," Ash said, his arm around her, getting her moving, leading her away. Down the corridor, saying, "Jesus! How in the name of everything sacred did he think he'd get away with a lunatic stunt like that? Sick!" He shook his head. "Annette's bringing up a change of clothes for you. Are you all right now?"

She didn't answer at once. She was thinking, watching Ash's mouth move, making words. She went with him into his office, feeling the foul wetness of the skirt as it slapped against her legs. Inside the office, she unzipped the skirt, stepped out of it, then kicked it into a corner. To stand in her shirt and tights, looking at Ash, her thighs damp. Rage boiling inside her.

"You let this happen," she said evenly. "All these months, you've known what was going on, but you did nothing."

"I couldn't—" he began.

"You could have," she cut across him. "You could have done so many things. But you were proving something, Ash. Using me. God! I knew it. I've known that right from the beginning. Using me to get yourself a leg up, to make yourself look good—the innovative producer, the daring one. Putting a woman on the show with that...that... Proving it could work."

"Wait a minute..."

"No." She shook her head. "I let myself be used because I loved the job. And I thought I could put up with all the rest of it because... You haven't *helped* me, Ash. So many times you could have. But you let this happen. I asked you to *care*."

"He's finished, Isabel."

"So what?" She was shivering, her whole body quaking.

"It's your show."

"So what?"

"Don't you *want* it?"

"Want it? What I want. It doesn't matter what I want. Is this my reward, Ash? Is my own show the reward?"

"Does it matter?" he asked. "Does it? Don't you want it?"

"So much to go through...all the ugliness, the politics, when all I ever wanted was to do my job...do something I liked. You started all this in the first place, dangling the spot in front of my nose. I don't understand how you could use me this way. I don't understand that. Can you make me understand it?"

"You're shaken up. Why don't you go home now? We'll talk about this later."

"Later after I do your show for you?"

"The sponsors have agreed. The management's agreed. It's yours."

"And if *I* don't agree?"

He lifted his hands helplessly. "You'd be crazy to turn it down."

"Stepping on my feet, bumping into me, stealing my notes. Now...*that!*" She shuddered, pointing to her discarded skirt. "Am I real to you? I couldn't be. Maybe," she said, her eyes still on the skirt, "maybe you've killed me. And maybe I let all of you do it."

Annette knocked and came in, round-eyed, handing Isabel a skirt. "I found it in wardrobe," she said, looking first at Ash and then at Isabel. "I hope it fits. What's going to happen now?" she asked Ash. "Jerry's gone off screaming, threatening lawsuits, murder."

"Not now," Ash said.

Annette deposited Isabel's handbag and overcoat on the sofa and went out.

"You're wrong, Isabel," he said, sounding worn out, sinking down into the chair behind his desk. "I've cared all along. A lot. But there's only so much power in the chain of command. You didn't complain, didn't ask for help."

"I thought adults were adults because they could see where the need lies and take responsibility without having to be asked or told. This is a kindergarten," she said, looking at the skirt Annette had given her, then stepping into it. She reached for her coat, pulled it on, picked up her bag, and went to the door.

"You're leaving?" he asked, sensing a dreadful finality in her movements.

"Going home," she said.

"But we really should settle this. I know you're upset, but..."

"When I decide, Ash, I'll let you know."

She opened the door.

"Isabel?"

She turned.

"I'm sorry about what happened. But you are wrong. About my motives and about how things get done."

"I'll let you know."

She couldn't seem to do anything, once at home. She stood for several minutes in the hallway, then went into the living room and sat down. To stare at the wall. She was still sitting there an hour later when, with a crash, two squirrels fell into the fireplace. She leaped up openmouthed, staring, slowly seeing that the squirrels were trapped inside by the mesh fire curtain that was anchored at the top and bottom of the fireplace. What should she do? God! Too much, too much. How am I supposed to think? I can't think. So many things happening. I can't just leave them in there, they'll starve to death, die. But she also couldn't open the screen and attempt to let them out. They'd do terrible damage to the house, or possibly even fly at her with those sharp, dangerous little claws. Horrendous damage squirrels were capable of doing.

She ran to the telephone, got the Humane Society number, called up, and tried to explain coherently about the two squirrels in the fireplace.

"We'll send somebody," she was told.

Feeling as if her nerve endings were popping through the surface of her skin, she paced up and down the front hallway, her eyes on the fireplace and the two animals trapped there, waiting for the "somebody" from the society to arrive; seeing Jerry gripping her arm, doing that to her. There was a stone stuck in her throat. She couldn't breathe.

When she heard the truck pull into the driveway, she threw open the door and gesticulated wildly at the slow-moving obese young man, urging him into the living room, pointing out the two squirrels. Thinking: I can't cope, can't. Please end this! Take care of this for me. It's all too much. No more. *Please!* No more.

"Two, uh?" the coveralled young man said, setting down a small cagelike box with a drop-front screen door. "This is gonna be tricky, you know. If I open the curtain, see, the one's liable to get out while I'm tryna get the other one. See? What I think, if you open the front door and move all this furniture'n stuff outta the way, block the other doors, then I open this screen here, and they'll make straight for the front door and out."

"I don't think that's a very good idea," she said, doubtful. "You can't be sure they'll go out the door and not..."

"Well, I can try'n get this here noose down inside the top of the screen, see if I can't get 'em one at a time that way. But it's harder'n hell gettin' the noose over their heads, you know."

She stared at the noose, shivering.

As he inserted the noose end of the pole down inside the fire curtain, the two squirrels seemed to go berserk. One flew scrabbling up the inside of the fireplace, its claws scratching madly on the bricks; the other ran around and around in terrified circles as the noose followed after it.

"I really don't think..." she began, when the squirrel suddenly ran straight up the pole, through the gap in the curtain, and darted into the room. Isabel flew out of the way, gasping. Hastily withdrawing his contraption from the fireplace, the young man waddled after the squirrel, which ran under the baseboard heating unit and stayed there. From the doorway, she watched as the young man pounded up and down the length of the baseboard unit with his fist, peering down underneath it as far as his bulk would permit, finally announcing, "That squirrel's disappeared, lady!"

"What do you mean, 'disappeared'?" she demanded breathlessly. "How could it have *disappeared?* It's *there,* under the heating unit."

"Come look for yourself," he snapped testily. "I'm *tellin'* you, that goddamn thing's *gone!*"

Trembling, positive the squirrel would jump out at her, she went near to where he was pointing, bent down to the floor level, to see that he was evidently right. The animal was nowhere to be seen. And it couldn't have gone anywhere else, because she'd been watching and would have seen.

"Where did it go?" she asked, absurdly frightened.

"Looks like it got itself down in there, see. Between the wall and this here flange thing, or whatever, that's holding the unit on the wall."

"Well, get it out of there!" she ordered.

"It ain't gonna *come* outta there!" he argued.

"You're supposed to know what you're doing!" she accused. "Get that squirrel *out* of there!"

"I'm *tellin'* you, it ain't gonna *come* out! It's too scared!"
"*Try!*"

Standing her ground, she waited while he made several trips back and forth the length of the room, banging his long stick—he'd reversed it, so the noose bobbed about menacingly in the air—on the wall. He bumped into a lamp and nearly sent it to the floor, but she threw herself forward and caught it. Setting it down gingerly, with numb-feeling hands. He kicked the furniture out of his way, leaving filthy footprints on the upholstery.

"That goddamn squirrel ain't comin' outta there! I told ya that! No *way,* lady!"

"What am I supposed to do?" she asked, outraged.

"It's probably gone down inside the wall to the cellar or something," he speculated.

She could feel her hands getting ready to fasten themselves to his throat.

"Take your things, those *things,* and get out!" she shouted. "Get out! *Get out!*"

He turned a bland yet belligerent face toward her, shrugged as if to say she was completely crazy, picked up his squirrel trap, and then, managing to make his movements insultingly insolent in a fatly quivering way, casually strolled out.

She stood in the living-room doorway staring into the room, utterly positive the squirrel would at any moment emerge from its hiding place in the wall and begin tearing either her or the house itself apart in an effort to find an exit. What to do? What? She was afraid to move for fear the instant she did, the animal would come out.

The second one had now returned to the floor of the fireplace and was sitting calmly on one of the andirons looking out at her. She backed away and went to the kitchen, to stand trying to think what to do, when she heard a high-pitched shrieking noise start up in the living room.

Shaking uncontrollably now, she ran back to the living room, to hear the one squirrel in the wall, scratching and chittering, and the other inside the fireplace answering, emitting a terrible severed-larynx sound.

I can't stand it! No more! No more! There has to be something, someone to help. Brian . . . In blind panic, she zipped apart her handbag, found the card he'd given her, ran back to the kitchen, and dialed the number he'd written on the back.

He answered on the first ring. Without bothering to identify herself, she launched into a hysterical description of what had happened.

"What should I do? What should I *do?*" she asked over and over. "I don't know what to do. It's in the wall, the one, and the other is just sitting there in the fireplace. They'll get out and *destroy* the place. They're vermin, you know. Rats, really. Tell me what to *do!* Please! I've got to do something. I can't just leave them in there. And the noise. They're making such a *terrible* noise. I can't stand it. Please, *please!*"

"Isabel! Listen to me for a minute! *Listen!*"

"I can't just stay here. I should go back and watch—"

"*Stop* for a minute, and *listen!*" he shouted.

She abruptly went silent.

"Put on your coat," he said in a more normal tone of voice. "Go out to the car, drive to the supermarket, and do your grocery shopping. Or buy some magazines. Anything. Stay out for a while. Take your time. Leave the front door open on your way out. Okay? When you've finished the shopping, have a nice quiet coffee somewhere, a sandwich. Then head back home. I'm going to take care of it. All right?"

"Yes. Okay. Yes. I'll do it. Okay."

She slammed down the telephone, snatched up her bag, pushed the scattered contents back inside it, found her key ring, and ran straight out of the house, leaving the front door wide open.

Brian put down the receiver on the private line, stubbed out his cigarette, and got up. Finally, there was something he could do for her. He was deeply gratified that she'd chosen to call him. And deeply disturbed by the incoherence and obvious stress, the panic of her call. It took a lot more than a pair of squirrels on the loose to send someone like Isabel into such a visible, tangible state of despair. That "everything" again. Something had gone haywire with the show. He'd watched, knowing. But whatever had gone wrong, she'd managed to carry the show with an apparent effortlessness. Apparent. Except for the hints of fear that had infrequently, throughout the show, left her smiling wordlessly for a beat or two. Before picking up, going on, getting it done. He couldn't help wondering what had gone on before the show, what had happened after.

In a state of frozen shock, she spent almost an hour going up and down the aisles of the supermarket, reaching for things, then replacing them. Thinking as she went. Tallying up the weeks. Four and a half months. Almost five. How long can she stay away? Does she realize how long it's been? No. I can't. Not anymore. Those animals. Probably destroying my house. I'll have nowhere to live, nothing at all left. Everything gone. Judy staying with Blake again tonight, spending more and more time with him. I haven't any claim on her, no right to presume upon her time, her energy. Jerry doing that. She shuddered, feeling again the wetness on her legs. Ash, how could you? I thought you cared, asked you to care, you were my friend. No friends in business—isn't that what you were trying to say?

Having managed to complete a full circle in the supermarket with an empty basket, she abandoned the effort and went to a nearby coffee shop, tried to drink a cup of coffee, but couldn't. Throwing down some money, she hurried back to the car and drove home, tortured by the idea she'd arrive to find her home ruined. As she was coming hesitantly through the front door, Brian called out, "If that's you, unload your stuff through the kitchen door. Stay out of here for just a few more minutes, okay?"

She turned away and went around to the rear of the house. She removed her coat, put her handbag down on the table along with her keys, and waited. Her head ached. After a few minutes Brian came into the kitchen, wiping his hands on one of the towels from the downstairs bathroom.

"Okay"—he smiled—"it's all over."

"How?" she asked, her forehead creased.

"There's a hole or two in the wall, but I'll fix that later."

"What did you do?" she asked.

"I shot them."

"You . . . shot . . . them."

He shot them. Dead. A gun fired inside this house. Holes in the wall. Dead animals.

"Excuse me," she said, moving past him.

He put down the towel and unrolled his shirtsleeves, assuming she was going to the living room to assess the damage.

Ruined, everything ruined. Her job overrun, her house, her mind. The child a runaway. Up the stairs and into the bathroom to open the medicine cabinet and reach for the vials, taking them all down, lining them up on the edge of the sink one after the other. Then picking up the first one, removing the lid.

"What are you doing?" he asked softly from the doorway.

Startled, caught, she closed her hands around as many containers as she could hold and tried to push past him.

"No!" he cried, catching her. "You're not going to do that. No!"

"I'll do what I want!" Her voice was high, out of control. "What I *want!*"

"No!" he insisted, his hands closing around her wrists. "Drop them!"

She shook her head back and forth, her eyes very round. "No, they're mine!"

"Isabel, let me have them!"

"No! Let go of me!"

"Please," he said miserably, tears filling his eyes, fear clawing his chest. "Please, let me have them! I don't want to fight you for them, but I will. I won't let you do this. I can't let you."

She looked at his suddenly reddened eyes, then down at his hands on her wrists, and tried to pull herself free, dragging him halfway across the room with her in the effort.

"I'm *not* going to let you have them! I won't!" He let go of her wrists, and for an instant she thought he'd let her go after all, but then he pulled her into a fierce bear hug, crushing her.

She stared at him, tried to move, couldn't, and opened her hands, letting the containers drop to the floor, because she'd need her hands to fight him. His viselike arms seemed the final physical manifestation of everything happening in her life against which she was powerless. She struggled, fighting him; twisting, kicking, grunting with the effort, screaming at him to let go of her. He wouldn't.

I'm going to win this round, he thought, determined. This time I'm in control.

They crashed into the furniture, knocking things off the surfaces; colliding with the bed where they fell, rolling about, each of them trying to outmaneuver the other. She strained away from him with all her might, but he was too big, too strong. Sank her teeth into his shoulder, and he yelped, then, between his teeth, said, "Fight clean," freed his hand, rearranged his grip, and inserted his forearm between her throat and his body in such a fashion as to prevent her from effectively moving her head or getting close enough to bite him again.

I won't let you die, he thought. I'll take those pills and scatter them all over your garden, grind them into the dirt with my heels, but I won't let you take them, I won't. "Go ahead!" he shouted at her. "Go head, *fight* me! Maybe it'll get some of the poison out of your system. You're going to have to kill me to get to those fucking pills!"

She fought with her legs and hands, her fists pounding against his thighs as she tried unsuccessfully to kick him. He didn't fight back, but simply protected himself, holding her trapped inside his arms. Her hair was blinding both of them, getting wet from her useless attempts to spit strands of it out of her mouth. She fought without words but with sudden fearful bursts of energy, attempting to pull her entire body free of his arms with one mighty heave. She couldn't get free. Her lungs ached with the effort of trying to breathe.

"*Let...me...go!*" she screamed, twisting her head from side to side, struggling to break his hold on her. "I don't want you here...don't want you...you don't...you have no right... *Let me go!*"

He refused. She couldn't break his armlock, couldn't escape. Shook her head back and forth, back and forth, infuriated, becoming exhausted. He was grinding her down. "*Get...out!*" she screamed, feeling her throat going raw. "*Let go of me!*" She tried to get more words out, but they wouldn't come; something was breaking in her chest, making her lungs hurt even more, making her throat throb. She stared down into his face for a moment, then collapsed, sobbing bitterly on his chest. She thought he'd release her now, but he didn't. Crying. It set her off all over again—snarling, kicking without connecting, pinching viciously at his thighs. But her energy was gone. The tears were taking it. She fell once more, weeping brokenly, slowly subsiding, her entire body shaken by the force of her tears.

He said nothing, simply held her until he sensed the fight was over; he'd won. Then he freed his arm from her throat and positioned her head on his shoulder, smoothing the hair away from her damp, flushed face, wiping her eyes and streaming nose with the edge of the sheet. He felt an extraordinary calm, an inner certainty. An enormous hunger.

She lay thinking of tricking him into believing her quiescent, then jumping up and hitting him with the lamp. But she hadn't the strength left. Drained in every way, she suffered his stroking fingers, his silent ministrations, becoming aware of his body, the awesome musculature of his body. And his scent. The scent of his hair and flesh, the identifying spoor of this Brian Connors. His alone, this combination of scents. Clean-smelling, fresh. Something he used on his hair.

"There's no point to letting it all build on top of you until the only exit left is death," he said, unlocking his other arm and turning, bringing her down on the mattress. The pillows were gone, knocked to the floor. The blankets and sheets were twisted and tangled, a floral-print heap. Her skirt was up around her waist, her tights ripped in several places. Several of the buttons were missing from his shirt, a large tear in the shoulder seam. She stayed where he put her, her heartbeat accelerating. Watching him, feeling stark.

He leaned on his elbow, spreading out her hair, smoothing it back from her forehead, caressing her face, causing her eyelids to droop sleepily. His touch was tender, too suspiciously soothing, but she couldn't resist it. He pressed his lips to her temples, her forehead. Her mouth readied itself. He kissed her eyelids, then paused to stroke her face some more before kissing her ears, the sides of her throat, her chin. Her mouth quivered. She began to cry again, unable to withhold her response to the delicacy of his touch.

"I care," he whispered, so that she opened her eyes, regarding him with renewed suspicion. "There's so much you can do. You're strong, you can keep going. Things'll get better, not worse. The only way to go from down here is up."

She was listening closely to every word, feeling something registering inside her; not sure whether it was the words or the caresses making the impact. But the fight was dripping out of her, going away.

"I care so much," he whispered again, as his hands began unbuttoning her clothing; unzipping, unsnapping, unfastening. She kept on crying, feeling his lips and fingertips making their way over her face and neck.

"You don't have to say any of that," she said hoarsely, humiliated by her burgeoning responses. "I'm not going to stop you."

"All your signals are crossed," he said sadly, taking off his clothes very matter-of-factly, looking not at all as if he was about to throw himself upon her. She lay tensed, waiting for him to proclaim himself the victor, claim her body as his prize. But why did he look so sad, so sorry?

He put his arms around her, and she found them merely heavy, not at all comforting. He put his mouth to hers at last, and she was aware only of the texture of his lips, their softness. He put his hands on her hips, bringing his body into line with hers, and she felt him growing against her and thought of the sameness, the eternal sameness of every confrontation, every man who'd pressed his body to hers and grown with the eagerness to place himself inside her. Her arms refused to hold him. He whispered soft words about her skin, her hair, her life. He held the hair away from her neck and kissed her below the ear, his hands moving up from her hips to her breasts. His touch still delicate. Kissed her mouth again, and the slightly increased pressure of his hands broke her reserve, conveyed his messages more directly to her interior. His tongue ran lightly over her lips, and she sighed, opening her mouth, finding herself all at once able to use her arms, her hands. Laid her hands against the sides of his face, learning the shape of his mouth, its potency. She sighed again deeply and held him.

He hadn't been wrong, knew it now. Bringing her out slowly, away from that wild craving for death. Away.

Keeping hold of her, her mouth more avidly joined to his now, he turned with her, his thighs closing around her, so that he was holding her as completely as he could. Yes, she thought, hold me! Yes! His hands traveled from her shoulders down the length of her back, curving into place over her buttocks as he rocked gently beneath her, creating a pressure at the apex of her thighs, causing her to move, rocking with him, heightening the sensations. She reached down around behind her to hold her hands over his, rolling steadily against him as his tongue in her mouth made her dizzy with wanting.

"So lovely," he murmured. "All softness."

How was it possible he could find her beautiful when she was at least a hundred years old? For every day Denny had stayed away, for every prank Jerry had played, she'd aged a year. She felt it in her bones, in her eyes, in her groin. Yet her ability to react to this stimulation, her capacity for self-lubrication, astounded her. How could she still be functioning sexually?

He was set on evoking responses that would pull her back. She could sense this. He'd prevented her from taking whole-hearted flight into the dead center of the void between what was actually real and what only seemed to have been real. If I can stop you, he thought, I will. Because you feel, I know you do; and you might even care, you could.

She was becoming very wet, and felt him shiver as he slid back and forth under her. Keep me, she thought. Hold me! *Hold* me! Make this something more.

She was very afraid he'd try to enter her too quickly; he'd plunge into her and spoil her ascent, her fragile appetite. She felt too afraid, too aware of the potential loss of this last of her alternatives. Trading in her death plan for a possible pregnancy, because she was in no way prepared to be doing this, had stopped taking the pills after her emergency visit to the gynecologist. There'd seemed no point then to going on protecting herself, when there was no one. She'd allocated Marshall to be the last of her lovers. The last. Not planning on a future. Yet, here was Brian telling her through her skin that love could be a life-giving issue. No one could touch her as he was touching her now without love.

He freed his hands from beneath hers, turning once more, making her gasp into his mouth as he teased her nipples, luring her just that little bit closer to complete receptivity. Turned again and carried her down beneath him, his mouth replacing his fingers on her nipples, turning them hard. His mouth on hers. His one hand on her breast, the other languidly investigating her inner thighs.

Was she damaged? she wondered, suddenly cooling. Would it hurt? Were there ridges of scars inside that might react with pain? But she couldn't think. His head moved down. He kissed her belly, pressing his face into her, both his hands relishing the smooth, hard curve of her hips. He moved down more. She murmured, "Good," opened her legs. His head dipped, her knees bent open, and she gave birth to him. His mouth, his tongue, his fingers all caressing her, so that she moaned, laboring, and opened still more; her face, breasts flushed, burning. She located the rhythm, and her hips led her into the dance, yet withheld, held back, luxuriating in the leisurely tempo.

Kissing her wounds better, communicating directly with old injuries; drawing out the venom, dulling the memory. His hands, open palms chafing her breasts; his mouth feeding, sipping, drinking from the offered vessel of her body.

Don't make me finish this way. I haven't the energy to take you more than this once at this time. Next time, she thought, surprising herself. Realizing: I will want you again if you'll read me correctly now. Because his body was smooth, new, hard. Yet deliriously familiar. Unlike anyone else's she'd known. Yet so right, so perfectly right.

She placed her hand lightly on the top of his head, and he stopped, coming up to lay himself down the length of her once more, and she took him between her hands, leading; taking him in, her breath held. This crucial moment, the temporary loss of heat, the suddenly renewed perception of danger. But no, he was tender still, considerate, coming gradually inward. No force, only a continuance of this pleasurable rightness, merging into her.

He looked down at her face, into her eyes.

"Do you know me now?" he asked. "Do you see me?"

She nodded, extending her legs. They felt miles long, and taut with excitement. Binding him to her with her arms, meeting his mouth greedily, a starving child. So slick with liquid, the excitement. He stirred inside her, then moved back, measuring her responses, then forward, and her hips lifted to meet him, her thighs spreading still more. Good. A new rhythm. He timed himself to her, to her slow return, the tightening band of her arms. Slowly climbing higher, increasing the pace; she was all feeling, all mouth, gone away with the pleasure; blind and deaf with the pleasure, the tremendous relief; revived in every pore, magnified; caught in the sun's fire. She could feel it beginning to happen, the steadily soaring approach to the boundaries of Saturn. Multicolored rings of brilliant, glowing intensity. Lifting toward completion, thinking: It's happening, happening. No demoralizing experimentation, no disappointments, no breaks in the flight pattern. Not just doing this for the later reward of being held for five minutes, having a short session of simulated closeness. This the reward, all of this. Months of pushing him away from her, gratified to see he wouldn't be pushed, would return and return, proving himself constant, proving himself genuine. All closeness, real, nothing simulated. This is real. It feels so real. I'm going to come, you're making me so close closer now. She groaned under the onslaught of this engulfing pleasure, this encompassing pleasure; rescued, when only minutes before she'd been on her way to a visit with death. Lifting herself as close as possible to his hard white thighs, his riveting presence within, his saving ways.

She cried out, tearing her mouth away from his for a moment to rake his face with her eyes; her eyes large and astonished, vulnerable. And he moved more quickly, knowing; wanting this gift from her, this sign of life, wishing to bestow gifts of a like nature, loving her. "I love you," he whispered, knowing she didn't hear, returning his mouth, to be met by hers hungrily, wildly; as she arched against him and held there trembling as he kept on, on, until she cried out again, sobbing. And convulsed so spasmodically, with stark starling cries, her body jerking, shuddering so explosively, he had to let his full weight down upon her in order to maintain the connection. He had to stay inside her, feel the totality of her response; feeling it, made humble by what they'd together achieved; jubilant.

He ceased moving, and she sank down, whispering, "You can't stop. Can't! I need you to go on, hold you now." She bent her legs around him, enveloping him, whispering, "I have to see your face when you come in me. I have to *know*."

"I do love you," he whispered. "I want you to believe that. This isn't a game."

He went forward once more, stunned by her shuddering response as he recommenced the motions. Their eyes now joined too, they watched each other until he stopped resisting, released them both, ending inside her. She felt his sudden stillness, then the ecstatic flow as he moved again, again; at last dropping down into her embrace as she wove her fingers into his hair, whispering, "Now I know."

"I'm going to split now," she told Cathy.

"Okay," Cathy said, shifting Tink so he was sitting astride her hip.

"I want to thank you, you know? I mean, it's been really good."

"I'm glad if it's been good for you," Cathy said. "It's been good for us having you. You're not the bad act you think you are, Denny."

"Yeah." Denise picked up her big new canvas bag. "I guess I really should like tell you," she said, feeling awkward for the first time in weeks. "You know that chick on the tube, the one you groove so hard on? That's like, uh, my, you know, mother."

"I got that," Cathy smiled. "A whole long time ago."

"You *did?* How come?"

"Well, for one thing"—Cathy's smile broadened—"you look like her. You know? And for another thing, I just knew. That's all."

"Yeah," Denny said, embarrassed. "Okay. Well, I guess I'll split."

Cathy leaned into Denny and kissed her cheek. "Come see us, okay, Den? We'll be here."

"Okay," Denny said, opening the door. "Say 'bye to Larry for me." She started down the steps.

"Denny?"

"Yeah?"

"Come *see* us." She smiled. "Like for real. Not just for say-so. And bring your mother."

Denise stood a moment, reading Cathy's expression, then smiled back.

"She'd probably do it," Denny said, lifting her hand, waving good-bye. "I'll call you."

"Don't forget!"

"No."

A long walk through the snow to the road. Good crunchy snow on the back road, but all slush and muck at the highway. All excited and up there, thinking about the look there'd be on her face when she opened the door. She was soaked and half-frozen by the time a car finally stopped.

Ten

He sat for a few minutes finishing his cigarette, watching her sleep, admiring the length of her back, the shape of her legs. His eyes moving up to the mass of her hair, her head. He couldn't see her face; it was turned away. The slow, even lift and fall of her back in sleep. His lips stretched, peculiar, as if he was trying to chew on something enormous that had been forced into the too-small interior of his mouth. He might bite down again and again but succeed only in breaking his teeth in his attempts to bite through this thing.

He wanted to gather her up in his hands—as if she was weightless—and somehow press her into him, make her part of himself. A giddy, greedy feeling. He'd felt it for the children when they'd been small. Holding Geoff inside his arm, tickling the little boy, seeing his gleeful response, he'd experienced this same delirious craving. To hold, keep on holding, never let go. Because the caring was so deep, so thick, it reduced his air supply, making it difficult for him to breathe properly. He'd only ever felt that way about the children, not their mother. What he'd felt for her had been quite different. A tender empathy, a pity—for them both—at her lifelong inability to commit her thoughts and feelings to the air flowing between them. She would go the end of her life with everything tightly hemstitched into the lining of her interior, revealing nothing. Just thinking of her, he felt the well-remembered sorry-sadness, the longing to try one more time to sit her down, tell her truthful things, and hope she might suddenly begin splitting at the seams, spilling out the treasure of her thoughts. But it was too late for that. And he no longer cared as he had at twenty. They'd still be married, still be silently making their way through time if Geoff hadn't taken one last trip down to the boiler room to huddle against the warmth of the big furnace and plunge a filthy hypodermic needle loaded with uncut heroin into his vein. He'd wondered forever about that, about how pure heroin came to be in Geoff's possession. Yet, was it unseemly, mad of him to feel a somewhat grief-stricken gratitude to Geoff? Because he was grateful. For better or worse, Geoff had smashed the family silence, broken the family itself. Freeing Brian for the infusion of these potent new feelings.

He wondered how far a trip it was from the walkway into madness back to the stream of everyday traffic. And how far along that path had she allowed herself to be taken? Do you come right back, or do you wander around in a daze for a time, saved but uncertain of your bearings? What monstrous vanity! he thought, thinking of saving people, reorienting them. I can't do a damned thing for you that you're not willing to have me do. And making love doesn't mean loving, doesn't mean you care. No matter how much I want it to be that way, I have too little, if any, effect on the direction of your affections.

He put out his cigarette, slipped off the bed, quickly collected the scattered pills and containers, and in his shorts and shirt went downstairs. To flush all the pills down the toilet, to crush the plastic vials between his hands before depositing their remains in the trashcan alongside the two newspaper-wrapped corpses. Then he washed his hands and prepared some coffee and sandwiches. It was just after one. It felt much later than that.

While waiting for the coffee to perk, he sat down at the kitchen table. Thinking random thoughts. If she'd come to his house, if she'd like it. It was suddenly important that she like the place where he lived. No matter if she never spent any time there. But it was so much his, so solely his. The only place in a lifetime that had belonged entirely to him. And he wanted to share it with her, have her see in the place what he saw, find the peace there he'd found for himself. He stopped himself. What're you doing? Making plans, planning the future, hoping for this, for that. You're a fool to do it. Too many variables. And the woman herself. "You don't have to say any of that." And she's right, I can feel it, but I needn't say it. Saying it to convince her, not me, because I've been convinced for months. But when you haven't anything else to offer, when gifts, or money, or the devious presentation of opportunities won't suffice, you offer yourself, your love. I might as well be poor. Because nothing I have to offer you will suffice. Except possibly the caring. Possibly that. I hope so. But even then, it's going to take a long time for it all to happen.

"I hate to eat alone," he said, stroking her back. "Wake up and keep me company."

She opened her eyes, to see him sitting on his haunches beside the bed, smiling at her.

"Food," he said. And she saw a cup of coffee sitting on the bedside table.

"You're still here," she said huskily, stupidly.

"Looks that way." He smiled. "Looks like we're both still here."

She sat up, keeping her eyes on him, and he put the cup of coffee into her hands before returning to the other side of the bed to sit beside her. She turned her head, watching him over the top of her cup, trying to think how she felt. She looked at his chest. He exuded strength. Like an aura. God! Sounding to herself like Marshall, thinking of auras, bubbles of bright light. She looked at his comfortably crossed legs, the shirt hanging open, the sleeves rolled above the elbows. Looked very carefully at his shirt. Custom-made. Custom-made? A policeman in a forty- or fifty-dollar shirt? That didn't make sense. And what about the telephone number he'd given her? I have no idea who you are, she thought. None. But you've done something to me, *done* something.

He passed her a plate with a sandwich, and she accepted it, continuing her inspection of his body, his face; feeling herself softening at the sight of him and the recollection of how well, how profoundly well he'd made love to her. Such a gift, that, the ability to take the time, make the effort to read the signs. Now, sitting here naked beside him, eating a sandwich, drinking coffee he'd prepared. Howard might have quietly provided her with food this way. Marshall would have expected her to do the providing. She remembered, and turned to look at the floor.

"I got rid of them," he said. "So don't bother looking. They're gone."

She turned back, her mouth too dry all at once.

"You didn't want to take them," he said reasonably. "Otherwise, you'd have waited until I left."

Was that true? Did I want him to rescue me? Did I have a dramatic scene in mind?

"Why do you look that way," he asked. "Are you going to be sorry now, appalled by where we find ourselves?"

She swallowed and returned her coffeecup to the bedside table.

"I don't know," she said. "I'm sticky. I'll take a shower."

"Why?"

"Why?" She regarded him with a puzzled expression. "Because Jerry Brenner...urinated...all over me this morning. He did that. And then we...I don't feel *clean.*"

"He did that, literally?"

"Literally, yes."

"Christ!" he said. "Is it all worth it?"

"I don't know anymore," she answered honestly. "I have to think hard about that. Do you *care?*"

"You know that."

She got up and walked into the bathroom.

"Will you leave the door open?" he asked, fearful of closed doors between them. "Please?"

She looked back at him, then did as he'd asked.

He sat finishing his coffee, watching her reach past the shower curtain to turn on the water; relishing the sight of her long body, the tangled black mass of hair cascading down her back, twin indentations sitting either side of the base of her spine. A tentative stirring. He pulled off his shirt, his shorts, followed her.

She seemed unaware of him for several minutes, busily occupied with bathing herself, unselfconsciously washing between her legs, then her breasts, scrubbing her arms, her face, finally standing directly under the water with her eyes closed, letting the water take the tangles from her hair before applying shampoo. He watched the muscles moving in her arms, back, and shoulders, fascinated by the white froth of soapsuds slithering down her breasts, her belly. She rinsed her hair, then stood slightly to one side, making room for him, watching him now. He looked so serious, holding his arms out to her, drawing her in. She couldn't close her eyes when he kissed her, so curious to see how he looked kissing her, his mouth very persuasive. In his arms, her eyes closing, she thought about the house, how silent it had been for so long. All the years since Howard's death. So many mornings when she'd come down the stairs to the music of voices, laughter in the kitchen. Then, after his death, years of descending the stairs to silence, entering the kitchen, to find Denny, who'd sometimes come in the early morning at the far end of the kitchen with her hands wrapped around a mug of coffee and her eyes fixed on Marshall as if she expected him to catapult himself across the room and attack her. And Marshall sitting happily with a stack of newspapers and a strange look of contentment upon his face. As if he'd thrived on Denny's animosity, her obvious dislike of him.

But the silence. She'd become accustomed to the silence. What else? she wondered. Events turning me passive. Brian was right. I've been letting it happen. Now you. Holding me so importantly. Am I going to go ahead and fall in love with you, just to keep this house alive? *Love?*—

She let her head rest on his shoulder, thinking. I don't want any more commercial travelers establishing temporary shelters in my house, my bedroom, my body. I don't. But am I supposed to gladly offer whatever's mine to this man, accept whatever's offered, and make do, keep on making do until it's too late to alter either my life or the compromise route I've chosen to follow? I don't know. I only know this house is too big for one person. Life. Damned life is too big for one person. But I won't love this man simply because I haven't anyone else. It isn't a good enough reason.

But what am I going to do about you? she asked herself, aware of his hands, the texture of his skin. What do I do with you? Men. I wish I knew why I go on wanting you, needing

you. Why? Not the sex. I can do without that. But the sound
of another voice, the knowledge of another presence. Why
can't I do without that? Why can't I be all I need to myself?
Why, why? It doesn't frighten me, the idea of living alone.
No, no. It's the idea of *dying* alone, of one day having two
men come to turn off the electricity or disconnect the telephone because the bills haven't been paid in months. They
come and find your moldering, reeking corpse on the living-
room floor or in the bathroom. Because you were so alone—
never mind being someone on television, the attendant celebrity, never mind any of that. You were so damned alone that
there was no one to notice if you stopped answering the telephone, no one to worry that your lights were never on, no one
to concern himself with your well-being. So, one afternoon,
two uniformed workmen come along, break into the house—
they have to break in, because you've taken to locking all the
doors and windows, the isolation having tricked you into
imagining all sorts of dangers waiting to befall you—and find
your putrefying remains.

"Are you planning to stay in here for the rest of the day?"
he asked above the rush of the water.

She pulled herself away and turned off the shower, climbed
out, handed him a towel, took one herself. Turned up the
thermostat. She felt half-frozen.

"Why are you here?" she asked, toweling dry her hair.
"Why?"

"Do you want me to go?"

"Please!" she said anxiously. "Don't answer questions
with question! I can't stand that right now."

"I *want* to be here," he said candidly. "Is that something
you can handle?"

"Can't you see I'm not handling anything? Telling myself
lies, little stories, making believe I'm in control. I'm not sure
I even know what control *is* anymore. Or if it matters. But I
hate the idea of being someone who has to cling for support."

"You want it all. You want to be a star, a martyr, a stoic.
You want to suffer through it all alone and walk off into the
sunset with a ramrod spine and your glowing dignity intact.

That's such crap, Isabel! It isn't going to make you any less than you are to admit you need a hand up, that you can't make it all the way through on your own.''

"But I should be able to. Other people do.''

"Maybe. But don't you ever wonder, though, where they're going as they march off into the fadeout? Have you ever asked yourself that? Home, maybe, to a can of soup and a boiled egg, a little TV, and then to bed. With an electric blanket to ward off the chill, because the nights are cold and the bed's too damned big.''

"Very poetic.''

"No. Truth, not poetry. Reality. If you want me to go, I'm on my way,'' He put down his towel.

"Don't pressure me. It's not fair to pressure me this way.''

"What pressure? Either you can tolerate having somebody around, or you can't. Either you're able to admit to needing or you can't. There's no pressure to that. You're either truthful about what you want, or you're not. I'm a big grown-up fellow, Isabel. I've seen pretty much all there is to see. There aren't too many surprises left. But you. I hadn't planned on you.''

"You think you'll convince me by telling me you love me.''

"Won't I?''

"I think you think you will. I think that.''

"I know better than that,'' he said. "I couldn't convince you of *anything* right now. We had our classic battle scene, followed by the classic surrender. I haven't any illusions. It was what you needed. It was what I needed for you. I'm not stupid enough to believe in my own importance.''

She picked up her hairbrush. "Isn't that an awfully sophisticated philosophy for a policeman?'' she asked his mirrored reflection.

"You've assumed I'm a cop. You haven't *asked* what I do.''

"What *do* you do?'' She turned to face him.

"I own a manufacturing company. Plastics. A family business.''

"Then what was all that other business?''

"I do stakeout work for the force. Because I care. Because if more people cared, maybe there'd be a few less kids in the cemeteries. Because it's my personal guilt trip. Okay? Because, like you, I've convinced myself I was a parental failure. Because maybe if I'd been doing whatever it was I was supposed to be doing, and doing it properly, my son wouldn't have been out shooting himself full of dope, trying to make the world look better. Because anybody with half a set of brains wants to know where he's failed and try to set it right. You're not different. You've hung yourself up on the notion that something you might've done differently could've prevented your daughter from taking off. It's a self-abusive exercise, Isabel, pointless. Not one of us can alter the way a child of ours handles life's situations. What happens, happens. Some kids cope, some don't. You do your best, hope like hell, and try not to let their misadventures throw you completely off the rails of your own life."

"That's a little existential. Do you really believe that?"

"Why labels?" he wanted to know, sitting down on the side of the tub, watching her drawing the brush through her hair. "Does it make it easier for you to accept the truth if it has a label attached?"

"Maybe. Don't you apply your own labels?"

"I try not to," he said. "With anything. Start sticking on labels, and you start categorizing your life, departmentalizing your emotions, slotting your reactions, putting captions to the things you think and do. You stick on the labels and risk alienting people outside who might be attracted to you, except that they're repelled by all the labels you've got all over you."

"But you're not scared off by me," she said, setting down the brush.

"Not a bit."

She walked out of the bathroom, picked up her coffeecup, and drank some of the now-cold coffee, then turned to look at him once more. Still sitting on the side of the tub, watching her.

"Keep talking," she said, dropping down on the edge of the bed, knowing she was going to make love to him again, wanting it so much her head and body hurt with it. I can't trust my body, she thought. I can't tell if it's *his* words or *my* need. I can't tell.

"I dislike games intensely," he said, his face set in serious planes.

"I have a need to hear."

He nodded and got up. As he approached, she lay back, trying to fight down the growing pain of wanting him. He stood looking down at her, then sat beside her, taking hold of her hand, turning her hand around, studying it.

"I'm selfish," he said, tracing the lines on her palm. "I don't want you to die."

"I can't say what you want to hear," she whispered, weakening at the touch of his fingertips on her palm.

"Say what you want."

So hard trying to get words out into the brightly lit air, with no darkness to shelter or diminish the impact of the words. Arms waiting to offer comfort from the blow of those words against the self. She might have those arms around her. Trying desperately to dredge up words and set them out in the air to hang before them both with unalterable finality. To put truth into the open was to risk so much.

"Do you thrive on seeing me struggling this way?" she asked thickly.

"I just want you to live. I love you." He said it so simply, so easily.

"A few weeks, a few months, and you love me," she scoffed. "You only want to keep on making love to me. And I don't even know why you want to do *that.*"

"Are you going to lie and tell me it isn't what you want?"

"I... I..." He was doing it again. Bringing her down—this time with words, holding her captive. She choked down her tears, feeling shamed by them now. She'd entered this with a degree of willingness, thinking it would be a way out of her thoughts, out of decisions needing to be made. But he'd stripped her so boldly, laid her down naked, and come spilling into her; in the process, concluding the long nightmare.

"I'll begin to depend on you . . ."

"Don't stop."

"No. It's no good. What happened to your family? Tell me."

"Joyce remarried. Joanna's in her last year of boarding school."

"Do you ever see them?"

"I fly over once or twice a year. We don't have too much to say to each other. Distance. And a death in the family. Jo's better off where she is, with her mother."

"I feel so guilty. Why do I feel so *guilty?*"

"I don't know," he said. "Why do you?"

"I didn't choose it. I didn't go through a catalog, pick out guilt, and send in a check with my order. I just can't seem to break it."

"You can," he said reassuringly. "You just stop. And let whatever's going to happen happen. I told you, you don't get any guarantees, Isabel."

"What's going to happen?" she said, closing her hand around his as she sat up, searching his eyes. "All these weeks," she whispered, "the truth... I did want you... to rescue me... A comic opera in my head. I do want you. We're talking, and I'm thinking about wanting you, trying not to. But looking at you, at your face. Oh, your face. It means something to me, the sight of you. I'm so afraid of trusting... how I feel. Those days when you weren't there, I couldn't... I wanted you to be there. *Want* you."

She was on her knees, looking directly into his eyes. He made a sound she understood—it was how she felt herself—and his arms came around her, his mouth meeting hers. Fear and a terrible hunger all pounding inside, falling back with him. The need. Terrible. Her hand slipping down to close around him. Needing this, pushing him down, turning to put her mouth on him, urgent, her hand spread flat on his belly. And as if she had no substance, no discernible weight, he lifted her over him, bringing her down to his mouth.

Wild at the first touch, he wrapped his arms around her thighs, rolling with her, holding her fastened to his mouth. She was already caught, spinning, her body writhing against him, his head moving between her thighs. His breathing as urgent as her motions. She closed her eyes, meeting the thrust.

She'd take him as he was taking her, take him to the end, make him, craving the madness, making it spread, two-headed four-legged monster, eating itself alive with hectic pleasure, they'd do this together, this tasting the measure of finality, the intense heat consuming.

She came first, leaving him for a moment. But awareness was sensory, all in the feelings, because she was determined to take him away with her, insistent, and they were two Roman candles, all circles, bursts of bright blinding light, fire, motion.

They fell away from each other, drawing air into their lungs in gulping spasms. Then his hand came down and descended onto her belly, and he was turning to lie face to face with her, his hand between her thighs, taking her down again into heat; before she had a chance to cool, he'd return her to the fire, bake her to the melting point. She hooked her arm around his neck, willing him to deliver her back. Go on, she thought, her leg bending, body turning, offering herself. Go on.

"I'll get pregnant," she said, sounding irrational. "You'll make me pregnant."

"I don't have anything," he said. "Do you?"

"No. I don't care. If it happens, it'll just be something else to take care of."

"What do you want?" he asked.

"What I want. I want you inside me again. Does your *love* take you that far?"

"I won't hurt you. I couldn't. I've never been able to hurt."

"How do you think it feels, taking you into me?"

"Tell me," he said.

"It feels," she said, "like a murder I'm committing on myself. Painless death."

"You feel so good to me," he murmured.

"This is all nonsense," she said, her expression suddenly clearing. "The half-sensible things people say to make sense of wanting to put themselves together. I want," she said, straddling him, "to watch you again, see how 'happy' I make you."

"I can't come on order."

"Then make *me*. I'm going crazy."

"You're not." He smiled, for the first time feeling optimistic. "You're on your way out of all that."

"Put yourself inside me," she urged, lifting, holding herself open above him. "I want you to, want to see you."

"Do you come this way?"

"No."

"I'll make you, then. Because it's very good for me this way. Hold still," he said, one hand on her hip, drawing her down over him, pushing steadily up into her, hearing her whispering, "Slow, slow," feeling her engulfing him. "Now," he said, easing her down on his chest. "Tell me. Anything."

"I can't." She hid her face against his throat.

"I'd do such a lot for you if you'd let me," he said, his hands skimming up and down her back. "All those weeks, wanting the telephone to ring, wanting it to be you. That night. Seeing you in that room. That fool screaming at you. I wanted to kill him. How... What happened? Will you tell me? I know that's a big part of your 'everything.'"

"I wanted to die," she whispered. "That was the start of it, thinking constantly of dying. Because there were no doors out, no answers. Making Marshall watch. I felt so sorry for him, having to watch, see." She sobbed, her fingers pressing into his arms. "He put his hand...his *hand* inside me. Those long fingernails. Hurt so... I couldn't cry. Weeks, weeks I wished I could, wanting to cry. But I couldn't. All dried out, too stunned to cry."

"Was it the worst thing that ever happened to you?"

"The worst?" She lifted her head to look at him, her face streaming with tears. He wiped them away. "That's a strange question."

"Was it?"

"Everything that's happened for months has been the worst thing that's ever happened to me. Bad. I can't commit myself to you, Brian. I can't be sure you wouldn't end up as some sort of burnt offering in a continuing atrocity."

"Dramatics again. Tell me about your husband. What sort of person was he? Talk to me, tell me. You can trust me."

"He was...in some ways, like you. Not your size or your coloring. I like the color of your eyes," she said, all at once caught up. "He had blue eyes. And such a sense of rightness, of time. Knowing when to offer himself. I second-bested with Marshall. It was romance. All romance. And metaphors. But I had to. Because... Truth. This is the truth: I was scared. Scared by the number of men who came to call, not because they liked *me*, but because they liked the look and shape of me and thought it might feel good to them to touch my body and fit themselves inside of me. At the end, I felt like a whore with Marshall. Full circle to that. Because I felt like a whore in the first place, allowing myself to be picked up in a parking lot. Teaching him. Do you know how humiliating it is, a grown woman having to teach a man? I haven't that sort of... I don't know what it is. Whatever it is a woman might possess that would allow her to instruct a man, without feeling minimized, shamed somehow. Not at the start. Later. Inside the relationship, yes. I could tell you. So strange. I *could* tell you. But this is the beginning, isn't it? And I don't have to tell you. You know."

He moved, thrusting slowly once, twice, then stopping.

"Caring," he said, his hand in her hair. "Wanting it to be just right. For both of us. The best it can be. That's the difference between what's real, what's alive, and what's merely fabricated, drummed up out of desperate need. I do love you. You don't want to hear it or believe it. That's all right. I understand why. But how could I stand by and let you die? Or make your display of intentions. You wanted to be stopped. And that night, when I sat down on the floor, put my arm around you, felt your skin, felt through your skin to the horror, I wanted you. You were so *bare*. Not the clothes. But stripped down, so naked."

"He said, 'I like your cunt, mama,'" she whispered. "I felt like a beast for being a woman, betrayed by my construction. I wanted to destroy him for doing that to me. Wanting to destroy Jerry for doing what he did. Different, but the same. I tried to kill him, my hands."

"I'm sorry for all of it."

"Why?" she asked with a sigh, moving against him briefly, then resting. "I'm not going to be able to keep on talking very much longer."

"I can't explain that. Why does one person become important to another? I could spend forever trying to analyze my feelings. But all I have to do is put my hands on you, look at you, and it all flies out of the window. There's no logic."

She sat up, and he stroked her breasts and belly, deriving a pleasure as intense as her own from the act.

"Tell me what you like, dislike," she asked. "Music?"

He smiled. "I play the flute sometimes. Do you like that sort of music? Have you ever heard Poulenc's flute concerto?"

She shook her head, touched.

"Jean-Pierre Rampal. Beautiful recording I'll play for you if you like."

"What else?"

"The season concerts. Dvořák, Scarlatti, Beethoven."

"Music. Chopin . . . Ravel. Do you know *The Pavane for a Dead Princess?*"

He nodded.

"Denise," she said softly. "I haven't been able to stop myself thinking about it." She swept her hand lightly over his chest. "Dvořák's Romance in F for violin. The Paganini violin concerto. It seems such a long time without music. Tell me more. All the things you like."

"Eggs Benedict." He smiled. "With truffles."

"Good."

"And kite-flying. The best on a Sunday afternoon in the summer after you've spent the whole morning in bed with the newspapers. Swimming."

"Lying in the sun."

"The theater?" he asked.

"Yes, absolutely." She stared at him, feeling it all coming back to her.

"I trust you," she said, looking bewildered. "So quickly." She pressed her lips down into the warmth of his neck, feeling the depth of his penetration everywhere in her.

Thinking for a moment of all the times she'd been in this bed with Marshall, all those times they'd made love. With such an awful absence of passion. Lust, yes. But passion, that great swelling of the emotions, had never entered their encounters. And it was here now, shaking her as she slowly allowed the sense of this man and the truth of him to come to her through her fingers, her mouth, her skin. Something vast, breathtaking in the sudden passionate attachment she felt. Passion that lifted her up and set her riding, her arms braced behind her, set her to dancing a slow, naked ride into oblivion. You knew what was needed, she thought. Knew. And pulled me out kicking, screaming. I don't feel ridiculous with you, don't feel a fool for needing you inside me. All those times before, Marshall and so many others. When she'd felt herself the ultimate clown-woman, letting herself be positioned, bent, and twisted in order to be penetrated in what had always seemed such intentionally demeaning ways. But now the need and desire were so unanimous, there was no room, no longer time for standing off to one side and looking down in dismay at the acrobatics being performed for the sake of their immediate satisfaction. I'm trusting you. Don't destroy me with it. Yes, do that; yes. Your hand do that, yes.

Eleven

In the later afternoon, she awakened from a second brief nap, knowing she'd have to call Ash.

"I want to do the show, but I'm scared," she admitted, curled against Brian's side, his arm around her. "I can't be sure I'll be left alone to do my job without there being something more. Not Jerry. But something else."

"There's always something else," he said. "That's part of being upwardly mobile."

"I hate phrases, expressions like that. I'm not concerned with mobility. I simply, truthfully only want to do something I'm good at, that gives me satisfaction."

"I saw the show this morning," he said, lighting a cigarette.

"You did?" She leaned on her elbow, looking at him. "You wouldn't ever consider giving those up, would you?"

"I might. I watch every morning," he said.

She laughed, pleased.

"You were gorgeous this morning," he said, folding one arm under his head. "Your hair down that way, plain clothes for a change. You looked . . . real. I thought there was going to be an on-the-air fracas."

"Could you *see* that?"

"I would hazard a safe guess and say everybody watching could see."

"How did it look to you Brian? How did it seem?"

"Nuts. Like the guy was completely out of control. And how controlled you were. You talk about not knowing what it is, but you've got it working for you."

"You actually think that?"

"It's a thing about television," he said, following a thought. "The way they want to make everybody look like everybody else. Punch-out paper dolls. You've been good all those other mornings. But this morning was . . . so real. Real people talking. You get so goddamned *much* out of those people!"

"I've got to phone him," she said, losing her smile.

"Do it. You know you're not going to give up now. Not when you've got a show of your own sitting in your lap."

"It has to sound funny, as if I'm being inversely vain or something, but it wasn't what I was after. It wasn't. I'd have been perfectly happy doing my segment. But Jerry. He wouldn't stop, couldn't see I wasn't competing."

"Sure you were," he said. "If you look at it from his viewpoint, you were damned well threatening. Anybody with ability, talent, is a threat to someone with little or none. Especially in a business where it seems to me everything's contingent on just how much flash and glitter you can manufacture. You happen to be beautiful, which works very nicely for you. You can just sit there being beautiful and let your looks and intelligence carry the flash-and-glitter aspect."

"You're making me sound like some sort of dummy," she warned.

"You're beautiful," he said, somewhat impatiently. "It's a commodity. And you damned well know it! What you can't know, thank God, is how well that beauty is *contained*. It isn't something that's so perfect it's offensive. You're just you, and you're great at it. Your brain's a bonus. Call the man and tell him you're going to do the show."

"Why?"

"Because you want to."

"Are you going to go away from here and say you fucked a celebrity?"

"I'm going to go away from here and say nothing."

"You think I'm cashing in on my externals."

"So what if you are? If it helps you get the job done, why not?"

"I think I should be offended," she said uncertainly.

"The truth shouldn't offend you."

"Are you going to go on forever working for the police?"

"I'll tell you a little secret," he said, his expression suddenly very intense. "For the last few years, I've hated my life. Oh, moments, you know. Moments, it's been all right. But in the back of my mind, I've been scouting out someone, something to motivate me out of my rut. I've felt just as crazy as you have. Women. All hair-sprayed and stiff. Situations you find yourself in without really knowing how you managed to get yourself into them. A lot of women. Like you, with the men you talk about. I don't know. Maybe it's something we've all got to get through. I don't know. I want to change directions, need to. I could lie here and make any number of proposals. Any number of them. So many things I'd like to have happen with you and me. And if you're wondering about the immediacy, I'll tell you a little something else. I'm almost forty-two years old. I don't have all that much time to waste. Neither do you, Isabel. If you want to play it out, do a lot of ground-testing, make sure I'm not another Marshall, that's fine. The idea doesn't thrill me, but I don't have a hell of a lot of choice. I'm committed, whether or not you want me."

"How can you be so sure?"

"I've got nothing to lose. You're what I want, need."

"You... I don't know..." She lifted the hair back over her shoulder. It was still slightly damp.

"Go make your call. I'll get dressed and go get us some dinner."

"Chinese." She smiled, leaning over him. "In a minute. I enjoy you too much," she said, kissing him, gratified by what she was coming to see as his consistent response. If she approached him, he reciprocated. His arm came out from under his head and over around her.

"Christ, you feel good!" he said, dropping his cigarette in the ashtray. "Do I feel as good to you?"

"Yes."

"Great!" He sighed, both arms around her now, one hand on the back of her neck, under her hair, the other hand spread over her buttock, his knee between her thighs.

* * *

Denise let herself in, dropped her bag beside the front door, listened for a moment, hearing no sound downstairs. Called, "Mom?" then ran up the stairs, "Mom?" Walked down the hall to see if she wasn't maybe in the shower. "Jesus Christ!" she exclaimed, disgusted, instantly angry. "*Another* one!"

Isabel turned, her heart knocking, thinking: Not this way! Oh, *God!* Why this way?

"Denise . . ."

"You just don't quit, do you?" Denny said, glaring at the two of them. "One after another, like fucking trains!" She whirled around and stamped down the stairs, to stand staring at her bag, trying to think what to do, the blood pounding in her ears. She could just go right back out to Oakbridge. Pick up her goddamned bag and split right this minute.

Isabel jumped off the bed, grabbed her robe, and went flying out of the room, down the stairs, coming to a sudden stop three steps from the bottom.

"Denny," she said softly, "don't sentence me without a hearing. I'm so . . . happy to see you. Denny?"

"I don't understand you! You know that? You don't make one fucking bit of sense to me. Who's *that* one?"

"Please! Could we talk quietly. Just talk. Brian's going to get some food. We'll talk. We have to, Denny. It can't go on and on this way. We're making each other miserable. I've been so worried about you."

"Yeah, I can see that. So worried, you've got to get it off at five o'clock in the fucking afternoon with some ape!"

"Don't!" Isabel came down another step.

"*Don't!*" Denny mimicked her. "What're you gonna do, give me some big hot story about how you weren't up there fucking away like there's never going to be a tomorrow? I'm not seven years old anymore, you know. I know where it's at."

"Denise, stop!" she said, still softly, advancing down one more step. Feeling the madness surging back at her.

"Man, I can't believe the pictures I had in my head! Fucking *fantasies* about good old Mom and the cozy goddamned fireplace. Come all the way back here to find you jerking off some gorilla! Jesus!"

She didn't know she was going to do it, couldn't have stopped herself in any case. Her arm flew out into the air, and her open hand collided with Denny's face. There was a moment of shattering silence. Brian stood at the top of the stairs watching, his breath held.

Denny's face contorted like a small child's. She raised her hand, then dropped it and fell into Isabel's arms, crying noisily.

"Denny," Isabel whispered, cradling her, "always so hurtful, saying the most damaging things you can think of. Please, let's stop it now. I can't take any more, and neither can you. You're such a little girl in so many ways. Isn't there some way we can talk to each other, make our meanings without drawing blood? I'm so tired of all of it, the years and years of fighting, arguing. Months of staying away, and I've been terrified you were dead. Have *I* done it to you? Tell me what I've done wrong. Tell me! How can I be what you need if you won't even meet me partway?"

I've gone dry again. Dry as sand. I feel like crying with you, but I can't. I haven't hit you since you were ten. Should I have? I never believed it would solve anything. But look! I did it, and it's brought you right into my arms.

"Come on," she said, "let's sit down and try to talk."

Denny allowed herself to be led into the living room. Brian made his way down the stairs, pulled on his topcoat, and quietly went out. Isabel listened to the door close and his car start up, and wondered if he'd come back. He probably wouldn't. The ultimate embarrassment, being caught in bed with somebody's mother. But it didn't matter if he didn't come back. He'd helped so much. It didn't matter. Did it?

"I'm okay," Denny said at last, pulling herself away, mopping her eyes on her sleeve before getting a pack of cigarettes and some matches out of her jacket pocket. She took her time lighting one, noticing the holes in the wall, then sank back on the sofa, slouching low, her legs stretched out in front of her.

"I'm sorry. *Okay?*" Denny said defiantly.

"Okay."

"Shit! Why do you just *accept* it that way?"

"Denny, what do you *want* me to do? What will satisfy you?"

"I don't know," she mumbled, puffing on her cigarette.

Suddenly spent, Isabel leaned sideways against the back of the sofa and closed her eyes. Fatigue whispering through her bloodstream like the faint rustling of leaves against a closed door. I've finally come to the end, she thought. I can't go any further.

"That ape," she said, "was here when I needed someone today. Sounds melodramatic, doesn't it, Denny? Preposterous. I wanted to kill myself, and you come home and find us making love. That doesn't add up. I'm sorry it doesn't. But that 'ape' has cared more about me the last few months than you have. And I *need* someone around who cares."

"How come you'd want to do a number like that?" Denise asked, aghast.

"Why not?" she said, massaging her forehead with her fingertips. "Why not?"

"Jesus!" Denny said, looking carefully at her mother, noticing the purplish circles under her eyes, the worn-down look of her. She kept on looking, and slowly began seeing someone else, someone outside herself. Another person. Another woman. Taking advantage of Isabel's closed eyes, the sudden awful intimacy, she whispered, "I had to get away. From Lane. He was wrecking me. Using me so badly. I just didn't think about how you might . . . Mom? Don't open your eyes, okay? Just . . . I have to . . . I've been watching you on the tube. And it was so . . . I was so . . . proud of you, you know? I didn't mean all that stuff. It just got to me, seeing, that's all. I had this picture all painted in my head, like how it'd be. It just wasn't the picture, you know? I mean, I know you're not that way, the way I made it sound."

Isabel opened her eyes. "I love you Denny. Does that hurt?"

"I don't know. It doesn't. I guess it's what I came to hear. I guess . . ." She floundered, began paying close attention to her cigarette. "Is it a thing with him?"

"He isn't Marshall, Denny. That's the only thing I can promise you."

"So how come he just split?"

Isabel overcame a sudden compulsion to turn around and look at the empty hallway, the door, as if to prove to herself he'd actually gone. She remained facing Denise, saying, "He'll be back. He went for food." And saying this, it hit her that it did very much matter if he came back. Please, she thought, don't be another runaway. I need your support in this. I'll lose her again if you run. Even if it's simply a token gesture, live up to some of the lofty claims you've made today. Don't take me down any further in her eyes.

"Where did you go, Denny?"

"Oakbridge," she said, feeling the warmth of the room penetrating the cold she'd collected inside during her afternoon on the road. "There was this couple. They let me stay."

"And?"

"And. I don't know. Maybe they rubbed off on me or something. No, I know. It was something that happened with Christy that did it. She fell in the kitchen. And Cath and I both jumped to pick her up. But Cath got to her first. I watched the way she like comforted Christy, the way she *mothered* her. And the weird thing was, if it'd been me who'd got to her first, I'd've done the same thing. It kind of scared me a little. Because I didn't know that was in me. And Cathy was so into your show, watching every day. I thought I was playing it so cool, laying back on who you were, and that whole time, she knew. You know how?"

"How?"

"Because she said I look like you. Jesus!"

"And that's bad?"

"Shit! Did I *say* that? I didn't *say* that. Don't be so goddamned defensive."

"Sorry. I'm just tired."

"No, *I'm* sorry. It keeps hitting my head what you said about trying to off yourself. It scares me. How could you get into that?"

"A lot of things. Too many things."

"And I helped," Denny said guiltily, knowing it was the truth.

"I just wanted to be dead, Denise. Wasn't that how you felt, taking all those pills?"

"Man, *no!* That was an *accident!* I didn't *do* that. I wouldn't ever! Lane gave me this whole Baggie full of pills, and I felt so sick, all I wanted was something to make me feel better. I never took more than a little something once in a while to get up a little or come down a little. It was an *accident,* Mom!"

"I'm glad to know that," Isabel said, easing down a little lower on the sofa. Her thigh muscles ached. Her breasts felt swollen, chafed. Her mouth rubbed raw. She thought of him, saw and felt him pushing into her, and wondered if she'd played her peak performance as clown-woman. So close to shame, this feeling. Monstrous shame if he failed to come back. She shielded her eyes from the light with her hand, remembering she hadn't yet called Ash.

"Denise, there's a phone call I have to make. You won't go, will you?"

Denise shook her head.

"Please stay. I have to call my producer. I'll explain when I come back. You'll stay?"

"I'll be right here," Denny promised, lighting another cigarette.

Feeling panicked again—talking to Ash was returning herself mentally to the scene of the crime—she went dizzily down the hall to the kitchen and dialed his home number.

"It's Isabel," she said.

"Are you all right?"

For some unknown reason, she laughed. "No, I'm not all right," she answered. "Are *you* all right?"

"Frankly, no. But are you *all right?*"

"I'll do the show, Ash. I wanted to let you know. I'm sorry I'm so late calling."

"It doesn't matter. As long as you're calling now."

"I think it's too much for me to handle on my own, though. That's the truth. I'm not a charmer, like Jerry. I can't bluff and bullshit and grin my way through two hours every day five days a week."

"We'll get someone to do the news, a spot here and there. We're all going to be taking it one step at a time. I've got a lot of faith in you, Isabel."

"Why didn't you ever *tell* me that?"

"I'm telling you now."

"Why?"

"I'm not big with words, Isabel. We all do what we have to. And this isn't going to hurt you, you know."

"Except in small ways."

"You pay for what you get."

"That's what Brian says."

"Who?"

"A friend. I'll see you in the morning. My daughter's here. I can't stay on the phone."

"Okay. In the morning."

"Ash, I think I should thank you."

"Wrong. I should thank you."

That made her feel suddenly lighter, more able to breathe.

"What's coming down?" Denny asked. "You look all up. Five minutes ago, you were coming unglued. What's happening?"

"Jerry's off the show. I'm going to be taking over."

"You're kidding! No lie?"

"No kidding."

"Boy, that's really something!"

"How do you feel about it?" Isabel asked.

"Well, it's terrific. Isn't it?" Denny looked unsure of herself.

"What do you want, Denny?"

"Want? Like when, how do you mean?"

"For your life, Denise. For you. What do you hope for?"

"I don't know." The old Denny surfaced defensively.

The doorbell rang. She swallowed hard, relieved and tearful again. "Would you let him in, please?" she asked.

"You're not sick, are you?"

"No, just worn out."

Denise got up and went to open the door. She couldn't get over it, her trying to off herself. That was too heavy. It gave her a creepy, weird feeling, as if her skin had shrunk or something, and everything inside was all squished together. She had this feeling of wanting to split, but another, stronger feeling of wanting to stay and find out what was coming down around here. One thing for sure, though, if this ape hassled

her, she'd be back on the road tonight, heading for Oakbridge.

Brian stood waiting at the takeout counter, his head so
filled with conflicting ideas he was unaware of anything but
the need to quickly filter through the largest of his thoughts
and decide how he wanted to proceed. It simply didn't occur
to him not to go back. The thought never came to his mind.
What did concern him was how to turn the situation to Isabel's advantage, so that she wouldn't appear small in the
daughter's eyes. Because her finding them that way had badly
rattled him. All he'd been able to think of that moment had
been how he'd have felt if it'd been Joanna. And he knew, if
it had been, he'd have felt low and contemptible. Because
that's how Jo would've been bound to see it. It was what you
saw, being a kid; not how you reasoned it through. See, react, lash out. No thinking, no stopping to consider what
might have gone before you happened on to the scene. Just
pure reaction.

Isabel twisting herself frantically out of his arms. And that
girl's eyes filled with anger and disillusionment, hurt. Her
eyes hard and unforgiving as flint. It could've been Joanna.
And he'd have done precisely what Isabel had: gone rushing
out after the kid, forgetting everything else. Because the two
of them, they didn't matter. They could deal with each other
later. The kid was the important one.

Now, he thought, how do I handle this? I'm going to have
to wait and see how Isabel's going to handle it, play by her
cues. What rotten timing. What god-awful, stinking timing.
But at least the girl came back. Remember that! It's the important part of all this.

He paid the cashier and carried the bags out to the car,
smelling the food, feeling its warmth permeating the paper
cartons, the bags; suddenly hungry. Things would work out.
The windshield had started to freeze over again. He started the
car, turned the defrosters on full blast, and lit a cigarette,
waiting for the windshield to clear.

Thinking about that terribly arrogant kid he'd been. He
could see it now, that galling arrogance. And the infuriating
good-natured tolerance his father had displayed, telling him

to "Take it easy, son. You're not going to change the world or the people in it. You're just going to ruffle everybody's feathers." Which had certainly been the truth. But Brian had seen it as a revitalization process—pumping fresh blood and adrenaline into the old company veins. Getting married to Joyce because she'd been the sensible, quietly good-looking type of girl who'd make a good executive's wife. Retrospectively pitiable, that brash, ambitious kid. Sure, he'd made the whole thing work. The company had turned cartwheels and started churning out rows of figures in black columns. But where did it lead him? To the morgue, and then to a crematorium. From there to a courtroom had taken only a matter of months. And then good-bye. Standing at the window in the airport watching the 727 take off, staring at the dissolving jet stream until there was nothing left. What had it all been for?

Thought of his father smiling and guzzling down the last of a fifth of rye, a pretty happy man going out. He'd never harmed a soul. He'd wasted one hell of a lot of money. But he'd made quite a surprising number of people happy, as evidenced by the dozen or so women of varying ages who'd shown up at the funeral home to pay their respects, all wearing expressions bordering on the beatific. Who was he to say it was a waste? And at least, he thought, pulling out into the street, I wasn't ever too stuffy to tell you I loved you. One small redeeming act.

Growing up without a mother. Maybe it was why he'd always been so fascinated by women, had always derived so much pleasure from the sight, sound, and smell of them; their ways, their habits. From a distance, though. Because he'd stayed loyal to Joyce, faithful to the end. And then, after she'd left, he'd gone a little berserk, playing at being a minor-league playboy, wining and dining more women than he could now recall, bed-and-breakfasting them like the proprietor of some exotic boardinghouse. Until his appetite had dulled, his palate jaded, and he'd turned to an involvement with the force and the rehab programs, the shelters. Like finding religion. But now allowing himself to be deluded into believing he was doing anything more than financing dormlike crash pads. Doing penance. Trying to find his way back to an appreciation of the simpler things, the real things. Some land, an old stone farmhouse. And his one indulgence: the pool. With its winter bubble. A near-Spartan existence that had gradually peeled the excesses of executive flab from his body and removed the city's dirt from the surface of his eyes. Relocating his essential health. All so that when he saw Isabel bent and debased on the floor of that rattrap, his senses had been sufficiently restored to enable him to come at once to the core of his responses and draw on the strength he'd managed to rebuild. To find someone in whose life he wanted to share. And have his own life and senses enriched in the process.

Whatever way you lead, that's the way we'll play it. It's selfish because it's for me. And not selfish because it's for you, too. If you'll accept it. Is it love because I want it to be? Or love simply because it is?

Isabel pushed serving spoons into each of the cartons while Denny laid plates and cutlery, napkins, on the kitchen table. Brian went off to the living room to get drinks, then returned to ask Denny, "What're you drinking?"

It surprised her, awakened her suspicions. Was he giving her strokes just to make himself look good with her mom?

"Any beer?" she asked her mother.

"I don't know," Isabel answered, watching the steam rising from the rice.

"I'll look," Brian said affably. "I wouldn't mind a beer myself."

He opened the refrigerator door, said, "Two left," removed them, and went about pouring the beer into two glasses, setting them down on the table.

"Isabel?"

She looked over at him. Her mind felt as if it was running a lap or two behind what was happening.

"Drink?"

"Scotch," she said automatically, sinking into a chair.

The silence held until halfway through the meal, when Brian, realizing Isabel was either unable or unwilling to clarify the situation, decided to see if he couldn't help her get started. "I'd like," he said, "to ask you a philosophical question, Denise."

She lifted her head. "What's that?"

"Your mother and I were talking earlier about labels, about departmentalizing emotions, categorizing one's life. How do you feel about that?"

"Why're you asking me?"

"I'd like to know what you think about it."

"You want a real answer, or something that's going to make you feel good?"

"A real answer," he said, splashing some soy sauce over his rice.

Isabel watched them both, wondering if Denny would now attempt to verbally assassinate him.

"What I think," Denny said. "I think, if you want to know, it's all that heavily categorized action that sends kids out in self-defense looking for something better, because they can't hack all the stock lines, the programmed responses. That's what I think."

"Am I that typical?" Isabel asked. "Are the words and feelings so stereotyped, you know just what I'll say and when I'll say it?"

"Did I say *you?*" Denny asked hotly. "It's a *philosophical* question, isn't it?"

"That's right," Brian said equably. "But is it what you think, Denise?"

"Sure it's what I think. I'm one of 'them,' remember? Okay, so she didn't hassle me. But she would've. I could feel it coming. Sooner or later, she would've started downing me. D'you have kids?" she asked him.

"One."

"Don't you lay that whole stock response item down on *your* kid?"

"I probably did," he said. "You're a tough little lady. Are you this hard on everyone?"

"I'm not tough," she said. "I just don't accept everything people tell me. And I really can't hack it when people start doing size numbers. I mean, if you're going to get into shit like that, man, I'll start calling you gorilla, ape. How does that grab you? I can't stand that shit, coming on to me with tough-little-lady crap because I hit you with a real answer to your goddamned 'philosophical' question."

"It wasn't intended to be an attack. You're being defensive."

"Fuck defensive! That's another one of those smartass, typically 'adult'-type cracks. You're just as fucking defensive as anybody. And if I've got defenses, man, it's because I *need* them. I need them because there are too goddamned many mouth-off artists around spilling a lot of shit for the sake of hearing themselves run off at the mouth. And you know damned well how much thoughtless spill-off garbage can hurt. So I'll be as defensive as I goddamned well like! There's always some dude out to hassle you. It'd be one goddamned beautiful change in the climate around this place if you'd climb off all that superior academic bullshit and tell me what the fuck you think you're *doing* here!"

"Denny," Isabel said.

"No," Brian interjected. "She's got reasons. I think we ought to talk about Denny's reasons."

Denny couldn't believe this. "What're you trying to *prove*, man?"

"Nothing. Everything. What're *you* trying to prove?"

"Have we finished in here?" Isabel asked.

"Don't try to cut this off, Mom!" Denny warned.

"I thought we might continue in the living room, Denise. I'd like to sit on something a little more comfortable than this chair. All right?"

"Okay," Denise agreed. Suddenly very excited. This was going to be very interesting. Why did these dudes always think she was some kind of mental featherweight? Such a piss-off, that. And such a turn-on to beat them out at their own word games. She could handle this one easily.

As they settled themselves in the living room, Isabel had the feeling that important issues were about to be aired, and her pulse was racing with both dread and anticipation. She didn't want to lose either of them, hated the idea of their alienating each other. Yet, Brian seemed so calm, so openminded about Denny. He was baiting her, yes. But in a way that was bringing startling responses out of Denny. The intelligence and the fire.

"Okay," Denny said, leaping in to her attack. "What're you doing here?"

"I want to be here," he said, lighting a cigarette, offering one to her.

"Thanks," she said, leaning forward to get a light from him. "Okay! That's evasive! *What're you doing here?*"

Brian looked at Isabel.

"Come on," Denny insisted. "Or is it you're just working a devious con to get laid, and you can't talk about that?"

"That's a minor part of why I'm here," he said, still calm, feeling he was risking nothing by being truthful. And what the hell did self-esteem matter?

"What's the rest of it?" Isabel asked, curious.

Denny was intrigued. A definite new, this. A dude who was going to maybe lay down some heavy-sounding truth. An old dude, at that. She couldn't believe he wasn't going to do the usual number, pretending he was here to play hopscotch with her mother.

"I'd like you to stay awake now that you're finally coming out of it," he told Isabel. "I couldn't stand that fool. What was his name? Marshall. What sort of imbecile was that? I listened to that childish retaliatory garbage he was screaming at you, and if he hadn't taken off, I'd have decked him. That wasn't your fault," he said sympathetically. "You had balls to go there in the first place. It took courage."

"Hey, wait a minute! What're you two talking about?"

"I went to that house to find you, Denise," Isabel said.

"Oh, Jesus! You *didn't!*"

"Marshall went with me. Your friend Lane wasn't there." Isabel's voice was fading. "But five of his friends were."

"Oh, wow! Leo?"

"Leo. And four others." Isabel nodded.

Denny covered her mouth with her hand, then puffed some more on her cigarette. "Oh, wow! Leo. He's such an *animal!* Oh, Christ!" she said, examining Isabel's eyes. "I think I know what you're going to lay on me."

Isabel simply stared at her.

"Tell her," Brian urged.

"With his hand," Isabel whispered. "They held Marshall, made him watch."

"Oh!" Denny felt sick. "Oh, Jesus!"

"Tell her the rest, Isabel," Brian said quietly. "I think Denise should be told."

"I can't!" she said, upset more now because Denny was.

"Tell her! Tell her about cruising the streets every night for months looking for her!"

"How did you know that?" Isabel asked him. "How did you know?"

"Judy and Blake. They trailed around after you, making sure you were all right."

Isabel shook her head, speechless. Denise sat motionless.

"Tell her about this morning, too," Brian went on relentlessly. "About Jerry Brenner pissing all over you. Tell her that! And tell her about how we had to fight over a number of pills it was in your mind to take."

"Mom?" Denise looked horror-stricken, ashen.

"It's been a good time, Denise," Brian said sardonically. "A great time. I'm telling you, because I think you should know you don't have any priorities on bad trips. I think it's about time you understood your mother's life isn't the happy-housewife fantasy you'd like to believe it is, with nothing more to do than lie down for a lot of 'apes' tramping through here for libido satisfaction, and a daily TV spot to keep her ego up there on a perpetual high. Whatever she has, she's paid for it. You included. What the *fuck* goes on in that head, girl? You think you're the only one who thinks, feels, gets hurt?"

"You're dumping on me," Denny began.

"He's *dealing* with you, Denny," Isabel said. "It's what I should have been doing. But I haven't done too well at it. I can't play pat-a-cake with you anymore, Denny. I'm too old, too tired. And I want something settled. When do we get together? When do the two of us climb down from our pile of grievances and deal with each other? I thought you were *dead!* You *knew* I'd worry myself half-crazy about you. You knew that! You've always banked on my caring, my love. Always. Relying on me not to strike back, but to just go on accepting your performances, your anger. I have my own anger."

"I can't believe this is *you,*" Denny sputtered. "I just can't *believe* it!"

"Believe it!" Isabel said, fully fired up now. "Whatever I was before, I'm not that now."

"I don't know this you," Denny said. "Laying all this heavy stuff on me. What'm I supposed to *say* to all that?"

"Maybe, just this once, I'd like some understanding from you. There's a little kid inside me, too, Denise. Inside all of us. The one in me's been interfered with lately in a lot of ugly ways. Make *me* feel better, for a change! I want all this to end! Months, years, watching you grow. For what? What? To have you run from me. Denise! Eighteen years of my *life!* I've been such a silly optimist, believing you'd come to me, want to know me, share yourself with me. Never. Not ever. I wanted more children. There couldn't *be* any. Because Howard couldn't. Something else you didn't know, Denny. He was dying for years, *years!* Why can't you just *accept?* Why do you have to come armed, always, ready to tear everything down? I'm not just your mother, I'm *someone!*"

"I care," Denny said lamely.

"You're so stingy with your affections. So mean with your love. Don't you love me, Denise?"

"I love you." She had this awful image of her mother upstairs trying to put herself away.

"Then come here, hold me, let me hold you! I *thought* you were *dead,* damn you!"

Denise went to her, confused by this mother, this Isabel, this one who could say all the things she was saying. So thin, she thought, feeling the bones in Isabel's shoulders and ribs, yet reassured by the familiar still-present softness of her breasts. The little-girl voice inside her head sighing: Mama.

"I don't want the impossible, Denny. I know you can't stay with me forever. I know that. It's inevitable that you go off, find your life. It's always saying good-bye over and over with the feeling that we've never said hello. I'm so tired, Denny. Don't go away without at least giving both of us a chance to know who we are. It's all I want. A chance." She held her tighter. "Give yourself a chance. There's a home here for you if you want it."

"I love you," Denny murmured. "You know I do. I guess it doesn't have to be . . . I just need room, that's all." Mom, the feel of you, the smell. I know you. That never changes, the way you feel and sound, your perfume. She pulled herself slightly away, to look again at this face, this someone familiar but new. "You have to work in the morning?" she asked.

"Yes."

Denise got up and stood looking at Isabel for a moment longer, then turned to Brian. This is it, kid. Be a big grown-up, act like one.

"I came on very strong to you," she told him, feeling the heat rising in her neck and ears. She hated sorry numbers. "I, uh, want to say, um, thank you, you know? About today, for Mom. I was way out of line." She held her hand out to him, and he took it, knowing what it had to be costing her to apologize.

"Anytime you'd like to discuss philosophical fine points," he said with a smile, "just let me know. You make a good argument."

"Yeah." Denny withdrew her hand, embarrassed but pleased. He really was kind of an okay dude.

"I'd better run along," Brian said, sensing a sudden awkwardness.

"What for?" Denise said surprisingly. "You don't want to. Mom doesn't want you to. And just to show you my head's together, I'll even make breakfast. I've been learning how to cook. You want me to crash in the garage?" she asked Isabel.

What was it that woman had said? Isabel tried to remember. Something about being women together finally.

"Wherever you like," she said, feeling genuinely hopeful for the first time in so long.

"Okay. I'll see you in the morning. G'night." Denny picked up her jacket, stopped at the doorway to retrieve her canvas bag, then stopped at the foot of the stairs. She felt really good. Weird, like some kind of natural high. But good. Like somebody'd just lifted his knee off her chest. " 'Night," she said again. And smiled. Not a bad dude at all, really. God-damned great to be home.

Take 3 of
"The Best of the Best™"
Novels FREE
Plus get a FREE surprise gift!

Special Limited-time Offer

Mail to The Best of the Best™

3010 Walden Avenue
P.O. Box 1867
Buffalo, N.Y. 14269-1867

YES! Please send me 3 free novels and my free surprise gift. Then send me 3 of "The Best of the Best™" novels each month. I'll receive the best books by the world's hottest romance authors. Bill me at the low price of $3.99 each plus 25¢ delivery and applicable sales tax, if any.* That's the complete price and a savings of over 20% off the cover prices—quite a bargain! I understand that accepting the books and gift places me under no obligation ever to buy any books. I can always return a shipment and cancel at any time. Even if I never buy another book from Harlequin, the 3 free books and the surprise gift are mine to keep forever.

183 BPA A2P5

Name	(PLEASE PRINT)	
Address		Apt. No.
City	State	Zip

This offer is limited to one order per household and not valid to current subscribers.
*Terms and prices are subject to change without notice. Sales tax applicable in N.Y. All orders subject to approval.

If you enjoyed the compelling drama of
New York Times bestselling author

CHARLOTTE VALE ALLEN

Be sure to add these stories to your collection:

#66030	DREAMING IN COLOR	$5.99 U.S. ☐
		$6.50 CAN. ☐
#66067	SOMEBODY'S BABY	$5.99 U.S. ☐
		$6.50 CAN. ☐

(limited quantities available)

TOTAL AMOUNT	$
POSTAGE & HANDLING	$
($1.00 for one book, 50¢ for each additional)	
APPLICABLE TAXES*	$ _____
TOTAL PAYABLE	$ _____
(check or money order—please do not send cash)	

To order, complete this form and send it, along with a check or money order for the total above, payable to MIRA Books, to: **In the U.S.: 3010 Walden Avenue, P.O. Box 9077, Buffalo, NY 14269-9077; In Canada: P.O. Box 636, Fort Erie, Ontario, L2A 5X3.**

Name: _____

Address: _____ City: _____

State/Prov.: _____ Zip/Postal Code: _____

*New York residents remit applicable sales taxes.
  Canadian residents remit applicable GST and provincial taxes.   MCVABL2

MIRA

Look us up on-line at: http://www.romance.net